ICE *Me* BABY

Ivy Cole

CONTENTS

Team Members

<u>Team Management</u>

General Manager: Nicholas Diaz (Nick)

Assistant General Manager: Aubree Roberts

<u>Coaching Staff</u>

Head Coach: Mason Fernandez

Assistant Coach: Jerry Robinson, Loren King

<u>Medical Staff</u>

Medical Director and Head Team Physician: Dr. Garfield Fulton

Head Athletic Therapist: Max Spencer

Assistant Athletic Therapists: Elizabeth Monroe (Liz, Lizzi) (Boys call her Roe Roe), Danni Phillips

Strength and Conditioning Coaches: Emma Rowlands, Stephen Navaro

Roving Strength and Conditioning Coach: Shane O'Donnell

Massage Therapist: Lorna Godwin

Sports Scientist: Joanne Stenhouse (JoJo)

Lead Performance Dietician: Andra Hill (Andi)

Performance Dietician, Player Development: Roy Davidson

Culinary Staff: Lakin Scott, Eliza Cordova, Isaac Iza, Rennie Peterson

Orthopedic Consultant: Nathan Hodge

Team Dentists: Alissa Butler, Omar Mills

ICE ME BABY

<u>Equipment Staff</u>

Head Equipment Manager: Bryant Collins

Assistant Equipment Manager: Conor McLean, Nia Ross

Equipment Assistant: Ronnie Mora

Assistant to the Equipment Staff: Marshall Perez

Hockey Team Line Up

<u>Forwards:</u>

1. (11) Dean Lewis (Lewi) - Center

2. (16) Ace Langlois (Lani or Langly) - Center

3. (26) Ives Perri (Perri) - Center

4. (28) Russ Coleman (Cole) - Center

5. (14) Bobby Tucker (Tuck) - Leftwing

6. (50) Corin Mercier (Merc) - Leftwing

7. (19) Jake Ford (Ford) - Leftwing

8. (10) Juste Travere (Trav) - Leftwing

9. (20) Max Gill (Gilly or Maxy) - Rightwing

10. (24) Philbert Rey (RayRay) - Rightwing

11. (27) Marshal Lynch (Lyn) - Rightwing

ICE ME BABY

12. (19) Raimond Victor (Vicy) - Rightwing

Defenseman:

1. (3) Guillaume Tremble (Tre)

2. (2) Mason Osborn (Ozzy)

3. (8) Aillard Tasse (Taz)

4. (4) Doug Fennimore (Fenni)

5. (5) Quintin Sameul (Samy)

6. (7) Simon Palmer (Pali)

Goalie

1. (35) Mac Oliver (Oli)

2. (30) Kemp Mann (Manny)

Players In Liz's Care

1. Mac Oliver (Oli) - Goalie 29yo

2. Dean Lewis (Lewi) - Center 27yo

3. Ives Perri (Peri) - Center 33yo

4. Bobby Tucker (Tuck) - Leftwing 23yo

5. Corin Mercier (Merc) - Leftwing 32yo

6. Max Gill (Gilly or Maxy) - Rightwing 29yo

7. Raimond Victor (Vicy) - Rightwing 20yo

8. Mason Osborn (Ozzy)- Defenseman 25yo

9. Doug Fennimore (Fenni) - Defenseman 30yo

10. Aillard Tasse (Taz) - Defenseman 22yo

Playlist

Yuri on ICE by Taro Umebayashi
Never Enough by Kelly Clarkson
Can I Have This Dance by Joshua Bassett, Sofia Wylie
Only Love Can Hurt Like This by Kiesa Keller
This Is Me by Keala Settle
Lady of Worlds by Miracle Of Sounds
Cruise – Remix by Florida Georgia Line, Nelly
Could Have Been Me by Halsey
Miss Me More by Kelsea Ballerini
Unconditionally by Katy Perry
What Was I Made For? By Billie Eilish
Traitor by Olivia Rodrigo
Are You With Me by Nilu
Lonely by Nathan Wagner
Ghosts by Nathan Wagner
Tattoo by Loreen
Classic by MKTO
Dirty Thoughts by Chloe Adams
Dibs by Kelsea Ballerini
Yeah Boy by Kelsea Ballerini
Pretty Please by Dutch Melrose, Benny Mayne
24/7, 365 by Elijah Woods

Dedication

To my readers. Dreams are fluid things. Don't be afraid to change and edit your dreams.

Dare to dream and change. Don't let fear hold you back.

You hold my dreams in your hands. Take care of them for me, my lovely readers.

"When you reach an obstacle, turn it into an opportunity. You have the choice. You can overcome and be a winner, or you can allow it to overcome you and be a loser. The choice is yours and yours alone. Refuse to throw in the towel. Go that extra mile that failures refuse to travel. It is far better to be exhausted from success than to be rested from failure." -- Mary Kay Ash.

Honorable Mention

Thank you so much Lorna and Natasha! You really helped me to make sure I stayed as true to hockey as possible. The number of times I made you re-read things to make sure they were correct was probably borderline needy.

CONTENT WARNING

Please advised. I may have missed some warnings but these are the ones that are mention:

- Stalking

- Betrayal

- Kidnapping

- Mental torture

- Physical abuse

Chapter One

When you're sixteen, dreams are everything. My dream? Make it to the Olympics. Be the next big figure skater. And I am on my way. The scouts are here to see Emmitt and me. We are the top skaters in our league, and this is the last year we can compete before they raise the senior division age limit. This is our last shot; we have to make it this year.

Emmitt bumps my shoulder with a smile. "You ready, Izzy?"

I smile back with a nod. "Ready as I'll ever be."

They always say never get involved with your partner. Keep it professional, they say. But I've known Emmitt since I was six. We met on the ice and have been inseparable since. He has never given me a reason not to trust him. But I didn't realize just how far he would go to become a star figure skater. How far he would go to avoid having to drag me along beside him. He wanted the spotlight. Alone.

We rocked our short program, and our long program is all that's left to do. It is the most important because it showcases our lifts. This is the program to show off our skills and make sure the scouts notice us.

I shake my hands out, trying to get rid of my anxiety.

Emmitt laughs as he looks down at me. "Got ants in your pants, Izzy?"

"I'm trying to get the nervous energy out before we step on the ice. I don't want it to ruin the routine."

Emmitt slips his hand into mine, giving it a squeeze. "I've got this. Trust me, Iz?"

I arch a brow at the ridiculous question. "Of course."

He nods. "Then don't worry."

Huffing out a sigh, I nod. "Right. We've got this."

Before we know it, it's our turn. We glide out onto the ice, and I can't help but smile at the rush I get from stepping on the ice and the feeling of freedom consumes me. We take our starting positions, ready for the music to begin. I take a few deep breaths before the music blares from the speakers, sounding like the beginning of my end.

I land every jump, and Emmitt holds strong for every lift. We had decided to save our throw-jump for the end. It is a risky move, but it increases the difficulty of the program. We've perfected the move, and I landed it every single time in practice. The points will be worth the exhaustion.

The moment Emmit grabs my waist, I know something is wrong. He isn't holding me in the same spot as we've practiced, but I'm already up in the air before I can do or say anything. He released me too high. My mind tells me not to overcompensate for the error. All of my training says not to try and fix the error. Just land as best you can. That's what I'm supposed to do.

My body decides otherwise. I try to shift my weight so when I land on the correct foot, I can then distribute my weight to my other foot once on the ice. In theory, it should have worked. In theory, lots of things should work. In reality, it didn't work.

My scream echoes through the rink as I land on the edge of my blade and fall. I slide across the ice, but the only thing on my mind is that my ankle hurts. The pain is unbearable.

Tears stream down my face as I force my eyes open and look down to take in the damage. My ankle... my... my ankle! It's wrong! It's so wrong! No. No, no, no, no, no!

When I look up again, I find Emmitt staring down at me, his face blank of all feeling and emotion.

"Em?" My voice trembles from the pain.

His eyes meet mine, finally. Then they widen as he takes in what happened. "I... I... I'm sorry. He made me."

My eyes narrow, and my breaths come quicker as I try to think past the pain. "What are you talking about?" There is something in his tone that I've never heard before.

"My dad. He told me to ruin you, so I could become the best skater alone."

My eyes widen and my entire body freezes. *He... he turned on me.* "You did this on purpose?" Medics begin to surround me, but I've grown numb from the shock. My best friend. My boyfriend... betrayed me? He ruined my life to ensure he got ahead.

"You did this!" I point to my ankle with a shaking hand the best I can. "You ruined my life, Emmitt! Why?!" I yell at him.

The medics try to calm me down, but there's no use. I'm making sure he knows exactly what he did. Unfortunately, I know there's no way to prove he caused the 'accident'. His parents are rich and can claim it was an accident.

As more people surround me on the ice, I watch him slowly back away. But I'm not done with him. I scream, "You have taken everything from me. I'll never be able to skate again! Never skate, Emmitt!"

"I'm sorry," he whispers before he turns and skates away. I watch as my best friend leaves me broken on the ice with the medics trying to put me on a stretcher.

I give in, slumping forward and allowing them to move me however they want. Tears continue to stream down my face as it fully sinks in that I'll never be able to skate the same again. I know my ankle is shattered. It will require pins for stabilization at a minimum. If it's as bad as I think it is, I'll need a plate put in as well.

I'll have no flexibility. No movement in that ankle. Sure, with years of physical therapy, I'll be able to do more. But that doesn't begin to touch the pain I feel from my best friend's betrayal. I choke on a sob as one of the paramedics looks down at me with a sad smile. "It will be okay, darlin'."

I shake my head as I cry, "It's over. My dream is dead."

The female paramedic on my other side shushes me. "Now, now, hunny. That's no way to look at it."

"Then how am I supposed to look at it?" I whimper. Everything I've wanted and dreamed of for so long, gone.

She gives me a kind smile as they load me into the ambulance. Hoping up beside me, she brushes a few strands of hair out of my face. "Dreams can change. They are a malleable thing, hun. You may not be able to skate like before, but that doesn't mean you won't ever skate again." I huff a heavy sigh. Like most sixteen-year-olds, I don't believe her.

But with a six-hour surgery that changed with the help of my dad. My days are spent in a hospital room, stuck watching TV most of the time. The only thing that catches my eye as I channel surf is hockey. I'm entranced as I watched them glide across the ice. Granted, I don't understand the game much, but the brawls the players get into are the only thing that make me smile. I believed that woman. Dreams could change.

It makes me wish I could take a stick to the side of Emmitt's head, but I figure that may be a little too violent. At least that's what my mom would say. My dad, on the other hand, loves that I have gotten into watching his favorite sport. When he isn't at work, he comes by and watches it with me. He happily explains the game and grins ear to ear when I ask questions.

We argue over our favorite teams. To be honest, mine changes depending on my favorite player at the time, at least that's what I tell my dad. Which I know irritates my father more than anything. Don't tell him, but my favorite team will always be the same as his. The Toronto Maple Leafs. My favorite player? Morgan Rielly of course, but don't tell my dad.

Now that I'm no longer skating, I have more time for school, and I put every bit of that time toward doing well. I do so well that I am on the road to graduating from high school early, and I take advantage of that. I've taken as many AP classes as I was allowed. If it were up to me, I would have taken more, but my guidance counselor said the workload would be too much.

My senior year of high school, I send my application to the University of Florida. It's the only school I want to go to, and I am determined to get in. I want to soak in the sun and visit the beach. As a figure skater, I didn't have much time to travel for fun, and most of the money my parents made went toward my dream. Vacations were never a thing in my family, so I am going to take advantage of it now.

I've always wanted to go to the beach and, this way, my parents will no longer have to spend all their money on me. I can get a part-time job if I have to.

"What's your plan if you get into Florida, Liz?" My mom's voice rings through the house from the kitchen.

I smile as I work on my homework at the coffee table in the living room. "What do you mean?"

"You'll be so far away," she whines.

I laugh. "Mom, I'll be fine. I'll get a part-time job to help with expenses. I'm sure they have an ice rink. Maybe, I can teach kids to skate."

She hums. "You shouldn't need a part-time job, hun. Your father and I can help pay. Your focus should be on school."

"Mom, you and Dad have spent enough money on me for a lifetime. I'll manage."

She pops out of the kitchen on a huff. "You are as bullheaded as your father. I won't argue with you because I know how to pick my battles. But if you need anything, we are only a phone call away."

"I know, ma. You worry too much."

She laughs as she walks back into the kitchen. "Yes. Well, it's a mother's job. Don't forget you have physical therapy tomorrow."

I groan in protest. "But ma!"

"No buts, missy! You will finish every session of physical therapy."

I frown, staring down at my homework, then eventually say, "It's too expensive, ma."

"I don't care. That horrible boy and his parents should be paying for this! But—"

I interrupt. "I don't want anything to do with them, ma."

"I know"—she sighs— "which is why you will complete every PT session and show that horrid family that you are better than them."

I smile. "Yes mama." I turn to the front door as my dad shuffles in. His bright eyes meet mine as I grin. "Hey, da. How was work today?"

"Work," he grunts.

I snort as I turn on the TV and switch it to the sports channel. The game should be on soon. My dad holds an envelope out in front of my face.

"This came in the mail for you."

I take it from him and release a loud squeal. He covers his ears with a laugh. "Good lord. I'm assuming that's a happy squeal."

I nod, impatiently ripping open the envelope and pulling out the letter. I have to read the words several times before I jump up from the floor. Pumping my arms in the air, I yell, "I got in!"

I'm immediately engulfed in my father's arms as he gives me a bear hug. "So happy for you, Iz."

I hug him back hard before pulling away. When I turn toward the kitchen, I find my mom standing there with a big smile and tears in her eyes. "Congratulations, baby."

Rushing over to her, I wrap her in a hug. She laughs and holds me close. "You are going to do great! I'm so happy you got in, baby. I'm proud of you."

"Thank you, ma," I whisper.

My father claps and announces, "This calls for a celebration!"

I shake my head, still smiling. "We don't have to do anything."

He waves a hand in the air. "Nonsense. My baby girl just got into the University of Florida. Go Gators! She's going to be the biggest and best athletic therapist in the National Hockey League one day."

"Da!" I shout and laugh.

He points a finger at me and says, "One day, every team in the NHL will want my baby on their team."

I roll my eyes. "If you say so, da."

Little did I know just how true his words would be.

CHAPTER TWO

I did it. I made it to graduation day! I received not only my bachelor's degree but also a master's in applied physiology and kinesiology. I'm graduating at the top of my class with honors. Fuck ya! Dammit... I am going to have to watch my language when I get home. Because I am going home. Well, home adjacent.

I've gotten so many job offers that I don't even know where I want to go. I've sat down, contemplating every single offer, and they blow my mind. I received three offers from the NFL, two for the NBA, and four from NHL teams. How is it possible that I got this many offers before I even graduated?

"A little birdie told me several of your teachers have sent out recommendations for you."

I arch a brow. "How do you know that?"

Jess snorts a laugh. "I'm the local gossip, girl. It's my job to know everything that goes on in this school."

I laugh. "Well, we graduate in three days. It won't be your school for much longer."

"A pity really." She laughs. "Do you know which offer you'll accept?"

I shrug. "I want to work with the NHL, so I'll have to decline the other offers."

Her eyes glitter with excitement. "Which teams offered you a spot?"

Pulling out the offers again, I list them. "Let's see. Tampa Tiger Sharks, Michigan Lansing Lynx, Missouri Mambas, and the Washington Wraiths."

She hums. "Those are good choices. Tampa's not that far away. You wouldn't have to move. You could stay in the sun and sand. Missouri is often called misery, so I'm not sure you want to go there. Michigan's hella cold in the winter, and so is Washington."

"I grew up in Washington, so the cold isn't a turnoff."

She arches her brow. "You do realize you've been here for five years? You are not cold-weather ready, girl."

I shrug. "It shouldn't be that hard."

She huffs before falling onto my bed in our shared dorm. "Whatever. I assume by your tone that you are heading up North. Michigan or Washington?"

My brows pinch as I debate. Though it isn't much of a decision. It would be nice to be close to home again. "I'm thinking Washington. I miss home."

"Whatever girl. I'm staying in the land of sun and sand."

"You're going with the NHL, too, right?"

She hums. "That's the plan."

"Well, don't leave a girl in suspense! Where are you going?"

She smirks as she says, "I got an offer with Tampa, too."

I laugh as I slap her arm. "You wanted me to choose Tampa, too, so we could get a place together."

She shrugs. "Can't blame a girl for trying. But I'll make sure to bug you when our boys meet on the ice." She holds out a fist for me to bump.

Bumping mine to hers, I say, "See you on the ice, then."

Looking out over the sea of students, I meet my classmates' eyes and finish my speech. "So get out there and do your best. Congratulations graduating class of 2025!"

Everyone erupts from their seats and throws their cap in the air. I can't stop smiling as I make my way down the steps and off the stage, being careful of my ankle. While working, I always wear a brace, but otherwise, I leave my ankle free and clear. My physical therapist says I don't need the brace anymore, but I want to avoid any more accidents.

In the years following that awful day, I slowly regained strength in my ankle, and I've since been able to get back out on the ice. I've been teaching the kids here in town how to skate, and each of them begged their parents to come to my graduation.

One of the little girls I taught for the last three years races up to me. Wrapping me in a hug, she squeals, "You did it!"

I smile and pat her back. "Yes, I did, Suzzy. Thank you so much for the hug." Looking around, I find several more of my students. One of the few boys shuffles forward, holding out a card he had hidden behind his back. "What do you have there, JJ?"

His smile is adorable, his front teeth missing, as he says, "We got you a card, Miss Liz."

Taking the card from the little boy, I say, "Thank you!" When I read it, I have to take a deep breath. It's a handmade card that reads, "We will miss you." I look at each of the kids. "I'll miss you all too."

Suzzy jumps up and down as she cries, "Open it!"

Biting my lip, I nod. When I flip it open, I see that each of the kids drew something small and signed it. My eyes burn as my gaze meets each child before shifting to their parents. They all look at me with teary smiles of their own.

"We appreciate everything you have done," one of the parents says.

I shake my head. "It was my absolute pleasure."

Another parent speaks up. "We know they didn't pay you much to teach the lessons, but we really do appreciate everything you did for our kids."

"We made a call to the rink in Seattle and the surrounding areas," Suzzy's mother says. "We told them you would be an incredible asset, and that they should reach out to you. I'm sure you'll be busy with the new job but still."

"No. I really appreciate the thought. Thank you." A hand squeezes my shoulder softly. I look over to find my dad standing there with a smile.

"We need to get going, kiddo."

"Right!" I nod and look back at the kids. "Alright, everyone! Remember everything I taught you, and make sure you get up, no matter how many times you fall."

All the kids yell a chorus of, "Yes, Miss Liz!"

I hold my arms out. "Okay everyone! Group hug!"

The kids squeal as they all squeeze in close. I make sure to pat each kid on the head, so they know how much I care. It's my mother who eventually says, "So sorry to ruin the group hug, but Miss Liz has a schedule to keep if she wants to get to work on time."

As much as I hate leaving these kids, there is a new life waiting for me. "Okay, kiddos, disperse!" I call with a laugh. They all squeal and rush back to their parents. My dad pats me on the back as I slowly turn toward the parking lot.

"You did good, Liz."

"Thanks, da."

He kisses the top of my head. "Let's get you settled in Seattle. It's going to be nice to have you home."

I nod. It will be nice to be home. There are only a few weeks left for me to get settled before I start my new job. It may be the off season, but that doesn't mean there isn't a job to do. I need to learn the players' names that I'll oversee and make sure I have a system down for treating the players before the regular season starts. Four and a half months before the season starts, then the real fun begins.

...I didn't realize that two of my boys would come to mean more to me than I was comfortable admitting. I oversaw ten men who would have my back no matter what. They were my boys, but I'd fall for not only one but two of them. The bonds I'd make with my boys would be stronger than I ever thought possible. Our friendships stronger than any bond Emmitt and I ever had. A love I never thought possible...

CHAPTER THREE

I've been staring at myself in the mirror for an hour now. *I shouldn't wear a suit, right? I mean... I already got the job. But... shouldn't l look professional on my first day of meeting them? I won't be dressed appropriately if I need to do anything physical, though, if I wear a suit. With a* groan, I twist back and forth. *Maybe I should just wear khakis and a polo shirt. I'd still look professional but be free to move and work if I need to.*

I run back into my closet and change—for the sixth time. Rushing around the apartment, I grab my coffee off the counter and shove a piece of toast in my mouth. *Coffee? Check. Food? Check. Keys... keys... check. Purse? Check.*

With everything I need, I rush out the door, somehow locking it without everything falling out of my hands. I make it to my car and throw my purse onto the passenger seat as I slide in. In my rush, I didn't notice the note stuck under my driver's side windshield wiper. Odd. Sliding back out of the car, I reach for the note. When I open the small piece of paper, I find scribbled writing.

A shiver runs down my spine as I look around; it feels as if someone is watching me. Nothing seems out of place, so I shake it off and get back into my car, tossing the note on the back seat. I don't have time for this. Shaking off the nerves, I finally bite into my toast as I pull out of my parking spot. Off to the first day of my new job.

I didn't expect to get to work thirty minutes early. So, here I am, standing in the parking lot, debating whether to go inside. *I don't want to appear too eager, but I don't want to look as if I'm not excited, either. Should I go in? I... should probably go in. Yeah. Yeah, I should go in.*

"Ma'am?"

I jump when I hear a feminine voice call out behind me. Looking over my shoulder, I squeak out, "Yes?"

She offers me a genuine smile before her eyes widen, her smile widening as well. "Elizabeth Monroe?"

I nod. "Yes. That's me."

"Oh my!" She shifts her small briefcase to her other side and holds out a hand. "Aubree Roberts! I'm the Assistant General Manager for the Washington Wraiths."

I immediately place my hand into hers. "It's so wonderful to meet you, Ms. Roberts!"

She laughs as we release hands. "You can call me Aubree."

"Elizabeth is fine. Or Liz," I say.

She gestures for me to follow her as she starts walking. "Come on inside! I'll show you around. Nicholas Diaz is our General Manager, but he's not here today. Nick is out promoting this coming season."

I nod as I follow her. She opens the door with a flourish and a grin. "Welcome to the Home of the Wraiths!"

My smile is huge as I step through the doors. This place is a dream. Aubree comes to stand next to me as she gestures to the left. "The offices are down that way. So HR, managers"—she begins ticking off fingers— "physicians, basically anyone who needs a desk lives down that way most of the time."

Pointing to the corridor in front of us, she continues, "The rink is that direction as well as the locker rooms and gym." Then she points to her right. "That way leads to another set of offices. But those are mainly for use by the medical staff. So that will include you. You'll find the other athletic therapists, stretch-training coaches, and massage therapist making camp there."

She points down the center again. "But you'll be mainly in this direction unless you need somewhere quiet to do paperwork." Her eyes meet mine as she smiles brightly. "Ready to meet everyone?"

No, not really. To be honest I feel like I am going to vomit. Instead, I nod. "Yeah. Let's go."

"Don't worry. It can be overwhelming at first, but you'll get comfortable. This will start to feel like a second home soon." She walks forward, gesturing for me to follow. "You will be taking over the care of players the previous athletic therapist worked with. I hope that won't be an issue."

I shake my head. "No. Of course not."

Aubree hums as her heels click-clack across the tile. "They are a rowdy bunch. Also, a warning, they are very excited to meet you. So please don't run if they start bombarding you with questions."

I chuckle. "I'm used to working with children, so it shouldn't be much different, right?"

She laughs. "No, I suppose it shouldn't."

We continue toward what must be the gym; I can tell because that's where the loud male laughter is coming from. She looks over her shoulder as we come to the door. "Hope you are ready for these crazy boys."

I smirk. "As ready as I'll ever be."

She nods and swings the door open. I thought I understood chaos, but what I had in mind doesn't begin to compare to what we walk into. Yelling, laughing, and loud music greet me as Aubree ushers me into the room.

They don't notice us until Aubree cups her mouth and yells, "Line it up boys! New therapist on deck."

Twenty pairs of eyes swing in our direction. The music stops, and they all mosey over to form a staggered line. Aubree holds out a hand in my direction. "This is Elizabeth Monroe. She's the new athletic therapist who will be taking over Doug's group."

She looks my way as she says, "I'll make sure you have a list with the names of everyone on the team as well as one with those under your care. But I'll quickly go down the line now, so you can start to match faces to names."

I'm really good with names and faces, but a list will definitely help me remember. I nod as she begins on the left side of the room. "Alright. First up we have Dean Lewis, Ace Langlois, Ives Perri, Russ Coleman, Bobby Tucker, Corin Mercier, Jake Ford, Juste Travere, Max Gill,

Philbert Rey, Marshal Lynch, and Raimond Victor." She stops a third of the way through the guys to look at me, brow arched. "Good?"

I nod with a smile. "I'm good." I point to my temple. "Got them all. Go ahead."

She smiles and continues her introductions. "Guillaume Tremble, Mason Osborn, Aillard Tasse, Doug Fennimore, Quintin Sameul, Simon Palmer, Mac Oliver, and Kemp Mann. You'll pick up their nicknames fast, and you will only oversee ten of these troublesome boys."

"Now come on, boss lady. We're not that bad," a deep voice rumbles from the left side of the room. If I remember correctly, that's Raimond Victor. He appears young, which may explain the mischievous look on his face.

Aubree smirks. "Vicy there is the most troublesome of all. He'll be one of yours. The ones who don't have families of their own live in a house close by. Nick owns two small houses near here that he used to rent out, but now he just uses them for these boys."

I nod as she continues to explain. "Danni Phillips is the other athletic therapist. Her boys live in one of the houses, and your group live in the other. Nick thought it would be easier to have them all in one spot in case you two need to check on them for any reason. The guys with wives and kiddos don't live far, either so, if need be, they can pop over to the house as well."

She takes a breath before continuing. "Max Spencer is the head athletic therapist for the Wraiths."

All the guys holler, "Pen-nay!"

Aubree laughs and gestures to them. "As you can see, Max is well loved around here." She taps a finger to her chin and says, "I feel like I'm forgetting something."

"The welcome party!" a man in the middle says. He also looks young. I think his name is Aillard Tasse.

She snaps her fingers. "Right! Thanks, Taz. The boys, though I told them to ask first, have planned a little welcome party for you. The office will throw a welcome party for you in a few days, but the guys you oversee wanted to throw you one at their house too. I hope that's okay."

I grin and nod. "Of course. It's no bother. It will give me a chance to see them in their natural habitat." I give them a wink as I say, "I'll see just how much trouble they are."

"No trouble at all, Ms. Monroe," one of the guys who looks to be closer to my age says.

I arch a brow. It takes me a moment, but I remember his name. "Is that so, Corin?"

He smirks. "Scouts honor. And you can call me Merc."

I laugh and shake my head; I doubt he was a boy scout. "Were you even in the scouts?"

His smirk widens, and he shakes his head. "Not at all."

Aubree laughs as she bumps my shoulder. "I should probably show you over to your desk, so you can get settled in."

I nod and turn back to the men. "It's a pleasure to meet you all. Oh, and you can call me Elizabeth or Liz."

"Nah. We'll find you a proper nickname. You're part of the team now," Vicy says with a grin.

"I look forward to it." I give them one last nod before following Aubree out of the gym.

"So, what do you think?" she asks with a smile.

I huff out a breath before returning her smile. "I'm excited to get started."

"Just so you know, your number has been entered into the employee database. We try to make everyone's number accessible in case of emergencies as well as easy communication."

"Understandable." Just then my phone goes off. Brows furrowed, I pull out my phone. Opening the screen, I see a text from an unknown number.

Aubree snickers. "That didn't take long." I look up at her in confusion as she points to my phone. "I'm sure that's the boys adding you to their group chat."

I open the message and click on the icon to see who all is in the chat. There is already a message waiting.

XXX-XXX-8525

> *Associate captain here! Raymond Victor AKA Vicy, also known as the greatest rightwing this team has ever seen.*

XXX-XXX-8327

> *If you hype yourself up anymore, Vic, you won't be able to play with that big head of yours.*

I quickly save the first number, so I at least have that one saved.

Vicy

> *That's Aillard Tasse, also known as Taz. Anywho, guess I'll introduce everyone in the group chat since our captain is a bit shy. He'll say he's antisocial, but I say it's the same thing.*

He makes me a list of all the players and the last four digits of their phone number, so I can add them to my contacts. I try to save each name and number as he sends them, not wanting to miss any.

Vicy

> *Along with being the best rightwing, I'll also be your favorite.*

I snort because I know several of the players can interchange positions. But that doesn't mean they don't have their favorites. Aubree gave me a list of the players along with their preferred positions. I'll make sure to add those to my notes in each of the players notebooks.

> *How do you know you're my favorite?*

Vicy

> *How could I not be?*

Gilly

> *I could be her favorite rightwing. You're not the only one in the group.*

It seems the others are checking their phones with the barrage of incoming messages. They will have to leave their phones in the locker room during practice, though.

> *He's right, he could be my favorite.*

Vicy

> *⊠ Blasphemy!*

Gilly

> *⊠ You're so dramatic. She literally just got here today.*

Vicy

> *So! I can still be her favorite!*

> *How about you're both my favorite for now?*

Vicy

...fine...

Peri

Stop acting like a child Vic. I'm sure she has work to do. Stop bothering her. Plus we need to get back to our workout.

Ozzy

He does have a point.

Tuck

Sorry to have disturbed you, Ms. Liz.

Just Liz.

Vicy

What about Lizzy?

⬚ Maybe...

Vicy

I'll take it!

Aren't you guys supposed to be getting ready for practice?

Vicy

Leaving now boss lady!

When I look up from my phone, I see that I've stopped in front of someone's door, and Aubree is looking at me with a knowing smile.

I feel my face blush as I put my phone in my pocket. "Sorry."

She shakes her head. "No worries. It's good to know they like you already." She shrugs. "As long as you get your work done, I don't mind you talking to them. We encourage you to develop a strong bond with the players, especially the guys in your group. You will be working closely together, and trust is very important."

She opens the door that leads to the offices and points to an empty desk in the corner. I notice that no one else has arrived yet. When she sees my questioning look, she smiles. "Everyone else is out for the day, either getting supplies or on holiday before the season begins. Time off is hard to come by once the season has started, so many try to plan ahead."

Nodding, I make my way over to the empty desk. There are several folders and envelopes neatly stacked on top. She points to them and explains, "Those are lists of your players as well as any notes from the previous therapist. You are more than welcome to go through them and get yourself settled. I'll be in the main offices if you need me or just send me a text."

She turns to leave but stops at the door and glances over her shoulder. "It was a pleasure meeting you. Welcome to the Washington Wraiths family, Liz."

"Thank you."

She gives me a quick nod before leaving. I look over the folders before taking a seat in the chair. With a deep breath, I begin flipping through the pages. It's time to get to work.

CHAPTER FOUR

W hat does one wear to a welcome party? *It's for me, so I can wear whatever I want, right? But it isn't an office party. This is being held at the house where the guys live. So maybe casual would be better, right? Ugh!*

I pull out my phone and immediately type a message in the group chat.

> So quick question, what does one wear to a welcome party?

> ⊠ What do you mean? Clothes obviously.

> ⊠Obviously. Is this a causal thing?

> Jeans and a tee are fine. Nothing fancy.

> Thank you! That's what I was asking. Clothes obviously ⊠

> Got ourselves a sassy one fellas! This is going to be fun!

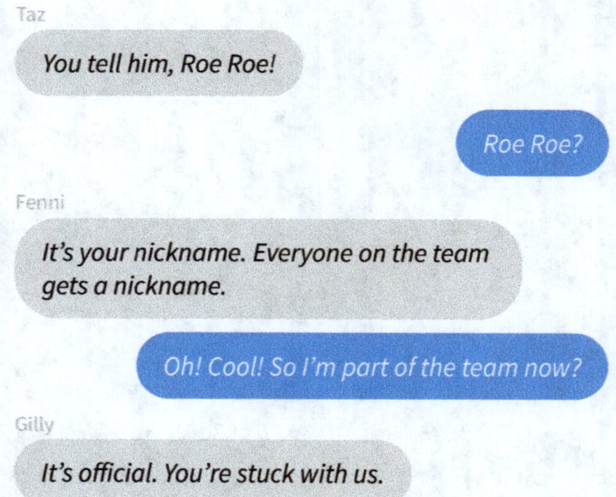

An audio file comes through, so I open it and can't help but laugh. It sounds like the whole team is together because there is a cacophony of male voices chanting, "One of us! One of us! One of us!"

I've only been with the team for five days, but I'll admit, I've never loved a job more. Well, other than teaching kids how to ice skate. But that doesn't count. That was more of a hobby than a job.

I send a quick text, then finish getting ready to head over.

Staring down at my phone for a moment, I realize there's one member in the chat who has been silent since I was added. The guys have been texting me all week while at work. Ironically needing to have their phones taken away because they were distracted. Their excuse? It was important they got to know their athletic therapist. Truthfully, the memes and gifs they constantly send have been making it harder to do my job.

Lewi is missing from the conversion now that I really look at it. The only time he said anything was when they all first messaged me their numbers. Odd. Is he not a talker, or does it have something to do with me?

Shaking my head, I pull on a pair of jeans and one of my favorite tees. It's a shirt my dad got me for my graduation. The front of it says, "If at first you don't succeed, try doing it the way your athletic therapist told you to do it the first time." It should get a few laughs from the guys.

I pull my hair into a pony and put an extra tie on my wrist. Then I slip into a pair of sneakers and grab my keys and wallet purse. I hate carrying a purse around, and I usually leave it in my car unless I actually need it. Tonight, it will be tucked in my center console and my keys will be clipped to my belt loop.

When I step outside, there's a note taped to my front door. *What in the...?* Peeling the folded note off my door, I open it.

I crumple the note and throw it on the ground. If this is someone's way of greeting their new neighbor, they are barking up the wrong tree.

Huffing out a sigh, I mumble, "Ha ha very funny, whoever you are. If you are going for creepy, you win. Leave me alone." I march down the stairs and out to my car.

Ten minutes later, I'm pulling up in front of the guys' house which, by the way, is not how I would define their house. Although, when I think of houses, my parents' small home is what I think of. This looks more like a mega house. I mean, it isn't quite a mansion, but it certainly isn't the type of house I had pictured, either.

It does have to house a lot of guys, though, so I suppose that needs to be taken into consideration. I park on the street, so I don't congest the driveway, in case any of the guys need to leave. Making my way up to the door, I go to knock but remember they said to walk in. Wiping my sweaty hands on my pants and taking a deep breath, I turn the knob.

What the... hell? The moment I walk inside, I'm greeted with a wide-open living space, but that's not what catches my attention. No, it's the three hockey players standing on the table, dancing and singing the Cruise remix by Florida Georgia Line featuring Nelly. Badly, may I add. Although, I'm not sure if they are actually trying to sing to the song or just playing around. I am going to go with playing. No one can dance or sing that badly.

No one seems to have noticed me yet, and considering how loud the music is, along with the general ruckus, I doubt they would be able to hear a bomb going off. Cupping my hands around my mouth, I yell, "Am I interrupting something?!"

They all turn to me and yell, "ROE ROE!"

I laugh, covering my ears until the music is turned down. "Seems like you boys are having fun. Hope I didn't interrupt."

Vicy grins from where he stands on top of the table and holds out a hand. "Want to join the fun?"

I shake my head, laughing. "No! Absolutely not. I am not a singer or a dancer. For good reason."

Taz does an overly dramatic shoulder shimmy and calls, "Come on. You don't have to be good at it to have fun."

I snort as I make my way to the kitchen area. "I'm still going to pass."

Vicy hops down from the table with a shrug. "Well, guess that leaves us to question you like crazy and eat."

I smirk. "I thought you guys questioned me already. You bugged me all week while I was trying to work."

"Lies," Taz says as he hops down and heads to the living room. He drops down onto the floor and gestures to the couch. "Sit. Sit. Time for questions!"

I look at him then turn back to the kitchen to admire the spread of food. As I look back at him, I point over my shoulder with an exaggerated pout. "But... food."

He grins. "One of the guys can bring you food. Sit. Sit."

I can get my own food, though, I don't need them to get it for me. Oli steps up beside me with a soft smile. "I'll bring you something to eat. I think Taz may bust a gut if he doesn't get to ask his questions."

"You sure?"

He nods, pushing me in the direction of the couch. "We have burgers or brats."

"Um... brat, please."

He nods. "Chips?"

"Sure. What do you have?"

He chuckles. "If you name it, we most certainly have it."

"Doritos?" I ask as I take a seat on the couch.

He nods again. "I'll get everything, and I'll bring the toppings over for you to pick what you want on it."

"Don't bother. I don't like toppings."

He looks over his shoulder with an arched brow. "No toppings?"

I shake my head. "I like a raw dog." I slap a hand over my mouth and feel my face burn red. *What the fuck did I just say? Why the fuck would I say that? Oh my god, kill me now!*

His eyes widen for a moment before he bursts into laughter and turns to head to the kitchen. "One raw dog coming up."

Embarrassment has me burying my face in my hands. After a moment, I feel the couch dip beside me, and I peek between my fingers to see who it is. Vicy greets me with a wide grin.

"I like you. You're funnier than our previous therapist," he snickers.

I groan, my hands still covering my face. My words come out muffled when I say, "This is such a bad first impression. Although, I suppose it's technically my second impression. Ugh! Either way, it's a bad impression."

"On the contrary; this is an amazing impression," Perri says from his spot on the chair next to the couch.

I peek through my fingers, looking at him as I ask, "How so?"

Merc speaks up. "The older guys"—he points to the four men who live outside of this house— "have learned to filter our words and watch what we say around women in the hockey industry. A lot of women are switching to this industry, which is great, but it means that what we say is often thought of as inappropriate."

Fenni builds off of Merc's thoughts. "We don't always mean for what we say to sound vulgar, it's just often how it comes out. The youngest ones here often have trouble with their filter. Which can cause issues, especially because our previous athletic therapist was male and, now, we have a female."

"The things we used to joke about when getting stretched or taped by our therapist were all in good fun, but they could come across as inappropriate if we said them to you," Gilly says with a sigh.

"Basically, these fuckers are saying that your mind appears to be as dirty as theirs," Lewi says, his voice ringing out behind me. I jump at the sound of his voice, not having noticed he was here. He has avoided talking to me all week, and now he chooses to say something?

I watch him make his way around the couch and take a seat on the floor next to my legs. *Interesting spot choice.* Oli clears his throat behind me, and when I turn, he hands me a plate piled high with food.

"What Lewi means is that it's nice to know you have a similar sort of humor. And that if we say anything inappropriate, you understand we don't mean to. Just let us know if you are uncomfortable with anything we say or do, and we will stop."

Lewi snorts, muttering, "I said what I meant."

Ozzy kicks him in the leg from his spot on the loveseat. "Be nice!"

Lewi groans, "I am."

"Try harder," Tuck huffs beside Ozzy.

As the tension in the room grows, I decide to squash it while I can. "Taz, you have questions for me, right?"

His eyes meet mine. Taking the cue, he nods. "Right. Um... let's see. Where are you from?"

I smile. "Here, actually. I'm from Tacoma. My parents don't live too far from here, which is nice."

"You're close to your parents?" Lewi asks.

The question catches me a bit off guard, and it takes a moment for my brain to compute. "Oh! Yeah, we are. My parents helped me get through school, even though I told them not to. I'm an only child, but not for lack of trying on my parents' part."

Oli hops over the couch and sits beside me. "Did you like being an only child?"

I shrug. "I didn't mind it. Made it hard to get away with anything, though. There wasn't a little sister or brother to blame stuff on."

Taz laughs. "I bet." He scoots a bit closer before leaning back on his hands. "Have you always loved hockey, or was this just the best offer type of thing?"

"This was a dream offer; I love hockey. I watched it with my dad growing up. I purposefully picked teams that he hated when I was younger. I'm pretty sure I almost gave him an ulcer once when I told him my favorite team was based on whoever had the cutest goalie that year."

The guys chuckle as Oli asks, "Why the goalie?"

I shrug. "My dad's favorite player was a defenseman. I thought it would be funny."

"And who is your favorite player?" Vicy questions.

I smirk as I press a finger to my lips. "That's a trade secret."

Merc laughs as he joins Taz on the floor. "Fine. Let's ask the most important question of them all, can you skate?"

I stiffen without meaning to. It isn't a secret. When Oli appears to notice, he raises a brow. "You good?"

Shaking myself, I force my body to relax again. "Yeah... yeah, I'm good. Um...yeah, I can skate."

Merc, seeming to realize that it is a sensitive subject, quickly changes it. "Well, guys, it seems we have a keeper. She gets our sense of humor, likes dirty jokes, and she can skate."

"She's pretty too," Taz adds with a grin.

Vicy hums beside me. "Mhm, that is a good point."

I playfully smack him with the back of my hand. "What's that supposed to mean?"

Vicy shrugs. "It's a good point is all I'm saying. The last guy was old, and now we have a pretty lady looking after us."

Narrowing my eyes a bit, I ask, "So you only like me because I'm pretty."

"I most certainly never said that."

"You implied it." I turn to Oli beside me, trying to hide my smirk as I say, "Didn't he? He implied he only likes me because I'm pretty."

Oli nods, continuing the charade. "He did. I heard it."

Vicy grins and says, "*Mange la merde!*"

I, of course, have no idea what that means, but it's clear everyone else does when they begin laughing. Taz must see my confusion and tells me, "He said eat shit."

I nod and try to repeat the words but, apparently, butcher them. Vicy just smiles. "You need to produce the sounds from the back of the mouth. But you did well on your first try."

I laugh. "You will have to teach me more French, so I can practice. Curse words are especially fun when no one understands you."

Taz smacks the floor with his palm as he laughs. "Ain't that the truth."

The guys continue with their questions, to which I gladly answer. They even answer a few of mine as well. As I sit there getting more comfortable with each question, I notice Oli lift an arm and rest it on the back of the couch behind my head. What gets my cheeks heated, though, is the way he shifts to get more comfortable by leaning closer to me. *Does he realize he's doing it?*

I peek over to find him laughing as he engages in conversation with Ozzy and Tuck on the loveseat beside us. He must feel my eyes on him because he turns to me. With a smile, he asks, "Everything okay, Chérie?"

Fucking hell. I can feel my face growing hotter. "Y-yeah... fine. I'm-I'm fine," I stutter.

His eyes rove over my face before meeting my eyes again. "Are you sure? Your face is red. Are you getting too warm?"

Oh my god! Is he serious right now? Does he not have a single clue as to why I may be blushing?

A snort from the floor by my feet has my eyes flicking over to a grinning Lewi. "If her face gets any redder, I think she may combust in your arms, Mac." He arches a brow as he asks, "Has a man never been that close to you before? You're blushing like a virgin."

If it were possible to die from humiliation, this would be the moment. My mouth drops open in shock as the room turns deathly silent. The last time I was this embarrassed was when Emmitt left me on the ice with a broken ankle. My eyes begin to burn with tears as the heaviness of the emotion falls over me.

Before anyone says anything, I jump up from the couch. My voice is low as I say, "I believe it's time for me to go." Without waiting, I rush toward the door, slipping from Vicy's grasp when he tries to stop me.

His voice sounds a little desperate as I run past. "Roe Roe! Don't leave."

Waving a hand over my head, I continue toward the door and yell over my shoulder, "It's been fun, but it's getting late. Thank you for having me."

I hear a thump behind me, then Perri's grumbled words. "*Connard!*"

With how thick his accent is, I assume that's another French word. I push through the door, closing it behind me and rushing to my car. I hate crying, and I hate it even more when it's due to embarrassment.

I hear the door open behind me and look back to see Oli rushing out after me. He keeps muttering, "*Putain*" loudly to himself—whatever that means. When he sees me beside my car, he rushes in my direction. "Please wait! Don't leave."

I huff a sigh and wipe the few tears that managed to fall before he can see them. I wait, because how the hell can I not? He's been nothing but sweet, and this isn't his fault.

"I'm so sorry," he rushes to say before stopping in front of me.

Good lord, he's tall. He's definitely got a foot and some change on me. I wipe another tear that escapes before replying. "You have nothing to apologize for."

He slowly reaches out a hand but then hesitates. His fingers curl into a fist before he lowers it back to his side. "I do. I didn't realize I was making you uncomfortable. Forgive me. I didn't notice how close I was sitting to you—it felt so natural."

My eyes finally meet his, and even in the darkness, I can still make out their almond color. They look pained though. As if he truly feels responsible for me running off. Biting my lip, I debate what to say as my eyes dart back down to his chest. "I-I didn't... feel...uncomfortable." Exhaling a sigh of frustration, I rub the back of my neck. "To be honest, this whole thing is new to me."

His keeps his voice soft as he asks, "Do you mind explaining?"

"I... I don't trust easily. It takes a while before someone can earn my trust. I was..."—I swallow thickly—"I was burned by someone close to me, and since then, I've found it hard to make friends," I say, rocking awkwardly on my heels.

When I look up, Oli is ruffling his hair, a frown on his face. He briefly looks back at the house, then back at me. "I promise Lewi isn't bad. He... well, he's been burned, too, and he doesn't take to new people well. He does his best to push them away before he can get attached. The guys and I—we—" He groans. "But that isn't an excuse for his behavior."

The smirk that pulls at my lips surprises me. "It wasn't his words that bothered me, to be honest. It was the fact he said them in front of everyone."

His brows knit together as if he doesn't follow. "Why does that matter?"

Groaning, I explain, "I'm trying to make a good impression here. I don't want everyone to think I'm crushing on you like a dang horny teenager. Relationships between the players and staff are frowned upon and, to add to it, I'm new."

He laughs but beams down at me. "So you crushing on me would be bad? Or are you saying I'm not handsome enough for you to crush on?"

"Yes, the crushing would be bad, and it would be easy to crush on you."

His smile widens. "So... you find me handsome?"

I roll my eyes but laugh. "Yes, you are handsome. As I'm sure the puck-bunnies have told you many times"

"But you could never have a crush on me?" His eyes glisten with mischief as he continues to grin down at me.

I pause before I mutter, "Correct." What is he getting at?

He takes a step back, then quickly boops me on the nose. "Challenge accepted."

He runs back into the house before my brain can reboot and make sense of what he said. *Challenge accepted? Wait... he wouldn't... would he?* He's inside before I can reply, but I yell anyway. "Wait. Wait! That wasn't a challenge!"

What did I just get myself into?

Chapter Five

The group chat with the boys has been blowing up all weekend. I debated turning my phone off, but that would probably have only made things worse. The owner of the local ice rink had reached out to me before I moved, asking if I had any interest in teaching the children's figure skating class. To which, I immediately said yes, on the caveat he understood that once the hockey season started, he would need to find another teacher to take over. I won't be able to make it every weekend. Between the amount of regular season games the team plays and the travel to and from away games, there's not a lot of time left in my schedule.

Saturday is spent filling out paperwork and skating on the ice to clear my head. Not that it helps. The boys continue to blow up my phone, and Oli's words still ring loudly in my head. *Challenge accepted.* Does he actually like me, or is this all a game? He can't possibly like me already; we met a week ago. Well, almost a week. But still.

Sunday greets me with audio clips in the group chat since I didn't answer their texts. Most of them are from Vicy and Taz. They are acting like little brothers, which I find oddly endearing and only slightly annoying. As an only child, I don't know if it is normal that I find their antics both irritating and hilarious.

When I press play on the first audio message from Vicy, there's a whine in his voice as he says, *"Roe Roe! Answer our texts. We are getting worried!"*

Rolling my eyes, I click on the next clip from Taz, who sounds equally disgruntled that I haven't answered. *"Yeah! Come on. At least let us know you are still alive!"*

As I'm debating whether to text them back or not, Oli's voice in the next message has me caving. *"Ignore them, Chérie. Text us when you have a moment. No hurry."*

Huffing a sigh, I send a quick text, refusing to send a voice message.

> I'm alive; I've just been busy.

It isn't a lie, but it isn't the whole truth, either. Truthfully, I'm not sure how to act around them now. I like that I am growing closer to the boys, but the fact that it's happening so fast has me second guessing myself. I should be acting like a professional instead of their friend. Almost as soon as my text is sent, I'm greeted with responses from Vicy and Taz.

Vicy

> She lives!

Taz

> Finally! We were getting worried Roe Roe!

> You're acting as if you haven't spoken to me in months. I just saw you on Friday at the party.

Vicy

> You ran out! We didn't get the chance to say bye.

Taz

Yeah. We wanted to make sure you were okay.

For the record, you two are acting like annoying little brothers.

Vicy

We heard there was an opening.

Taz

How would you know what a little brother acts like? You said you were an only child.

It's how I imagine little brothers would act.

Vicy

Do you mind?

Taz

Yeah. We aren't making you uncomfortable, are we?

I can't help but smile as I look at the messages from these two. To be honest, I love it. The banter with the pair has made me feel more welcome in their group. I don't feel as much like an outsider joining in. I feel like I'm already one of them.

I don't mind. Brothers are cool right?

Vicy

The coolest! I'll be the favorite of course.

Taz

Connerie!

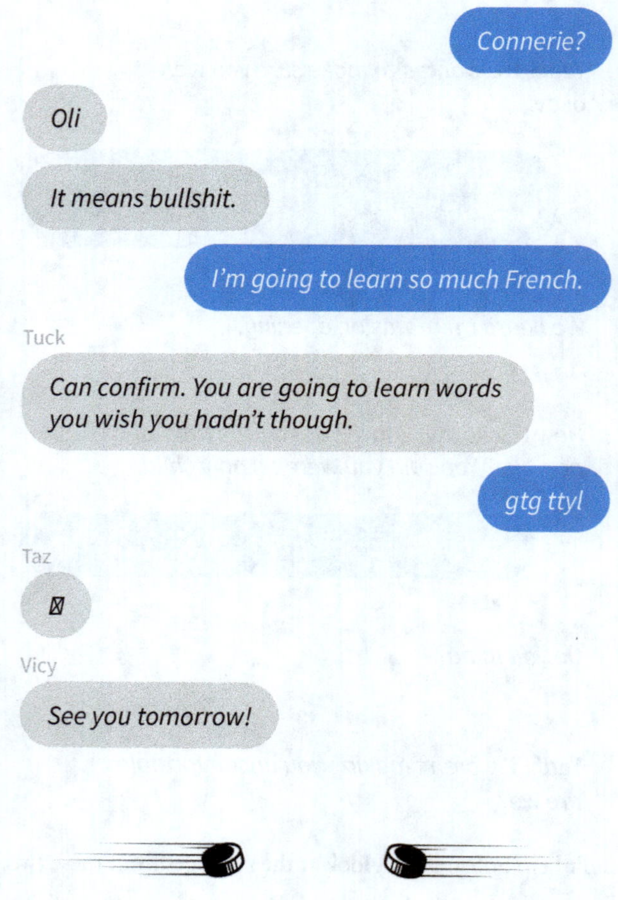

Monday. I hate Mondays. With a groan, I drop my head to rest on my desk. No amount of coffee can make a Monday feel less like a Monday. *Why do Mondays suck so much?* I still have a ton of work to get done. There are lists to be made. Medical records to review. Plus, I was greeted with another creepy note this morning. I didn't get one all weekend but, apparently, my hope that they had stopped was in vain.

I shiver as I remember the words scrawled across the small note.

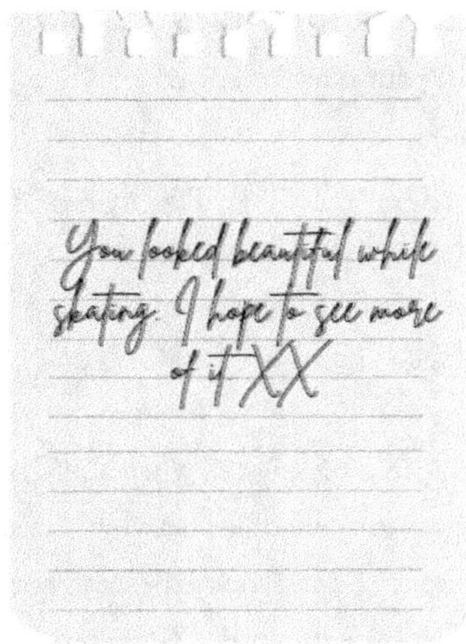

Whoever this person is knows where I have been and has obviously been watching me. I never noticed anything odd, but that just means I need to be more observant when I'm at the rink now. I also need to pay better attention as I drive to see if anyone has been following me.

Jerked out of my thoughts by a knock on the door, I lift my head and call, "Come in."

A man, who definitely has the silver fox look going for him, pokes his head through the doorway. He smiles and raises a hand in greeting. "Thought I should come by and introduce myself. I'm Max Spencer, the head athletic therapist. I'll be working with you and Danni."

I go to stand, but he stops me with a wave. "You don't have to get up." He laughs as he slips farther into the room. "I know Mondays can be a bitch. There's coffee and snacks in the break room. I just wanted to make sure to stop by before you are bombarded by the team."

I tilt my head and blink at him a second before my office door is suddenly flung open again. I let out a squeak of surprise when it hits the wall and reveals Taz and Vicy standing there panting. Max chuckles and points at the door as if to say 'told you so'. "Case and point. Boys, you shouldn't scare your new therapist."

They both mutter, "Sorry."

Max shakes his head but nods to me. "I'll leave you to it then. I'm sure they will all be here soon." He slips out of the door right as Oli shows up. Oli nods briefly to Max before turning to look at me. He smiles as if to say 'hello', but it looks as if he's dragged someone along behind him.

I'm about to ask what's going on, when a different man is shoved through the doorway into my office between Taz and Vicy. My eyes widen when I realize it's Lewi. I look expectantly between the four of them, waiting for someone to explain. When no one does, I hesitantly ask, "What's all this about?"

Vicy and Taz have huge grins on their faces as Oli says, "Lewi has something to say."

My eyes fall on Lewi as he straightens and unruffles his jersey. He looks everywhere but at me, rubbing the back of his neck. I peek at the others again before leaning back in my chair. "What is it that you need to speak to me about?"

His eyes quickly flick to mine before they drop to the ground. When he speaks, his voice is barely audible. "I shouldn't have said what I did on Friday."

Crossing my arms over my chest, I say, "Agreed."

He runs a frustrated hand through his hair while glaring up at the ceiling. "I'm sorry for what I said. It won't happen again."

It's odd to see this normally grumpy smartass look completely uncomfortable in my presence. I'm sure apologizing isn't something he normally does. "Are you sorry that you said it, or are you only apologizing because the others dragged you here?"

His eyes finally meet mine, and his dark-chocolate pits, usually filled with anger, have changed to a soft milk-chocolate full of insecurity. "I'm doing it because I want to not because I have to."

I slowly stand from my chair and move toward him, pausing once I'm in front of him. He stiffens in response. What does he think I am going to do? Offering him a soft smile, I say, "Thank you for apologizing. You mind if we start over?"

He looks at me quizzically for a moment as if unsure of my motives. "So, you forgive me?"

My smile grows, and I hold out a hand. "Hey! My name is Elizabeth Monroe. You can call me Liz or Lizzy. Izzy is off limits. I'm the new athletic therapist. I've heard you're one of the players I'm in charge of."

He stares down at my hand for a moment as if confused. His eyes meet mine, and he tilts his head to the side with a small grin but then reaches out and shakes my offered hand. "Dean Lewis, but the team calls me Lewi. I'm one of your centers."

The way he says *'your'* seems like he's implying something more. Ignoring the flutter in my chest his words give me, I go to slip my hand out of his, but he tightens his hold. Brows knitting, I watch him step closer. He bends to whisper in my ear, "Thank you."

Lewi steps back, releasing my hand in the process, then turns to the others, his face shifting back into his normal grumpy profile. "There. I've apologized. She forgives me. Can we go back to working out now?"

The others shoot me a quick look, and all I can do is shrug. "We're good." Shifting my gaze back to Lewi, when he looks back at me, I can't help but ask, "Right?"

He nods. "We're good, Lizzy."

My face heats at the use of the nickname. He must notice my blush because a small smirk pulls at his lips before he turns back to the others. "Let's go, fuckers! She's got work to do."

"I was expecting more bloodshed. That was disappointing," Vicy whines.

Taz hums in agreement. "I thought she would at least punch him in the face."

Oli chuckles. "You two are bloodthirsty."

I laugh. "Sorry to disappoint, boys. Now, get out of my office, so I can get some work done before you blow up the group chat."

Vicy and Taz both groan as they make their way back down the hallway. Oli gives me a smile and says, "You should come by the house again. We have a few cheat days left before the dietitians crack down on us for the start of the season."

"So, what you're saying is there may be ice cream?"

He shrugs. "Possibly."

Shaking my head, I laugh. "I'll see what I can do. May bring some of my work with me, though. I need to make sure I have every note on you guys that I could possibly need before the season starts."

"If you need help, let me know." He gives me a wink, then says, "Sounds like a date."

"Not a date, Oli."

He hums as he leaves the room. "Debatable."

I wish I could yell that it *isn't* up for debate because it isn't a date. But then everyone else in the building would hear, and I don't need that headache. So I settle for growling, "Not a date."

Lewi snickers as he heads to the door. "There's no talking him out of things once he has made a decision."

"Come on, Lewi, you gotta help me out here."

He shakes his head. "We've been friends for years. There's no way I can talk him out of it. He's got his sights set on you."

I lean against my desk as I pinch the bridge of my nose. "What's that supposed to mean?"

His eyes gleam with laughter as he smirks. "It means, be prepared."

"Gonna need a little more information than that, Lewi."

He raps his knuckles against the doorframe before saying, "He tends to attach himself to people he feels needs a little extra... care." He's silent for a moment before clearing his throat. "Anyway, I'll leave you to your work. See ya tonight."

I offer him a nod, and he turns to leave. I didn't know Lewi and Oli were that close, though, I suppose I should have guessed. Their personalities are completely different. Shaking my head, I sit down and get back to work. My phone dings with a notification, and I glance down to find a personal message from Oli. Odd. Clicking on it, I feel my cheeks burn as I read his sweet words.

Oli

> *You look beautiful today. Don't overwork yourself, and if you need help let me know. Also, drink water. Coffee doesn't count* ⊠

Why does this man have to make me feel like a teenage girl again? Huffing out a heavy sigh, I decide to reply. The man needs to stop making my heart flutter and my cheeks hurt from the constant smiling.

> *Thank you, but I bet you say that to all the girls. You have a large fan base. Also, coffee does count, it has water in it.*

Oli

> *I don't pay much attention to my fans. Plus, they only like me for my body or my money,*

so I'll pass. Coffee does not count. Go drink water.

What if I'm out for your money? Coffee helps me stay awake, water will not. Coffee for the win.

Oli

You would never. Ozzy is headed your way with water.

You're making Ozzy walk all the way here to give me water? Seriously, I can get it myself.

Oli

I'm not making him. He offered. Would you have actually gone and gotten water your-self?

...yes...

Oli

⌧ If you say so, Chérie. Ozzy should be there soon. gtg.

There's a knock at my door, and I look up to find Ozzy smiling and holding out a bottle of water. "As requested, one water hand delivered to our favorite athletic therapist."

Rolling my eyes, I say, "I haven't been here long enough to be your favorite."

He shrugs, setting the bottle on my desk. "My statement still stands. Oli said you are going to stop by tonight."

"I told him I *may* come by tonight."

"How can we turn the may into a solid coming over tonight?"

Tapping on the pile of files I need to get through, I say, "Well, I need to get through all of these files. We'll see how long that takes."

With a nod, he backs toward the door. "Then consider me gone, boss lady. I'll make sure the guys don't bug you through the group chat."

The lengths these boys will go to just so I'll agree to come over. "Fine. I'll be there tonight."

He shoots me a wide grin as he leaves my office. "Good! See you tonight."

It's absolutely too easy to say 'yes' to these boys.

CHAPTER SIX

I double check that I've grabbed everything before I leave for the night. *Ten notebooks? Check. Different colored pens? Check.* Okay, I should have everything. My phone buzzes and somehow, I juggle everything and manage to pull it out of my back pocket. Huffing out a sigh, I open the group chat. Surprisingly, it's from Lewi.

Are you still coming over to the house tonight?

That's the plan. I just finished packing all my stuff up. I'm headed out now.

Need any help?

Should be good.

Let us know when you get here.

Is there a reason I'm letting you know when I'm there instead of just knocking on the door?

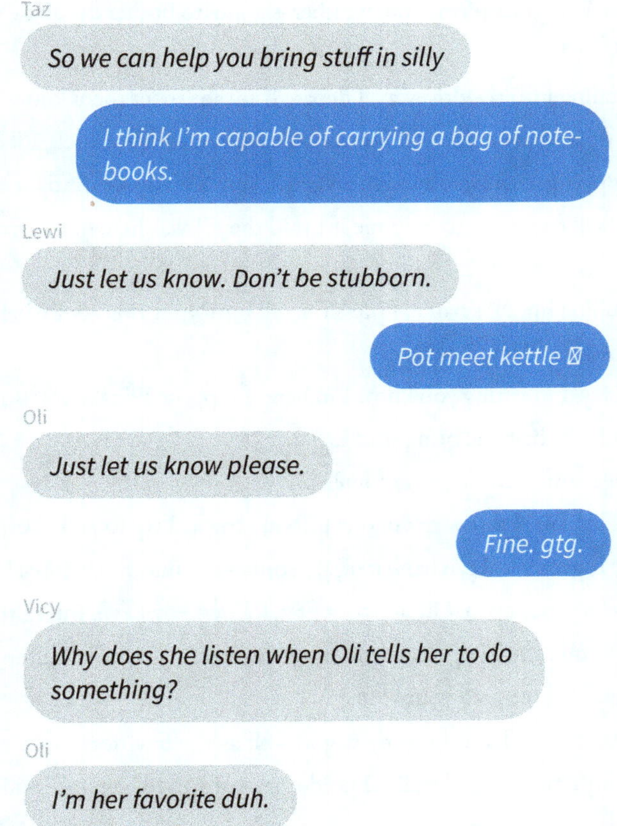

I laugh, putting my phone away as I walk out to my car. A sharp pain shoots up my leg, and I wince. Leaning up against the car, I lift my leg to wiggle my ankle and groan. As I'm rolling it around, I look up at the sky. Appears the weather is about to change. Spending so much time in Florida made me forget how much my ankle hates the cold weather changes.

Once the pain dulls to a manageable ache, I slowly increase the weight on my foot while I get everything into the car before slipping in myself. Taking a few deep breaths, I start the car. I'm going to need to stock up on aspirin if the weather is going to bother my ankle this badly.

Pulling into the driveway, I debate if I want to let them know I'm here or not. My ankle still hurts a bit and, knowing my luck, I'll end up tripping with everything in my arms. I can already see the fight over who will come out to help me if I told them I was here in the group chat.

Pulling up Oli's name, I press the call button. It rings twice before he answers, "Hey, Roe Roe."

"Hey, I'm letting you know I'm here. I suppose I'll take you up on the offer to help me bring stuff in."

He snorts. "Be out in a moment."

"Thanks." I throw my phone into my bag as I try to gather everything together so I can hand it off. It's only a few minutes before I hear the front door open. Oli steps out first, followed by Lewi. Interesting.

Oli smiles as he opens the door for me, holding out a hand for my things. "Let me grab your stuff."

I smirk as I hand him my bag as well as the few notebooks that wouldn't fit. "I didn't realize I needed two of you to help me inside."

Lewi shrugs as he waits for me to step out of the car. "We made a rule to always have a buddy with us no matter what. Keeps everyone out of trouble."

With a nod, I stand, trying to suppress a wince as I sidestep to close the door. Lewi must have seen the wince though because he arches a brow. "You good?"

"I'm fine."

He crosses his arms over his chest, and his eyes narrow. "Lizzy?"

Exhaling a sigh, I begin shuffling toward the front door. I know I can't completely hide my limp from Oli or Lewi.

Oli rushes to jump in front of me, which forces me to jerk to a stop to avoid bumping into him. He looks down at me with an arched brow. "Did something happen today at work? You didn't have that limp earlier."

Rolling my lips between my teeth, I try to avoid his gaze but cave when he continues to stare at me, waiting for an answer. "It's the weather. Just an old ankle injury, nothing new or crazy," I say, groaning.

He hums. "Nothing crazy?"

I nod. "Nothing crazy. Can we go inside now?"

He backs away, turns, and heads to the front door. "Yep. Come on inside. You can sit on the couch, so you can put your feet up."

With an eye roll, I follow him. "I don't need to do that. I'm fine."

"Just put them up," Lewi says from behind me. "You can't argue against us. We've all had ankle injuries. What would you tell us to do if it were the other way around?"

Scrunching up my nose, I huff out, "Elevate and rest the ankle."

He laughs. "Exactly. So, take your own advice. You're planning to work on paperwork anyways."

"Fine," I growl out. He's right, but I don't want him to know that. And my ankle is starting to ache more with each step. Sighing, I make my way over to the couch and do as I'm told; I sit and prop my legs up on the arm of the couch.

Lewi lifts my legs and places a pillow underneath my feet before sitting beside me on the couch. Oli holds out my bag and my loose notebooks. "You may be our athletic therapist, but we are going to take care of you just as much as you take care of us."

I smirk as I take my things from him. "So, you're only taking care of me because I'm your athletic therapist?"

He boops me on the nose before walking away. "You know I'll take care of you for other reasons."

My gaze meets Lewi's, and he gives me a wink, then mouths 'told you'.

Rolling my eyes, I focus back on my notebooks. I still need to make a few more notes about some of the players. It's not until I hear my name being called that I realize I've zoned out. Looking up from my paper, I see everyone around the room staring at me. "What?"

Taz laughs. "What has you focused on your work?"

I look down at the pages in front of me before looking at him. "I'm writing things down about you guys. Each book is dedicated to one of you."

Taz arches a brow as he asks, "Which player are you working on right now?"

I flip the page around to show him. "You."

"Me?" He shuffles closer to me. "What kind of stuff do you have in there?"

I shrug and return to writing. "I have stuff about all past injuries. What injuries I need to keep an eye on for this season. What allergies you have. Stuff like that."

He hums. "You got any personal notes in there?"

"Like what?" I ask absentmindedly.

"Like my favorite color or my favorite candy."

Without thinking, I say, "Your favorite color is green if I had to guess, and I've seen you sneak M&M's when you think no one is watching." I realize then that it's silent, which is odd considering their conversations had been my white noise for the last hour or so. I flick my gaze up again to find the guys all looking at me with deer-in-the-head-light eyes.

"What?"

Taz shakes himself before answering. "How do you know all that?"

Shrugging, I say, "I watch you guys practice on a daily basis, and I've picked up on things while I've spent hours a day observing you guys." I point over to Ozzy with my pen. "He favors his left side when he hasn't done enough stretching. Which is something we will be working on this week, by the way."

He gives me a sheepish smile. "I wasn't favoring my left side that much."

I arch a brow. "If I noticed it, you were."

"Well, you seem to know so much about us, but we know next to nothing about you," Vicy points out.

Closing the notebook, I say, "Well, ask me whatever you want."

Vicy taps his chin. "We should ask her something hard to answer. None of those easy questions."

Surprisingly, It's Lewi who speaks up. "How do you see yourself in life?"

Stunned by his question, it takes me a moment to form a reply. "How... how do I see myself?"

He nods like it's a totally normal question. "Yeah. Are you where you want to be? Doing what you want to be doing? Do you still have dreams you want to strive for? That sort of thing."

It takes me a moment to really think about my answer. Tapping the pen to my cheek, I say, "You guys know how waiting rooms work?"

They all nod as Lewi says, "Yeah."

"So, it was like I'd been stuck in a waiting room. I was waiting and waiting for something to happen. You're not sure if it's going to be big or small, but you know something is going to happen. You're just stuck waiting until it does."

"You say, it was not is. Do you not feel that way now?" Oli asks from his seat on the loveseat behind me.

Looking down at the notebook on my lap, but not really seeing it, my brows furrow. "I feel like I'm no longer in the waiting room, instead I'm stuck behind a glass wall. I can see all these amazing things happening. One by one everyone's dreams are coming true."

"But your dream hasn't come true, Roe Roe?" Taz asks.

I shrug. "I'm here as an athletic therapist for the NHL. It's been a big dream of mine, and here I am. But..."

"But what?" Lewi pushes.

My eyes meet his as I say, "I'm still stuck behind the glass wall. I'm too afraid to let go of my past dream. As if it was never a dream at all. A forgotten dream, part of a forgotten past." My eyes drop back down to my lap. "I don't mind forgetting the past, it's the dream I'm not ready to let go of."

"Then don't," Oli says from behind me, as if it were that simple.

I meet his eyes and say, "But I'll be stuck behind the glass wall. I'll never be able to move forward."

He shrugs. "Who says you have to let go of past dreams to move forward? And even if you're stuck behind the glass wall, you won't be stuck forever."

"How are you so sure of that?"

He gives me a crooked grin as he says, "Because I believe in you. You'll make all your dreams come true."

I feel my cheeks heat. "I'm not so sure about that."

He laughs. "You're not alone anymore. If you need some help along the way, you have us." His eyes soften as he says, "You've got me."

Chapter Seven

J uly has finally arrived, and Saturday is officially my favorite day of the week. I wave goodbye to the kids, and they enthusiastically wave back. The song Set It All Free by Scarlett Johansson plays in the background. It has become one of the kids' favorites to skate to. I've officially started teaching an ice-skating class at the local rink. As the last child leaves, the mom gives me a nod and walks through the door. I look around the rink and realize that the children helped clean up more than I expected. The clock on the wall reads six-fifteen, which means I've got some time to play if I want. *Should I get some skating time in?* With how busy everyone's been preparing for the season, I haven't had many chances lately.

Maybe it will help with the stress of someone leaving me random notes. Every day there is a new note waiting for me, but the one I found the day after hanging out with the guys was the most disturbing.

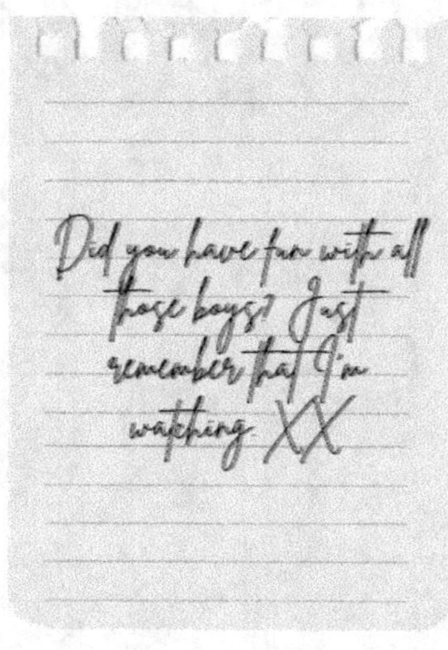

As a shiver runs down my spine, I look around the rink but find that I'm alone. At least, I think I'm alone. Trying to shake off the feel of invisible eyes, I glide across the ice and reach over the edge to grab my wireless headphones. I disconnect my phone from the rink's Bluetooth speaker, so I can connect it to my headphones. Scrolling through my playlist, I find my favorite song from my favorite anime; Yuri on ICE by Taro Umebayashi. The piano makes my heart race each time I listen to it. My favorite scene in the show is when he skates to this song.

I wait till I'm in the center of the ice to tap play. It may have taken some time, but I've been back on the ice practicing these last ten years. Re-learning what felt natural to my body. The first two years were hell, but I never stopped, never gave up. I remember Yuri's routine to this song, each jump and spin. I remember practicing when I was younger. How badly I wanted to imitate Yuri.

Landing jumps still gives me trouble, but I wouldn't let that stop me from trying. I spin to press my toe pick into the ice for a quadruple toe loop, double toe loop combo. I have to remind myself to use my right foot with jumps but always land on my left. It still feels odd to do things backward, but I can't land on my right leg anymore. Not since the doctors repaired my ankle.

I wobble a bit as I land, but I did land it. With a smile, I continue moving through the choreographed steps I've practiced so often. My chest feels lighter with each move I make. My smile grows as I feel true freedom, flying across the ice. I've felt like a bird with a broken wing for too long. I've felt the sun's rays, and the wind on my face, but it's not the same as flight.

The quadruple salchow is next and, surprisingly, I land that as well. My breathing comes quicker as this is the longest I've skate on my ankle since that disastrous day. I feel the slight twinge, but I can't stop. After a triple flip, I stick my landing and spread my arms wide just as the music slows. My face is turned toward the ceiling as if looking up to the sky.

Everyone tells me I have nothing to prove. But I do. I have everything to prove! I *have* to prove it to that sixteen-year-old girl who lost all hope. I need to prove to that girl that just because I was injured doesn't mean her love for skating will ever die.

To prove that—though her dreams of making the Olympics may be dead—the ability to skate will never die. All the years she struggled to get through physical therapy were worth it! The pain of re-learning how to walk on that leg was worth it!

My eyes begin to burn as I scream at my sixteen-year-old self. *It's worth every broken step! It will be worth it all to get to this moment!* I need to prove that what the female medic said was true. Dreams are fluid things. They change, adapt, and grow with you.

It's coming... the triple axel. I could hardly land it in practice after my injury, no matter how much I tried, but I need to try now. For her. For me. A bubble of laughter slips through my lips as I land it.

Not perfectly by any means, but I landed it. As I seamlessly move into the quadruple toe loop, I can feel the ache in my ankle. I know I'm overdoing it, but I can't quit. Not now.

It's getting harder to control my breathing, but even with the burn in my chest, I refuse to quit. *Triple axel, then move into a single-toe loop. Now triple salchow.* My left ankle almost gives out on me, but I manage to keep going.

I can feel tears streaming down my face as I continue. The pain in my ankle has turned into a pulsing throb. *Don't stop now! You can't stop! Prove to little Lizzy that Emmitt didn't break you. He didn't shatter your dreams! Prove it to her!*

Burying the toe pick into the ice, I do the triple lutz, then move into the triple toe loop. *I'll prove it! I'll prove it to them all!*

I don't mean to, but a scream bursts out of me as I attempt the quadruple flip and land it. A sob bubbles out, but I continue the routine. My chest is heaving when I pause in the final position. *I... I did it. I fucking did it!*

My ankles finally give, and I fall to the ground. I twist on the ice and lie spread eagle as I pant heavily. My eyes blur with the tears dripping down my face. The song switches to Never Enough by Kelly Clarkson, and my body jerks in surprise when I hear another pair of skates cut across the ice. I look up to find Oli racing toward me.

"Liz! You, okay?" The look of concern on his face makes me smile. He never looks that worried.

My head falls back to the ice. "I'm fine, Oli."

"You fell so quickly. Are you sure you are alright?"

I lift my head off the ice again as my brows furrow. "How long have you been here?"

His cheeks flush pink as he stutters, "Um... well... you see. I... shit! I didn't mean to watch, but when you started skating, you looked so beautiful. I had to watch."

I smirk. "Is that so?"

"I came by to look at the hockey lessons sign-up sheet. You happened to be here, and I may or may not have seen you teaching the kids. I stuck around for a bit and was planning to leave, but then you started skating, and I couldn't look away." He huffs out a sigh and ruffles his hair. "I had no idea you could skate like that, Roe Roe."

I hold out a hand to him. "Can you help me up?"

He nods, reaching out a hand for me to grab. "Yeah, of course."

He lifts me easily, and I wobble a bit on my tired legs, so he scoops me back up into his arms bridal style. I let out a squeak of protest. "You don't have to carry me, Oli."

He shakes his head. "You did something to your ankle. Let's not make it worse."

I can't stop the blush that heats my cheeks as the song ends and switches to Can I Have This Dance by Joshua Bassett and Sofia Wylie. Trying to cover my embarrassment, I huff out a sigh. "You're probably right. I shouldn't have skated like that; I'll need some ice."

He nods before yelling, "Lewi! Get some ice!"

My head jerks up, and I look around. There he is. Standing at the edge of the rink, staring wide-eyed and mouth agape. I groan and cover my face with my hand. "Please tell me he wasn't watching too."

"If I did, I would be lying, Liz."

A shiver races down my spine at hearing his deep voice say my name. It's odd, but I like it when they call me by name. The nickname makes me feel like I am part of the team, but him using my name makes it feel like we are friends. When he said my name, it sent a flutter of delight through me.

"Thank you, Mac," I whisper.

His cheeks pinken, and he gives me a nod. "No problem."

He sets me down on the bench and begins to unlace my skates. I should have worn a brace on my bad ankle, but then there would have been no freedom of movement in my skates. I was too constricted in my brace for skating. Oli's eyes meet mine as he holds onto my left skate. "May I?" he asks softly.

I nod.

He gently removes the skate and sets it aside before removing my sock, so he can get a better look at my ankle. He presses softly on the now-puffy skin, looking up at me to gauge my reaction. With a soft smile, I say, "It doesn't hurt too badly."

He hums. "It's a little swollen but shouldn't be too bad. You should probably put some ice on it just in case." He moves onto my other ankle and gingerly pulls off that skate too.

When he removes it, I can't help but hiss out a curse. *Shit. This isn't going to be good.* He's gentle as he removes my sock, and I watch his face when he takes in my foot first. I definitely overdid it. My foot is already swollen and bruised. With his thumb, he softly caresses the swelling as he turns my ankle to the left. His eyes widen when he turns it to the right, taking in everything. He slowly rolls the edge of my leggings to mid-calf before meeting my gaze again.

His dark eyes meet mine with an unspoken question. "Liz?"

As I'm about to answer him, Lewi races up with a bag of ice. He holds it out to Oli, but then his eyes widen as he takes my ankle. "Fucking hell, Roe! What happened to your ankle?"

I huff out a sigh; I suppose they will eventually find out anyway. The scars aren't extremely noticeable, but I usually wear pants, so they are always covered. The scars healed well, considering how badly I'd broken my ankle. The amount of work they had to do to fix it... yeah,

I was lucky. I'm lucky to be out on the ice at all now. But to a new pair of eyes, the scars look a bit extreme. On either side of my ankle, there's a scar that runs from the bottom of my ankle bone up to mid-calf.

"So, this is the old ankle injury I was talking about."

"You said it was nothing crazy," Oli points out, clearly disagreeing with my definition of crazy.

True. I did say that. Damnit. "I... I was in an accident when I was a teenager."

Lewi squats down next to Oli and gently runs a finger over one of the scars. "What type of accident?" he asks quietly.

My eyes shift to the ice before meeting Oli's soft gaze. "I used to be a figure skater."

Lewi snorts. "Used to be? You looked fucking amazing out there."

I smile softly. "I'll never be able to skate professionally, though."

"Why not?" Lewi asks.

Oli interrupts before I can answer. "She no longer has the flexibility to do so. She no doubt looked amazing out there, but she's not using the foot she's meant to land on."

I smirk. "Impressive; you could tell all that?"

He lays the bag of ice on my ankle as he says, "You are right-leg dominant. I can tell you often overcompensate when you walk and regularly lean to your left side." He looks out at the ice before looking back up at me. "You had to re-learn how to skate. You had to ignore what felt natural."

I nod. "I've been working at it the last few years. It hurt too much to be on the ice after it happened."

Oli stares at my ankle for a moment before his eyes narrow. "This type of damage wouldn't have happened if you had been a single skater. A solo skater knows their body well enough to avoid landing in a compromising position that can break an ankle this badly."

Always so fucking observant. "You would be correct. I wasn't a single skater. I had a partner."

His eyes narrow as they meet mine. "What happened to your partner?"

I shrug, trying to ignore the pang of hurt that still lingers long after Emmitt's betrayal. "Not sure. Probably a big-shot skater by now, I'm sure."

"Wait! Wait, wait, wait"—Lewi pinches the bridge of his nose as he tries to understand—"you were a paired skater, and your partner *could* be a big-time skater, but you're not sure. How do you not know?"

Oli doesn't hesitate to say, "Because he's the one who did this to her."

Lewi turns to Oli with a brow raised. "Why the hell would someone do that to Lizzy?"

I grin at Lewi calling me by my other nickname. He doesn't do it often, but when he does, you know he's taking something personally on my behalf. "He said his father made him do it. Not really sure if that was true or not, but it didn't change the outcome." I wiggle my toes, letting out a hiss of pain.

Lewi's eyes widen. "He broke your ankle on purpose?"

Leaning back against the wall, I shrug. "Physically? No. He didn't come up to me and break my ankle. He botched a throw, and I landed wrong."

"Throw?" Oli asks.

Humming, I reply, "In pair skating, there are certain requirements. One of them is a throw jump. Your partner lifts, twists, then throws you. The move involves a lot of practice and trust."

Lewi arches a brow. "So your partner literally throws you across the ice?"

I snort. "I mean... they don't throw you that far. It's more like a toss."

"Seems dangerous," Lewi grunts.

I giggle. "Says the man who enjoys getting slammed into the glass and hit with sticks."

He shrugs. "The devil you know and all that."

I huff out a sigh and wave a dismissive hand. "Anyways. Enough about that. I pushed myself more than I probably should have today. I will regret it in the morning."

"What do you miss about it?" Oli asks as he gently massages my foot.

The question catches me off guard. It takes me a moment to gather my thoughts together. "What do you mean?"

He gestures with his head toward the ice. "The pair skating. What do you miss about it?"

"The lifts," I answer with zero hesitation.

He arches a brow. "The lifts?"

I let out a wistful sigh as I nod. "They were my favorite. It felt like I was flying." The two share a look, and something passes between them that makes me wonder what they are up to. They both nod before turning back to me.

"I've got to look at the sign-up sheet really quick. I'll be right back." Oli shifts, so Lewi can take my ankle and hold the ice in place.

"You two seriously don't have to stay. I can get myself home."

Lewi shakes his head. "I rode with Oli. I can drive you home. You need to keep the ice on it, so your ankle isn't worse tomorrow morning for work."

Arguing with these two would be pointless, so I shrug, closing my eyes as I lean against the wall. I peek through my lashes when I feel soft fingers massage my foot. Lewi is looking down at my leg with a frown.

I barely hear him whisper, "Fucking idiot... didn't deserve you anyways."

CHAPTER EIGHT

Mac 'Oli' Oliver

Making my way over to the sign-up sheet, I think about every-thing I learned today. Liz had been breathtaking with the kids. The smile on her face was soft and friendly. She looked happy. I'd only planned to skim the sign-up sheet for hockey lessons before spending a little time on the ice myself. I didn't realize she would be here teaching a class of her own.

I would have gone the moment the kids left. At least, that was the plan, until I saw her fly across the ice. Fucking hell. I have two sisters who love ice skating. There is something about female grace when it comes to watching them on ice that has always mesmerized me. My sisters are beautiful and talented, but Liz… she was breathtaking. I was surprised she hadn't noticed me or even Lewi, for that matter, when he came barging in.

"The fuck you hiding for?"

I grab him quickly, covering his mouth. "Shut up!"

He grumbles and struggles until his eyes land on her. I can tell he's just as mesmerized as I am when he sags in my hold. Fucker is just as smitten by her as I am. I stiffen at the thought… smitten? Shit. I am smitten. I like her. We are friends, yes, but I want to be more than that.

Well… fuck. I look over to find Lewi watching her with soft eyes. In all the years I've known him, the man had never had soft eyes for a single woman. With Liz, though, he will test her patience but will never fight her. He listens and does what she asks.

My eyes dart back to Liz when I hear her scream. She's still skating, but tears are streaming down her face. Lewi tries to pull out of my grasp, but I hold him back. Something tells me she needs to finish her routine.

"Not yet. Let her finish." The look on her face says that this is impor-tant. Whatever demons she's fighting, this moment is important. We watch on bated breath as the song ends, and she finishes, breathing hard. Then she falls.

I don't hesitate. I race onto the ice, leaving Lewi behind.

I turn away from the sign-up sheet to head back to Lewi and Liz, pausing for a moment when I see Lewi massaging her foot, his gaze narrowed. He mutters something I can't hear from here, but when my eyes shift to Liz, I see a wide grin on her face and her eyes closed.

The music switches to a song I've heard only once, mainly because I have younger sisters. Could Have Been Me by Halsey. There's a flutter in my chest as I walk over and sit next to her on the bench. The lyrics remind me of the conversation we had at the beginning of the week. I can't help but ask her, "So, do you still feel like you're standing behind the glass?"

She lets out a soft laugh. Turning my way, she opens her eyes just enough to peek through her lashes. "I believe I've finally made it to the other side."

I can't stop the smile that spreads across my face. "I knew you would." I bend to take my blades off when she touches my forearm. Turning to face her, I arch a brow. "Need something?"

"Were you planning to skate?"

I shrug as I turn back to finish removing my blades. "I was going to skate for a bit after I checked the board, but it's fine."

She taps my arm again. "Go skate, Mac." My eyes meet hers, and she gives me a smile as she gestures to the ice. "Go. I'll be fine. I don't mind waiting if you both really feel the need to make sure I get home."

My jaw tightens before I give her a nod. "As long as you're sure?"

She smiles as she pokes Lewi with her other foot. "Go put your skates on too. Have some fun."

He rolls his eyes and continues to massage her foot. "I don't need to skate, Lizzy."

"If you don't go get your blades and have some fun, I'll tell the dietitians to take away your cheat day."

His eyes widen before he glares at her. "You wouldn't."

With a grin she takes out her phone. "I'll text them right now."

He growls before lowering her foot to the ground. "Fine," he grunts, then marches off to grab his blades.

She snickers as she puts her phone away. I can't help but chuckle. "You would really take away his cheat day?"

She shakes her head. "No, but he doesn't need to know that."

Shaking my head with a laugh, I step out onto the ice. It's only a few minutes before Lewi joins me. We do a few laps around the edge before I hear Liz yell, "You two should race!"

My eyes meet his, and he grins wildly. "You think you can keep up, goalie?"

I snort a laugh. "I can skate circles around you."

"Then you better catch me!" he yells as he takes off across the ice.

"Fucker!"

I hear Liz laughing as I chase after Lewi. Her laughter causes a flutter in my chest, and a grin spreads across my face when Lewi looks toward her too. He yells over his shoulder, "Come on, slow poke! All that time guarding the net has you falling behind!"

I let out a playful growl. "Fuck off!" I don't know the last time I had this much fun. However, I have a feeling it has something to do with a certain raven-haired, blue-eyed woman sitting on the sidelines.

CHAPTER NINE

Elizabeth 'Liz' Monroe

I slowly make my way up the steps to my apartment under the ever-watchful eyes of Oli and Lewi. It took twenty minutes of haggling for them to agree to stay behind. Lewi had made for the steps after handing over my keys. He was nice enough to drive my car home while I caught a ride with Oli.

The glare I sent him when he tried to follow me must have convinced him otherwise because he slowly backed up with his hands raised. I didn't take my eyes off him until he climbed into the car with Oli.

Rolling my eyes at the pair, I continue my slow climb up the stairs. I have my keys ready to open my door when I see yet another note attached to my door. My body stiffens for a moment before I let out a defeated sigh. Body sagging, dread pooling in my stomach, I peel the note off and open the door.

Throwing my keys into the bowl next to the door, I open the piece of paper, already dreading the contents.

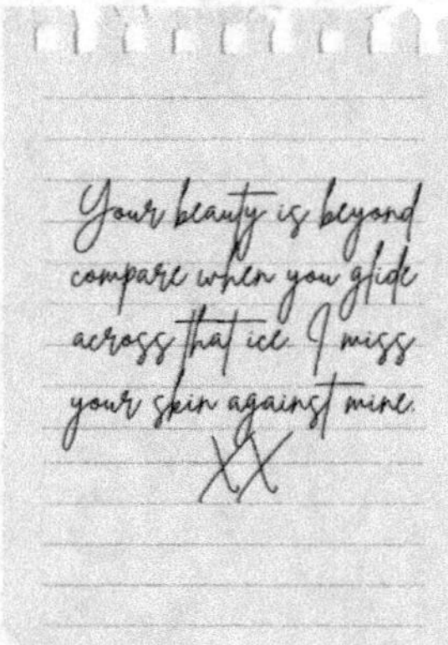

I freeze as I stare down at the note. *Your skin against mine? Who the fuck is this person?* I jerk out of my frozen state and rush across the room to throw the crumpled note in the trash. My hands start to shake, and my breathing grows labored. My vision narrows as my eyes dart around the room, and I realize I left my front door unlocked behind me. Running back over to it, I slam against the wood and snap the lock into place. Leaning back against the door, I slide down till I'm sitting on the floor, my vision blurring as I start to hyperventilate.

I'm being stalked... I... I have a stalker... oh God! My movements are jerky but, eventually, I manage to fish my phone out of my pocket. I can't see the screen through the tears sliding down my face, so I'm not sure who I've called until a bright, happy voice greets me.

"Roe Roe! How's my favorite athletic therapist?"

"V-Vicy..." I sob.

His voice immediately turns serious. "Liz? Liz, what's wrong?"

"I... I... I'm scared," I whisper as I huddle against the door.

I hear rustling in the background. "Where are you?"

I'm frozen in fear when I hear the scrape of boots outside my door. I whimper into the phone and scramble across the floor to hide in the corner.

"Sis! Sis, you need to tell me where you are." His words are muffled as he yells, "Get your shit on boys, our girl needs us!" His voice is soft when he says, "Come on, sis, you're annoying little brother needs your location."

I let out a wet laugh, but my eyes never leave the door. "Home. I'm at home. Oli and Lewi just dropped me off," I finally manage to say.

"Good. Okay. I'll make sure they turn around and head back. Don't you dare hang up, okay?"

A fist pounds loudly against the door, and I let out a scream.

I hear doors slam in the background on his end as he asks, "Liz! What's going on?"

My voice is low as I swallow and reply, "Someone is banging on my door."

"It's locked, right?"

"Yes," I whisper.

"Oli and Lewi should beat us there. They aren't too far away. We are coming, okay?"

I struggle to control my breathing as the pounding continues, but I feel like I'm going to hyperventilate. I'm right on the edge of passing out when I hear him ask, "What's your favorite anime?"

"W-what?"

"What's your favorite anime?" he repeats.

Surprised by his question, I ask, "Uhm, how do you know I like anime?"

He chuckles. "You do realize that you were humming the whole time you worked on those notebooks, right?"

My cheeks heat with embarrassment. "That doesn't mean I like anime."

"It does when you hum multiple anime theme songs."

Huffing out a breath, I realize that the distraction helped. I can breathe a little easier, and I'm no longer about to pass out. But the knocking continues. Thumping my head back against the wall, I say softly, "Thank you, Vicy."

"Your thanks isn't necessary when I want to know the answer to the question."

I manage a chuckle as I cover my other ear to block out the pounding. "My favorite anime is *Yuri on Ice*."

He hums. "I've never seen it. I'll have to check it out."

"What's yours?" I pull my hand away from my ear and realize the knocking has stopped. I slowly stand from my huddled position against the opposite wall.

"Does Vox Machina count? If not, I like Fairy Tale."

I let out a squeal when a deep voice sounds from the other side of my door. "Liz?" My relief at hearing the familiar voice has my shoulders dropping and my breaths coming a little easier. I rush over to the door and rip it open. Oli's dominating figure stands right outside my door, panting as if he ran all the way here.

"Chérie? Are you o—"

Before he can finish his question, I'm jumping into his arms. He immediately lifts me, my legs wrapping around his waist, and I hold him in a death grip. I sob into his chest as I say, "You're here."

"Of course, Chérie." He holds me close, and I soak in his warmth and protective aura. Muffled shouting reaches us, and I realize Vicy is still on the phone. I bring the phone back to my ear and apologize. "I'm so sorry. I didn't mean to leave you hanging like that."

"I just wanted to make sure you are okay. We are almost there, so I'll see you soon. Bye, Roe Roe."

I wrap my arms back around Oli and sag at the feeling of safety. His chest rumbles as he says softly, "I got you, Chérie. You're safe now."

"I couldn't find anything," Lewi says, panting. Oli just grunts in response and holds me closer.

My eyes water again as I whisper, "Dean…"

Lewi jogs over to and lifts a hand to cup my cheek. "Are you okay?"

I begin to nod, but then it turns into me shaking my head 'no'. A few tears escape as I choke out, "You're here."

His brows furrow, and he brushes my tears away. "Of course."

When I hear doors slam, I jump but then relax when I see it's the boys rushing up the stairs. Vicy bulldozes his way inside and wraps me and Oli in a hug. "Fucking hell, Roe Roe, you scared me."

He pulls away and points at me with a no-nonsense look. "You are staying with us until further notice!"

I shake my head. "I can't do that."

Taz is suddenly beside Vicy, grumbling, "That was a statement, not a question. You *are* staying with us until further notice."

"Don't make me get Peri, Merc, Gilly, and Fenni down here," Ozzy chimes in behind the guys.

Tuck huffs out a laugh as he points between Vicy and Taz. "If you thought younger brothers were annoying before, I can guarantee that having four overprotective, older ones will be worse."

"Don't drag them away from their families," I argue.

Vicy shrugs. "Then don't argue."

"Fine," I grunt out. "I need my keys and purse, though. And I'll need to pack some clothes."

"Only grab the essentials for tonight. We can come back tomorrow to get more stuff." Oli says, walking into the living room.

He carries me down the hallway and lowers me to my feet outside my bedroom door. He waits in the hall as I walk inside to grab what I need. I arch a brow when I notice he hasn't moved. "Are you going to wait out there?"

He nods. "Not leaving your side, Chérie."

Warmth fills my chest. I nod and move to my closet to grab a few things for the night. I will feel better if we come back during the day. Less places to hide when there are less shadows.

Chapter Ten

As we pull up to the common house, a horn sounds, and three figures rush out the door. I groan as I watch Lewi park my car in the driveway, Oli and me pulling in behind him. "You called the others? I told you guys not to bother them."

Oli shrugs. "You must have missed the text in the team chat."

I shake my head but pull out my phone. I forgot I had silenced the notifications for the team group chat. Now, I only get notifications for the chat with my guys. It's hard to follow twenty guys chirping back and forth. Danni and I were both added to the team chat to 'keep an eye' on the boys. I'm pretty sure Danni silenced her notifications too.

There are several unread texts in the chat. I usually open them just to get the notification number back down to zero. Huffing out a sigh, I open it and see the text Vicy had sent.

DocDanni

Shit, she okay?

Vicy

Not sure yet. I'll keep you updated. But I need our boys outside now to go get her. I just want to make sure everyone knows what's going on.

DocDanni

Keep me updated! I'll make your life hell otherwise Vic!

Vicy

Roger that!

I exit the team chat and find several missed messages in my guys' group chat along with one from Danni. I check the group chat first since that is just me and the boys, and it's blown up with messages.

Perri

How's our girl? Need an update. On the way to the house now.

Vicy

What did you say to the Mrs?

Perri

I told her there was an emergency at the common house that I needed to check on. You know Karen loves you guys, but she also knows how much trouble you cause.

Merc

I need an update! I can't get away from the house. We're in the middle of the twin's bed-

time routine, and I'm on story duty. Cheryl told me to go, but you know how crazy they can get.

Vicy

Yeah. We are on our way now.

Gilly

Fenni and I are on the way.

Ozzy

How are the wives?

Gilly

They are doing fine. Pregnancy looks good on them.

Vicy

lol I can't believe they got pregnant at the same time.

Gilly

That's what happens when you and your best friend marry identical twins.

When my door opens, I pause my reading and look up. Oli holds out a hand as he asks, "You ready?"

I nod and slip out of the car but wince when I try to put weight on my foot. Shit. I didn't ice it when I got home.

Oli doesn't hesitate to lift me into his arms, bridal style. I huff a sigh but don't argue; there would be no point. Tapping the screen of my phone, I ask, "Gilly and Fenni married identical twins?"

He nods as maneuvers around the car. "Yeah. A few years ago. Dannielle and Samantha both got pregnant a few months back and insisted the four of them live together."

"That's pretty cool." When I've finished catching up on messages, I scroll to the bottom of the chat. It doesn't look like anyone has given poor Merc an update yet. Nope. Not a single text on the way to the house. So, I send a quick text in both chats.

> I'm fine everyone. The guys have insisted I stay at the common house for a bit.

It doesn't take long for my phone to blow up again, but I don't have a chance to respond when we are stopped by Perri, Gilly, and Fenni.

"Are you okay!?" Perri's wide eyes take me in, looking for any injuries, while Oli holds me.

I nod. "Yeah, I'm fine."

"You are not fine," Oli grunts.

I roll my eyes as I smile at Peri. "I'm fine. Thank you."

"She needs to get inside and elevate her foot. So move," Oli grunts.

I slap him on the chest. "Be nice." It's odd seeing my normally soft cinnamon roll so grumpy.

He huffs. "Can you please move, so we can get her inside? She hurt her ankle, and needs to take care of it before it swells anymore. She'll need to be able to walk on it in the morning."

The three large men jump out of Oli's way, so he can carry me into the house with no problem. I pat his chest and smirk. "There we go. I was worried you swapped personalities with Lewi there for a moment."

He snorts. "I'm not sure that's possible. Lewi is a dark cloud."

I laugh when Lewi grunts. Oli gently sets me down on the couch, but before my feet hit the cushions, Lewi sits and lays them across his lap. I shoot him an arched brow, but he lets out a grunt and avoids my eyes, pretending to spend all of his concentration on untying my sneakers.

Oli heads toward the kitchen and yells, "I'll get the ice."

I'm about to tell him I'm fine when Lewi removes my socks and begins to massage the swollen tissue around my ankle. I let out a hiss when he hits a tender patch of bruised skin. His eyes snap to mine, and his hands freeze. "That bad?"

My head thumps back against the arm of the couch as I groan. "I knew going that hard on the ice was a bad idea."

Oli returns, hovering over the back of the couch as he hands Lewi a gel ice pack. "Let's agree that you won't go that hard on the ice again, alright?"

I smirk. "No promises."

Vicy is sitting on the floor next to my head, his voice soft as he asks, "What's he talking about, Roe Roe?"

Oli and Lewi both chuckle as I groan. "Yeah. Tell Vicy why your ankle is bruised and swollen, Roe Roe," Lewi playfully scolds.

I send him my meanest glare before I turn to Vicy. "I worked on an ice-skating routine I've been practicing."

Vicy arches a brow in confusion. "Why would that cause your ankle to swell that badly?"

My gaze shifts to Oli, then Lewi, who gives me another raised brow as if challenging me to share what happened to me with the guys, but he stays silent as his thumb teases the edge of my pants near my ankle. I debate if I want the others to know my secret. It's not a secret because I'm ashamed of what happened, more so that I hate the looks of pity I get when people see the scars.

Taking a deep breath, I let it out with a heavy exhale and give Lewi a nod. He removes the ice pack before gently rolling up my pant leg to the bottom of my knee. My scars are now on full display. They, admittedly, look worse with the dark purple of my bruised skin.

There's a unified hiss from everyone in the room. Gilly is the first to shuffle closer to the edge of the couch for a better look. He reaches out his hand but pauses and looks up at me. His eyes ask for permission to touch.

I give him a nod, and his fingers softly caress the pale scar that runs from my ankle to mid-calf. His brows pinch when he looks up at me. "You're a figure skater?"

I give him a sad smile as I say, "I *was* a figure skater."

"You *are* a figure skater," Oli growls. My eyes meet his as he continues. "Just because a hockey player retires or gets injured doesn't make him any less of a hockey player. Why is this any different?" He taps a finger to my chest. "It's here. You are a figure skater in here. It's in your blood."

My eyes blur as I shift my gaze back to Gilly. "I was a professional figure skater."

His eyes shift to Oli, and a silent conversation passes between the two before his eyes narrow then meet mine as he stands. "Who are we killing?" Gilly demands.

I laugh wholeheartedly, my heart a little lighter from his sincere concern, but I shake my head. "No one. They're not important anymore."

Fenni comes up to stand next to Gilly. "Why does he sound so pissed? What does being a figure skater have to do with her ankle scars?"

The others follow suit and crowd around the couch, looking down at me. Not going to lie, it's extremely intimidating to have nine pairs of eyes on you. I try to placate them by letting out a forced laugh, then say, "It's not a big deal. Accidents happen, you know."

Gilly points at my ankle and grunts. "That injury doesn't happen if you're a single skater. And I can see in your eyes that you don't believe it was an accident. So tell me, Roe Roe, who am I killing?"

I see the moment realization dawns in their eyes, and I close my own. I don't want to see their pity. Not before I catch a glimpse of Oli and Lewi's faces, and they looked way too satisfied by the guys' reactions.

"Some guy did that to you?!" Taz screeches. I wince because, holy shit, I didn't realize a man's voice could get that high-pitched.

Understanding fills the guys' eyes when Tuck says, "You were a pair skater. Which means you had a partner you trusted."

"He betrayed you," Perri quietly adds.

I nod as I whisper, "Yes."

"I'm with Gilly on this. Who are we killing?" Vicy growls.

Wanting to get off the subject of my ankle and Emmitt, I grumble, "He's not important. Can we just watch TV or something?"

The guys all share a look before letting out sighs of their own. Vicy settles back down beside my head on the floor. "*Yuri on Ice*?"

Excitement bubbles in my chest as I nod, "Yes please!" I need the distraction, and the guys probably need it just as much. I hate thinking about Emmitt or being reminded of him in any way. *Yuri on Ice* is the perfect distraction. Plus who doesn't love watching Yuri and Victor? Psst, a little secret between you and me; I shipped the two of them so hard and had the biggest crush on Victor.

CHAPTER ELEVEN

I'm jolted awake by a gentle jostle to my shoulder. "Wh-what? Did I fall asleep?"

When I open my eyes, Oli is in front of me with a soft smile. He nods. "Yes. It seems everyone fell asleep." He points toward my feet.

I look to find Lewi asleep in a very awkward position. He still has his hand on my ankle as if he fell asleep mid-massage. His neck is tilted to the side, which looks extremely uncomfortable. Then I take in the room and see everyone else is sporadically lying on the floor asleep. "We should probably wake everyone else up too," I whisper.

Oli gestures over his shoulder. "Fenni and Gilly will wake them up before they leave. Perri left an hour or so ago." He leans over to shake Lewi awake. He groans sleepily and rubs his face. Oli snorts. "Go to bed."

Lewi nods and slowly lifts my legs off his lap, so he can shuffle off the couch. He looks half asleep as he makes his way around the couch and down the hall.

I let out a squeak when I'm suddenly lifted from the couch. I instantly wrap my arms around Oli's neck. "Oli! I'm more than capable of walking on my own."

He just shrugs as he follows Lewi down the hallway. "Your ankle still needs time to rest; plus, you don't know which room is yours for now."

His cheeks turn pink, and I can't help but ask, "Whose room will I be staying in, Oli?"

He looks down at me briefly before turning to the door on the right. "Lewi and I volunteered to give up our bedroom. We plan to clear out one of the other bedrooms we use as storage for you, but until that happens you can stay in here." He shrugs and sets me down on the bed.

The room is large, though, I suppose it would have to be with two hockey players sharing the room. Two queen-sized beds sit on opposite walls, as if the room is split in half. "Where will you guys sleep until you clear out the room?"

"We will bunk with one of the other guys. Clearing out the other room shouldn't take too long."

I run my fingers over the silky-smooth bed sheets and smile as I look up at Oli. "Whose bed is this?"

He rubs the back of his neck as he looks away with bright pink cheeks. "It's mine."

I chuckle and snuggle into the blankets on the bed. I inhale and can't help but relax as his scent engulfs me. It's a combination of snow and the woods. Like standing in the middle of a forest after a fresh snowfall. A yawn overtakes me as I close my eyes.

"Sleep well, Chérie."

I slip a hand out from under the blanket to snatch his wrist. My eyes open just enough to see his surprised expression. "Don't go," I whisper.

He turns to kneel beside the bed. "Chérie, I will be a shout away. I won't be far."

My eyes burn as I whisper, "Please, don't go, Mac."

His eyes soften as he leans forward and presses a kiss to my forehead. He pulls away and whispers, "As if I could deny you, Chérie." Pointing over his shoulder to Lewi's bed, he says, "I will be right over there. I won't leave the room."

When he begins to pull away, for some reason, panic builds in my chest, and I remember why I'm here. My grip on his wrist tightens as I plead, "With me." I tug on his arm. "Please. Just for tonight. I just want to feel safe."

"Are you sure?" he asks.

"Please."

He nods before slipping into the bed behind me with all of his clothes on. I can't help but ask, "Do you normally sleep in all of your clothes?"

Oli chuckles as he settles in beside me but keeps a respectable distance between us. "No, I do not, Chérie. But I think stripping down to my underwear with you here would be inappropriate."

My cheeks heat, and I nod. We lie in a comfortable silence for a few minutes before I gather the courage to shuffle closer to him. I lay my head on his chest and feel him stiffen beneath me for a moment, but then he relaxes. He wraps an arm around me, pulling me closer to his chest. "Are you okay, Chérie?"

His steady heartbeat helps me even out my breathing, and my body starts to relax. Being wrapped in his arms makes me feel safe. "I am now," I whisper into the silence of the room. I feel the tendrils of sleep grasping my mind as I relax further into him. I barely hear his words before sleep takes hold.

"Je veux te tenir près de moi comme ça pour toujours, Chérie."

Mac 'Oli' Oliver

Of all the people she could have reached out to... she chose me. Though, I suppose having been frightened out of her mind, it makes sense for her to seek comfort. As much as I enjoy having her in my arms, a nagging feeling keeps prickling the back of my mind. There is someone missing.

Dean. Dean is missing. I've seen how he looks at her. Briefly looking down at her sleeping form, I reach over to grab my phone from the side table. Pulling up his name, I send a quick text.

> Hey, get your ass in our bedroom.

Lewi

> Seriously man? I just got comfortable.

> Stop complaining and just get in here.

Lewi

> Fine.

I can't help but smirk because I know he's rolling his eyes as he snatches his pillow to shuffle over here. He hates moving once he's comfortable and ready to sleep. I hear him stomp down the hallway before he reaches the door to the room and quietly slips inside.

"Why am I here?" he asks, groaning as he moves over to his bed.

I keep my voice low as I reply, "It feels weird to be in here by myself."

He looks at me with a raised brow. "You don't look alone to me."

I huff out a sigh and roll my eyes. "You know what I mean."

He climbs into bed as he says, "Do elaborate."

"Why do you have to be so difficult?" I groan.

He snorts a laugh and turns on his side to lie facing me. "It's a character flaw that you knew I had when you declared me your friend. You're stuck with me now."

"As if I'd get rid of you." I scoff. I love the guy like a brother, but that doesn't make him any less difficult to deal with. "As I was saying, it felt weird in here without you."

"So... what you're saying is you love me?"

God help me. "Dean..."

"Mac."

This conversation is leading nowhere. May as well go in for the kill. "Do you like her?"

His eyes widen in the darkness for just a moment before he masks his face. He cocks a brow. "Her? There are a lot of women in the world, Mac. You need to be more specific."

My eyes narrow on him as I scoff, "The only 'her' I'd feel the need to mention."

His gaze flicks to Liz before turning back on me. "It wouldn't matter if I did. Girls always go for you anyways."

I balk at his tone. "Me? I haven't dated in years."

"Doesn't mean girls haven't tried." He sighs before shifting to lie on his back. "Girls like you more than they like me. Can't blame them, though. You have that soft, doughy attitude, and I'm all anger and sharp edges."

My chest aches for my friend. He hasn't lived the easiest life. Letting people in to see the real him is hard. Many give up before they learn how amazing and loyal he is. "She's different, though. She doesn't shy away from you like the others did."

He huffs a sigh. "Yeah... well we can't both have her."

"Why not?" I challenge.

He flips back onto his side, eyes wide. "Why not? What do you mean, why not?"

Peering down at the beautiful woman asleep in my arms, I can't help but smile. "She deserves all the love she can get in this world." My eyes shift to him as I add, "Why not us? We could give her that."

"Are you proposing we share her?" he asks defensively.

"No. Nothing like that. It would be like..." Well shit, how do I explain this? Then I remember an old friend of mine. "Hunter. You remember Hunter?"

He gives me a look that says he doesn't follow. "Hunter? The mixed martial arts fighter dude?"

"Yeah. He owns that mechanic shop in Lindberg."

"I remember him. What does he have to do with this?"

I try to shimmy out from under Liz's body, careful not to wake her, so I can sit up. "Him and three of his friends are dating one girl."

"So... they share a girl?"

I shake my head as I try to explain. "Yes, but no. The way I understand it, each of them have a relationship with her. They have their individual relationships, and then they have a group relationship." I point to Liz's sleeping form. "We would both have separate relationships as well as one together... if you'd like."

He's quiet for a moment before hesitantly saying, "So we wouldn't be sharing her?"

I snort. "No, Dean. We wouldn't share her; she's not a hockey puck we pass back and forth. We'd have to work as a team."

"A team," he hums, considering the possibilities. His gaze flicks to the sleeping form of our guarded therapist. "How will we convince her to take a chance on us?"

My eyes shift from my best friend to the woman beside me. I reach out and brush a black curl off her cheek. "We give her what she needs most."

Dean's voice is hushed as he asks, "And what's that?"

My eyes meet his. "Someone who will choose her."

Eyes narrowing, he nods. "We will show her she can trust us. That we won't betray her."

I hum, turning back to stare at our therapist. I'm not sure how to pull this off. There are rules against players and staff dating. And I know Liz well enough now to know she will deny herself happiness if it means not breaking the rules. "We can start by showing her friendship and go from there. She won't jump into a relationship after what happened in her past. I have a feeling her relationships, if any, have been fleeting."

Dean grunts. "The stalker thing doesn't help, either."

The thought of her stalker hunting and scaring her makes my blood boil. I'm normally a chill person, like water off a duck's back. It's hard to ruffle my feathers, but it seems that when it comes to our sunshine therapist, I don't have the same outlook on life. "We protect her," I say with determination.

He snorts. "Duh."

Chapter Twelve

Elizabeth 'Liz' Monroe

The words play on repeat as I try to wake myself from this night-mare.

"I miss your skin against mine." The voice sounds deep and distorted.

"Go away!" I scream at the same time a fist beats against the door again. I want out of this nightmare. Someone... anyone. Help me! Then I hear my name, as if it's an echo.

"Liz? Liz, wake up."

At the moment, I don't care who's calling my name as long as it gets me out of here.

I wake with scream, and my arms fling out as if to protect myself. I hear a thump, then a groan as my vision slowly clears. Looking around, I realize I'm in Mac and Dean's room. Wait... I'm in their room? I roll over to find Dean next to me on his bed, his eyes wide as he bites his lip.

With a grin, he says, "You've got a solid right hook on you."

I groan and crawl to look over the side of the bed. Mac is lying on the floor, a hand over his cheek, his eyes squeezed shut. He must have landed in an awkward position when fell off the bed. Or, I suppose, was punched off the bed.

"I am so sorry, Mac!"

He waves his free hand in the air as he replies, "All good, Lizzy. I now know never to get on your bad side or wake you up from a nightmare."

Dean busts out laughing. "Or at least stay a safe distance away."

There's a knock on the door before it swings open. I groan, covering my face when I realize the others are about to come in, having heard the commotion. That seems to make Dean laugh even harder.

"Why is Oli on the floor?" Taz asks.

Which is followed by Ozzy blurting out, "Holy shit! Who the hell gave you that shiner, man?"

I peel my fingers away from my eyes just enough to see Dean howling in laughter as he points to me.

I turn to the boys in the doorway and watch as Vicy's eyes widen, then narrow on his friend on the floor. "Did he touch you inappropriately? Is that why he's on the floor with a bruise forming on his face?"

Taz and Ozzy stiffen before they converge on Oli. I scream, "No!" That makes them freeze. I wave my hands in front of me. "No! He didn't do anything inappropriate! I was in the middle of a nightmare, and he tried to wake me up." I gulp down a breath as I explain. "I didn't know where I was at first so my arms sorta..." I trail of as I make a punching motion.

"She knocked him on his ass!" Dean says through laughter.

I narrow my gaze on him and growl. "Stop laughing! You're not helping."

"So let me get this right..." Ozzy says, almost hesitantly, while rubbing the back of his neck. "You had a nightmare, and Oli tried to wake you up."

I nod in confirmation as Vicy points to me and then to Oli on the floor. "So... you punched him?"

"On accident," I whine.

Taz stares at me for a moment before blurting out, "He was sleeping in the bed with you." Not a question, just an observation.

"What?" I squeak.

He points to the bed, then the floor. "That's the only way he could have landed on the floor like that. He had to be next to you in bed." A smirk grows on his face. "Does our Roe Roe have a thing for our goalie?"

"No!" I screech out. God damn this frustrating man.

"Well now, that hurts more than the punch, Liz," Mac says, still on the floor.

"That's not what I meant," I say, throwing up my hands in defeat; I can't win with these boys. I look toward the man in question and find him with a smirk on his face. I grab the closest pillow and throw it in his face. "So not funny, Oli."

He chuckles and catches it before tucking it behind his head. "So much better."

I roll my eyes, and my stomach lets out a loud growl. I feel the flush in my cheeks reemerge. Oli grins and rolls to stand. "Alright, boys, time to get our girl some food and coffee."

I start to get up when he turns and points at me. I freeze. "What?"

Oli points to my ankle. "You stay right there until Lewi can wrap your ankle. You have a full schedule today, and we don't need it swelling more than it already will."

I want to argue, but I know he's right. So, with a sigh, I settle back on the bed. "Fine. But I'm only agreeing because I know how bad my ankle will hurt by the end of the day if I don't. Plus, I didn't pack my ankle brace."

He arches a brow. "Not because you know I'm right?"

"Nope." I pop the 'p' which earns me a smirk.

Shaking his head, he lets out a soft laugh as he heads for the door. "Be a good girl for Lewi now."

"I doubt the woman knows the meaning of good girl," Lewi comments with a snort as Oli and the others file out of the room.

"I know how to be a good girl!" I argue defensively. That earns me another raised brow, and my cheeks heat when I realize what I just said.

Lewi smirks and grabs a small box from under his bed. "Sure you do, Ice Princess."

I bristle at his use of the nickname. I've always hated when guys called me princess, as if I need someone to take care of me or to pander after. "I'm not a princess."

He kneels in front of me with a box of medical wraps, giving me a look that says 'are you sure about that?'. He picks out the purple wrap and says, "That's the only thing you took away from that sentence? The name princess?"

"I hate when people, men especially, call me princess. It's like you're using a derogatory term." I huff.

He rolls up my pant leg and begins to stabilize my ankle with K Tape. "Wait, how is princess a derogatory term?"

I'm quiet for a moment, taking in the normally grumpy man who is kneeling before me. Not only that, but he's taking care of me. Did I make that much of an impression on him that it made him like me, and now he no longer feels the need to hide behind his mask of anger? Though, now I'm curious as to why he's so angry and how Mac, the gentle giant, and he became friends.

I must be quiet for too long because Lewi's fingers pause on my ankle, and he looks up at me with a questioning look. "Liz?"

Shaking myself, I answer his original question. "When guys call me princess, they are usually trying to get into my pants. They think I'm weak and can't take care of myself." I lower my voice as I try to impersonate a guy, "Don't worry, *princess*, I'll take care of you."

He hums but continues his task. He has clearly done this before because he does it like a professional. "I can see that. But I don't mean it in that way." Adding one last strip, he lightly squeezes my ankle. When he stands up, he gives me a lopsided grin and says, "You're the princess of the ice. The queen actually. You're strong and independent, and there's nothing wrong with that."

He reaches out, brushing a stray strand of hair behind my ear as he softly says, "But it wouldn't hurt to let someone take care of you for a change. Letting people help and take care of you doesn't make you weak."

I huff out a sigh. "I've had to rely on only myself for so long; I don't know how to let anyone help."

He boops me on the nose before bending to pick up the box. "Well, it's a good thing you've got us then."

"Us?" I ask as he walks over to his bed to put away his supplies. After, he turns to face me.

"The guys and I are a team, and now you are a part of that team. We take care of each other. We're not joking when we say you are our girl." Lewi shrugs as if that should be obvious.

I shiver at his use of '*our* girl'. The way he says it makes me think he means I'm his and Mac's girl, but he's using it as a term of belonging among the guys on the team. Even though I'm ignoring the pull toward him and Mac, I can't quite deny the butterflies that flutter around my stomach anytime I'm near them. The thought of belonging to the two of them, being theirs, would probably be the best mistake I ever made.

Lewi interrupts my spiraling thoughts when he moves toward the door. He stops, looking over his shoulder as he says, "You're part of the family now, Lizzy. Once you're in, you're stuck for life"—he turns away, rapping his knuckles against the doorframe—even when you try your hardest to fight it."

Before I can reply, he's out the door. What did he mean by that? I stare out the door, trying to figure out the enigma that is Dean Lewis. He has a story, and I want to read it. I want to learn as much as I can about him and Mac, even the others. Because I'm starting to realize that he's right; they've adopted me into their family. I need to learn to rely on them, no matter what. Because they'll take care of me whether or not I like it.

Right now... that doesn't sound too bad. My mind drifts back to last night when I found the note, and heavy hands pounded on my door. My fingers tighten in the blankets before I push my stalker from my thoughts and jump off the bed to change for the day. Thankfully, this room has a small en-suite bathroom, so I grab my clothes before heading to the shower.

I still need to wash yesterday off me. Maybe my disturbing feelings will wash down the drain as well. Once the water is warm, I hop in. As I stand under the shower head, I let the water cascade over my skin, and I slowly begin to relax. I look for body wash and find both Dean and Mac's.

Biting my lip, I debate if I should use their soap, before huffing out a sigh. I grab one and open the cap to sniff. I hum at the smell of winter and pull it away to read what scent it is. It's a combination of pine and peppermint. It must be Mac's.

I put it back to pick up what I assume is Dean's. I do the same thing and find that his smells like a warm summer night. A combination of earth and campfire smoke. I debate between the two bottles and then sniff them together. It's an odd combination, but it smells good because it reminds me of them.

Having made my decision, I wash using with both, so I'll be surrounded by their scent all day. As I rinse off the last of the suds, I feel my mind calm and my muscles relax. I like the smell of them on my skin.

So far, I've done a horrible job of distancing myself from the pair, but I'm not sure how to pull away when they make me feel so... safe. Shaking my head, I turn off the water and get ready for the day. Just because I feel safe with them doesn't mean I want to jump into a relationship with them. We can just be friends. There aren't any rules against the staff being friends with the players.

I slide into a pair of dark-wash jeans and a pale, baby-blue blouse. I have paperwork to finish, so I'll be in my office and don't need to dress in my normal uniform of khakis and a team polo. I'm glad they don't require us to wear anything super professional because I hate dresses and skirts.

Putting on the bare minimum make-up, I give myself a nod in the mirror. Time to get this long day started.

Chapter Thirteen

With a long, tired groan, I bang my head against the desk again. I love my job, but I hate paperwork. I also hate having to work on the weekend. Why did they have us come in again? It's Sunday; I should be chilling on the couch reading or watching TV.

Exhaling a heavy sigh, I look at the stack of paperwork I still need to get through. The team held a voluntary practice, and the guys decided to go, but it mainly consisted of the guys who live in the common houses. The players with families usually wait until mandatory practices are held. I keep hoping one of the guys will randomly bust through my door. I never thought I'd wish for them to distract me from work, but I offered to come along because there's always paperwork to do. Routine logs of the players are normal but mine? I'm extremely detailed and efficient, which is great when you are in charge of ten men, so you don't forget things. Downside? There is paperwork for ten men. Which is *a lot* of paperwork.

I've ensured my boys are in top shape for the start of preseason. My notes are so detailed that I can pinpoint if there have been any changes in how they navigate both on and off the ice. That also means I need to keep my notes organized in a way that makes them easy to find. Why must I girl boss so hard?

I put in my ear buds with the hope that it will help me get through the daunting task of organizing my horde of notes. Clicking the Spotify app, I let it shuffle through my main playlist.

The first song to play is What was I made for by Billie Eilish. I remember hearing this song for the first time. It reminds me of the day a shattered ankle destroyed my dreams. I had put every piece of myself into skating for so long, I didn't know what else I could do. It's hard to think of the future when your soul withers away alongside your dreams. When you watch everything you worked so hard for go up in smoke.

I can't help but replay the song and sing along while I do my office work. After the accident, I didn't know what my reason for being was anymore, but after months and months of physical therapy and watching hockey, I knew I was made for the ice. The ice is a part of my very soul, and no matter what happens, I will find a way to be a part of it.

The last lines of the song pass over my lips, and I can't help but smile. I might have forgotten how to be happy for a while, but I've finally found happiness again. During a pause between songs, I hear a knock on my door.

I look up to find Taz and Vicy standing there, mouths agape. My cheeks heat as I remove one of my ear buds. "Uh, how long have you guys been standing there?"

Taz swallows before shaking his head with a wide grin. Though the smile looks forced; it doesn't quite reach his eyes. "Long enough to know that you are coming to karaoke nights from now on."

Embarrassment fills me, and I groan. I'm not saying I'm a bad singer, but I'm by no means a professional. "And when are these karaoke nights?"

"Monday nights after practice," Vicy answers, still looking a bit shocked. He wipes a hand down his face before adding, "We won't take no for an answer. We will drag you if we must."

I hum as I try to gather a bit of my dignity. "Right... anywho. Is there a reason you knocked on my door? Shouldn't you two be in practice?"

Taz nods. "We ran a few drills, but coach could tell we were distracted. He knows about your whole situation and let us go early, so we can help move your stuff out of the apartment."

I'm speechless and not entirely sure how to respond. Vicy seems to know what's going through my head because he adds, "The whole team helped. Don't worry we didn't go into your stuff or anything. Danni packed up your room."

Taz snorts. "She's quite the packing queen. She's already talked to Max, who is trying to find somewhere closer to our place since your stalker obviously knows where your apartment is now. Your current building doesn't have much in the way of security, so Max is looking into a place somewhere a little safer."

Vicy doesn't let me get a word in as he adds, "We were able to get all your stuff in the basement of the house. Tuck and Ozzy stayed behind to clear out one of the extra rooms and get it ready for you. We got your essential stuff with Danni's help."

I'm silent for a moment, trying to process everything. I could have easily moved my stuff to my parents' house while I tried to find a different place. But it seems the team has taken it upon themselves.

"Roe Roe?" Taz asks hesitantly.

I shake myself before saying, "Yes. Um... okay. That's a lot to process. Everyone didn't have to do that."

Taz shrugs. "We wanted to. You're part of the team, which means we take care of you, the same way you take care of us."

My eyes begin to burn, and I pinch my leg to prevent myself from crying. There is no way I am going to cry about this right now in front of people. Maybe when I'm in the shower and by myself. "Right… okay." It's then that I notice the box in Vicy's hands. I point to it and ask, "What do you have there?"

He lifts it as he answers. "Danni found it in the back of your closet. She said to tell you she was sorry, but her curiosity got the best of her."

I sigh, realizing exactly what that box holds. "Did you guys look?"

They both shake their heads no. Vicy walks into my office and lays the box on my desk. "The look on Danni's face told us that it was private."

With a chuckle, I reach for the box and open it. Inside holds the memories of my ice-skating career. Every video my parents took, along with pictures of Emmitt and me. I look up to find Vicy and Taz trying to peer into the box, curiosity painted across their faces.

I snort as I pull out a few pictures and lay them on the desk so they can see. I also take out a few CD's that contain the music from each of my competitions. The guys immediately grab for the pictures.

I search for the CD with my last competition on it. The moment I find it, I let out a deep sigh. I haven't watched the video. I never wanted to see the moment my dreams shattered across the ice like my ankle.

"Roe?" Pulling myself from the dark thoughts, I look up to find Taz with an arched brow, pointing toward the CD in my hand. "What's that?"

Biting my lip, I stare back down at the small square case that holds the worst day of my life. "It's the video of my last competition," I answer quietly.

"The one where you broke your ankle?" Vicy asks.

I nod but keep my eyes on it, debating if I want to finally watch it. I suppose I could watch it alone, but that would probably lead me down a spiraling rabbit hole of trauma I don't want to revisit. "I'm debating if I want to watch it or not."

"You've never seen it?" Taz asks quietly.

"No, I... I couldn't watch it after what happened. To be honest, I forgot about the box until now."

"Well... shit," Vicy says. "Sorry, Roe. We can put it back; we didn't mean to bring up horrible memories."

I wave my hand dismissively. "No. It's okay. I should probably watch it. It's been long enough."

"Do you—" Taz starts hesitantly. When I look up, I find him rubbing the back of his head. "Do you want us to watch it with you?"

I point to the two of them using the CD case. "The two of you?"

Vicy shakes his head. "No, the team. Well, your team," he says with a smirk. "We can make a night of it. Make some popcorn, and you can tell us about all the amazing songs you've skated to."

Taz bumps Vicy with his shoulder. "We can even trash talk the dude who hurt you." He raises a brow at me and asks, "Are you ever going to tell us his name?"

I chuckle darkly as I put all the stuff back into the box. "You'll find out when we watch the video. They introduce us before we skate."

"Nice," Taz says as he high fives Vicy. He points at the box filled with the memories of my old life. "You hold onto that. We'll go tell the guys the plan."

Vicy points at me as he backs out of the room. "No take backs! Meet us out front, Roe Roe."

I glance at the stack of paperwork I still need to get done. "But I need to finish all of this."

Taz clicks his tongue. "A problem for tomorrow. Let's bounce!"

Looking back down at the paperwork, I debate. But it doesn't take long for my brain to say *a problem for another day.* Huffing a sigh, I push away from the desk and grab the box. Vicy and Taz turn to find the others. I cup my free hand around my mouth and yell out behind them, "I want adult beverages for this!"

Vicy throws me a thumbs up as he turns the corner. Taz shakes his head and chuckles but follows. I'm not joking; I want alcohol for this. The memories of that day are still seared into my brain. Watching them play out in HD won't be much better.

The gang has all gathered at the common house—the guys I'm in charge of anyways. The guys' Danni oversees have already left. Perri, Merc, Gilly, and Fenni somehow managed to convince their wives they were needed at the common house for a few hours. I suppose the life of a hockey wife means accepting that your husband is often gone more than home.

Vicy takes a seat beside me on the couch, pouting slightly because he's the only one not old enough to drink. Legally anyway. Taz and Ozzy work together to make me a fruity drink, stating that it will blow my mind. I'm not sure if that's a good thing or not, but if it helps me get through this video... I'll take it.

While Oli and Lewi get the popcorn ready, Tuck sits down on my other side and bumps my shoulder. I look up from where I was staring down at the CD still in my hand.

With a soft smile, he asks, "What was your favorite song you ever skated to?"

I smirk, welcoming the distraction. "My favorite song? I suppose it would have been Lady of the Worlds by Miracle of Sound. We had really cool outfits for that one. It was a fantasy-themed skate."

He hums. "I hope you have the recording of that one in your box too. It sounds like an amazing routine."

I nod as I look back at the disk in my hand. "It was." I groan but get up to put the disk in the DVD player. Once it's in, I return to my seat between the guys. A bowl is placed in my lap, and I look over my shoulder to find Oli.

He shoots me a wink before handing me a glass as well. "I hope Taz and Ozzy didn't make it too strong."

I give the drink a tentative sip before I grin. "It's good."

He nods and takes a seat on the floor in front of us, leaning back against the couch. "Let's get this night going!"

Lewi hits play, and the screen comes alive. I'm pulled in by my parents cheering in the background. This was our short program, which was the one we did amazing in. It was going to be our ticket into the big leagues. At least that's what I thought at the time.

All I can do now, is sit and watch the skater I used to be as she flies across the ice, unaware it would be the last time she'd ever skate like that. The screen reflects all of my dreams that slipped through my fingers like melting ice. Don't get me wrong, I love my new job and my new dreams. I've accomplished so much. But you never forget your first dream. You don't forget the pain of watching them disappear.

Old wounds, long healed and forgotten, reopen as I watch the younger version of me. A head rests on my shoulder, and I know it's Vicy. He has a way about him that he can't help but try to make people feel better. To reach out and attempt to spread some of his happiness to those around him. It's often infectious, but right now, it can't break through the old hurt.

His voice is gentle as he says, "That's you." It doesn't come across as a question. More like an awed observation.

All I can do is nod as I keep my eyes glued to the TV. The short program wraps up, and the video switches over to our long program. The one where I broke my ankle. I can't tear my eyes from the screen as horror builds within me. I know what's going to happen, but *seeing* it happen offers a different perspective than experiencing it in the moment.

Vicy's voice is hesitant as he continues, "And... that's the guy who botched the throw and caused your injury?"

I nod again as silence fills the room. The guys know his name now. I noticed they all stiffened when he was announced at the beginning.

"You looked happy," he whispers.

"I was," I reply. Holding my breath, I watch as Emmitt tossed me into the air, and it's clear that he botched the throw on purpose. He knew what he was doing; it was no accident. I watch the teenage version of myself slide across the ice while panic builds in the crowd. The camera is moving sporadically, and I can tell my dad is rushing down the bleachers, having forgotten that he's still recording.

I admit something that I never thought I would reveal to anyone. A secret I've kept all these years. "Do you know what hurt more than my broken ankle?"

Vicy lifts his head from my shoulder and asks, "What, Roe Roe?"

"Being betrayed by the one person you trusted more than anything." My eyes slip from the screen to look at Vicy. Screaming and yelling is all you can hear in the background as the recording stops, and the screen turns black. "He was my soul mate of a different kind. We might have dated, but we were friends before that. He was a part of my very soul. We knew each other on a deeper level than many experience in a lifetime."

He looks devastated by my admission, and I'm afraid to look at anyone but him. "Roe?" His voice is a quiet question.

I tilt my head, giving him a sad smile. "It's hard to cut off a person who is part of your very soul. But I suppose that's why you can have more than one soul mate. At least... that's what I hope."

His fingers twine with mine, and he gives my hand a reassuring squeeze. "I'll make sure you find the perfect soul mate and get the happy ending you deserve."

My smile is real this time as I squeeze his hand back. "I know you will." I finally gather the courage to look around the room and find all they guys watching me. "If it makes you feel better, I'm happy now. And this alcohol is kicking in. So... I'm feeling great."

There's a round of snorts and laughter as Vicy steals the remote. "Time for some anime." Can't argue with that. A night can't end badly when anime and alcohol are involved.

Chapter Fourteen

Monday morning rolls around too quickly, and I groan as I turn over in bed. I'm not sure how I got here, but I barely remember anything after the sixth episode of *Yuri on Ice*. I rub my temples, squinting and trying to figure out where I ended up last night.

I'm not familiar with this room. It's not Mac and Dean's. I take it in with wide eyes as I realize the space is furnished with all my stuff. Everything that had been in my apartment is now in this bedroom. My mouth gapes when I notice it's set up as best they could to replicate my old area at the apartment.

I bite my lip as emotions swell within me. They went to all this work for me. To make sure I felt safe and at home. I'll need to figure out a way to thank them for this. A knock at the door startles me out of my thoughts. Clearing my throat, I say, "Yes?"

"Oli wanted me to let you know that we are headed out," Tuck calls from behind the door.

I grab my phone to check the time, wondering why my alarm didn't wake me up. I have to squint at the bright screen to make it out. Then I look out the window to see that a blush of morning light streaming through to softly light my room.

Why are they up so early? As if reading my mind Tuck continues. "We have to go in early this morning, so don't be alarmed when you get up and find no one here."

I groan as I say, "Thanks for the heads up."

There's a soft chuckle before Tuck says, "There's a glass of hangover juice on the counter. Make sure you drink it."

"It tastes like shit," Taz yells. "See you in a bit, Roe Roe."

I can't help but snort and call back, "Thanks! See you guys there."

It doesn't take me long to get ready and head down to the kitchen. I find the cup on the counter and make my way over. When I look closer at the liquid inside, I frown. Why does it look like muddy water? Picking it up, I take a hesitant sniff and gag.

"Shit that smells like sweaty feet." Looking around, I see they also made me a cup of coffee. I take a deep breath and shotgun the disgusting-smelling liquid.

I gag again but manage to keep it down as a shiver runs up my spine. Rushing over to the coffee they left me, I take a swig to wash out the gross taste on my tongue. "Ugh, I hope this crap works for hangovers, or I drank that for nothing." Another shiver runs up my spine as I recall the flavor and texture of the questionable liquid.

I huff a sigh and grab my keys and wallet before making my way out the door. That better help with my hangover. I'm not sure how much work I'll get done with my head pounding like a jackhammer.

Karma must know I'm in need of some good luck because I hit every green light on my way to work. My headache turns to a dull ache as I step through the double doors of the hockey rink.

I walk over to the upper sitting area, so I can make notes about my players. I purposefully sit in the higher stands, so they don't see me while they practice, which makes it easier to take notes. They are less likely to hide things if they don't know I'm looking.

After a few hours of noting anything of importance, I head to my office. I need to make sure I get the notes added to the correct notebooks. Being extremely organized has its benefits and downfalls. Though, if Danni ever needs to take over for my players for any reason, she won't have a problem making sure they get the appropriate training. But it also means that I have hours of additional writing to do for each player.

After what feels like several hours have passed, there's a knock on my door, and I look up to find Taz and Vicy. It's odd that they are always the ones to come get me or find me in my office. It makes me wonder why Mac and Dean don't. I could have sworn they wanted to but... well... maybe I was wrong about them wanting to get with me.

Giving them a smile, I ask, "What's up?"

Taz taps on his bare wrist. "It's time to leave."

Raising a brow, I ask, "And I need to leave with you guys because ...?"

Vicy snorts. "She already forgot. It's Monday night, Roe Roe. Monday nights are karaoke nights at the bar. Remember?"

"I thought you were joking. I don't want to go to a karaoke bar. I hate singing in front of people," I complain with a whine.

"It will only be us. Come on! It'll be fun, I promise," Taz begs.

"Yeah. If you don't like it, you don't have to come next week," Vicy adds.

I huff as I stare at the pile of paperwork still on my desk. I don't have much else I need to do right away. Turning back to Vicy and Taz, I find them pleading at me with puppy-dog eyes. I can't help but laugh and, of course, give in. "Fine."

They let out a hoot of excitement. Shaking my head, I start gathering my stuff. My thoughts can't help but drift to Mac and Dean. The question that's been bothering me slips out before I can stop it. "Did I do something to upset Oli and Lewi?"

The guys share a look before sending me a quizzical expression. "What do you mean?" Taz asks.

I shrug as if it's not a big thing. "Just seems like they've been distancing themselves the last few days, compared to how they were when I first showed up."

Vicy gives me a grin full of trouble and teases, "Do you like our forward and goalie, Ms. Monroe?"

Picking up a sticky-note pad, I throw it at him with a huff. "I didn't say that!"

Taz shoulder bumps Vicy. "I bet it's because we found her in bed with Oli."

My cheeks heat as I hiss, "Nothing happened!"

They chuckle, lifting their hands in surrender. Vicy continues to smirk as he says, "Knowing Oli, he probably doesn't want to overwhelm you. You've had a lot happen the last few days."

"He's will try to win you over, no doubt. But he's not going to take advantage of you while you're staying with us until you find a new place," Taz adds.

I raise a brow as I walk over to them. "What do you mean, win me over?"

Vicy chuckles and throws an arm over my shoulder. "The man likes you, Roe Roe."

I feel my cheeks heat again, and I elbow Vicy in the side. "Whatever."

He laughs as he tugs on my ponytail. "When it comes to Lewi, I never see that man laugh or smile. But he does with you."

"And that means?" I ask.

Taz throws an arm over Vicy's on my shoulder, then whispers conspiratorially, "The man rubbed your feet and ankles, girl. I'm pretty sure he is enamored with you."

I snort. "Enamored?"

He grins and nods. "Yep. Enamored. People still use that word, Roe Roe."

I roll my eyes as I try to squirm out from under their arms. When I finally get free, I jog a few paces in front of them before turning to walk backward. I point between the two of them. "I'm your athletic therapist. I'm not starting a relationship with any of you."

Vicy sends me a teasing smirk. "So why did you ask about Oli and Lewi, then?"

My eyes narrow. "A momentary lapse in judgment, I assure you."

Taz laughs as he shakes his head. "Deny it all you want, but you don't always have a choice when fate is involved."

I halt my steps as they continue toward me. "What's that supposed to mean?"

Taz ruffles my hair, messing up my ponytail in the process. "If you're meant to be with those two, you will."

Vicy bumps my shoulder. "Plus, Oli has us as wingmen."

I throw my hands up and turn to follow them. "What about me?"

Vicy winks at me over his shoulder and replies, "Someone has to chip away at that icy wall around your heart."

Taz snorts and adds, "What better way to chip at that heart of yours, than having two annoying hockey players who are like brothers."

I roll my eyes and make my way to the double doors that lead outside. "I don't need anything chipped away," I grumble. "My heart is just fine. And you two were already acting like annoying brothers." I sigh and push open the doors. My breath hitches as my eyes immediately lock on the two men we were just talking about.

Oli is still laughing as he ruffles his damp, wavy hair, leaning against a parked car. Lewi is next to him, shaking his head in amusement as his lips tilt into a soft smirk. How do these two take my breath away and make me feel like I'm sixteen all over again?

I'm jerked out of my reverie when Vicy bumps my shoulder. I look up to find him tapping the side of his lips. "You've got a bit of drool there."

"You may want to close that mouth of yours. You'll start catching flies," Taz teases, but they both jump out of reach of my swatting hands.

"Get back here!" I screech as I take off running after them.

CHAPTER FIFTEEN

I follow the line of cars to the karaoke bar, and I'm the last one to walk through the doors. Well, Oli and Lewi were nice enough to wait for me while Taz and Vicy took off, rushing through the door first.

I snort out a laugh as I catch up to Oli and Lewi. "Why are they so excited to get inside?"

Lewi rolls his eyes, and Oli smirks. "This is sort of their thing."

"And we get dragged along," Lewi finishes for him.

I chuckle as we file through the doors and move through the semi-crowed area until we see a hand waving near the front of one of the stages. The stages are sectioned off where several people can relax.

I fight my way through the bodies until I reach our section. I sigh as Oli pushes me to sit near the front. I look behind me to give him a raised brow, but he just chuckles and sits a few seats down at the long table.

Whatever song Taz and Vicy were singing when I walked in must already be over because the crowd is giving a slow golf clap. Looking up at the stage, I see the two exchange a glance, then a nod.

Taz scrolls through the song list before selecting one. Vicy sends me a wink as the song starts, and I recognize the beat as Classic by MKTO.

I can't help but smirk as Taz throws up his hands. "Let's go!"

Vicy grins and sings the first verse, but he's singing directly to me. Pointing at me, he crooks his finger in a 'come here' gesture, telling me to join them on stage. I shake my head with a laugh, but then Taz comes down the steps and holding out a hand while joining Vicy in the pre-chorus.

I take his hand and let him drag me up on the stage. Taz spins me as they sing the chorus. When he lets me go, I'm standing between him and Vicy, and I can't stop laughing as Vicy waggles his brows at me. They hip bump me before somehow coordinating a spin as they switch sides.

Taz belts out the second verse, making dramatic moves as he gets down on one knee. I snort when he takes my hand and kisses it before finishing the last line. These boys are having way too much fun. He stands back up and sings along as they spin again and repeat the chorus.

I'm getting into it now, as I hip bump both of them, getting into the beat of the song. I'm sure I'm grinning like an idiot, but I'm having so much fun that I don't care. The beat drops and the verse begins, and I can't stop from singing along with them.

They each wrap an arm around my shoulders as they belt out the last line. When the song ends, they are breathing hard, and the team stands with a cheer. I'm still laughing as they press kisses on my cheeks.

"Your turn to sing!" Taz announces.

I shake my head. "I don't sing in public."

Vicy snorts and hands me the microphone. "You sing better than we do. One song?" he begs with a whine.

With an eye roll, I take the microphone. "Fine." I look through the list of songs available and grin when I see Miss Me More by Kelsea Ballerini. Considering what I've been through lately, this seems like the perfect one for me to sing.

Taz and Vicy's eyes widen as the first notes play from the speakers, huge grins on their faces. I sing the first verse, and I see the team's surprise. Seems the boys didn't share my little secret. I am by no means a professional singer, but I can carry a tune pretty well.

I start the pre-chorus and have to hold back laughter when Taz and Vicy sing backup vocals. I guess they know this song too.

When the song reaches the part about a snare drum, they come up beside me and act like they are playing drums. As I sing, I can't help but get into it more with the two of them as my back up.

I stare back into the crowd and find Oli and Lewi still staring with shocked expressions. A smile creases my face, but I keep singing. Taz and Vicy don't miss a moment of the backup vocals. A bit of my anxiety and stress from the last few days fades away as I lose myself in the song. As it draws to an end, Taz and Vicy sandwich me in a hug.

Through my laughter, I somehow manage to say, "You guys are squishing me!"

They chuckle and release me. Laughter shining in their eyes. Taz tilts his head and asks, "You feel better?"

I nod. "Much better."

Vicy yips and says, "Good because you are going to sing another song, and we get to pick which one this time."

"I just got done singing," I whine.

Taz rolls his eyes while he scrolls through the song choices. "You know you had fun. Just one more song."

Huffing a sigh, I relent. I am having fun. It's nice to forget about the crazy waiting for us for a little while; I think everyone needed a good laugh. "Fine, I suppose I can sing one more. Why do you get to pick?"

Vicy's face turns mischievous as he says, "Just because we are Oli and Lewi's wing men doesn't mean we can't help you out a bit too."

I look down at the screen, but I don't have enough time to protest before the song starts to play. Dirty Thoughts by Chloe Adams blasts through the speakers, and I have seconds to start the first few lines.

Glaring at the guys, I sing. Assholes. When I look toward the team, I see several of them trying to hold back laughter. My eyes drift to Oli and Lewi, and I didn't realize their eyes could even get wider. But their mouths are hanging open as shocked eyes meet mine.

Well, I'm already singing, may as well get into it. I send them both a wink, and Oli is the first to recover. He shakes his head with a smirk and sends me a wink back. Lewi, on the other hand, still seems too shocked to do anything.

I can't tear my eyes from the two men as sing. The beat drops, and I repeat 'I get dirty thoughts'. With each line, I see Oli's eyes darken and his smirk get wider. I can't meet their eyes anymore, so I look at the other guys as the song draws to an end.

My cheeks flame, and I give them a bow before heading back to my seat. I am done singing for the night. The moment my butt hits the seat, Oli leans over and whispers, "You sang beautifully."

"Thank you," I whisper back.

Taz clears his throat, and all eyes land on him as he gestures to the crowd. "I think it's only fair that the mysterious man himself gives us a show tonight."

Whoops and hollers explode around me as my gaze lands on Lewi. And I find him already looking at me. It appears a battle is being waged but, eventually, he huffs and stands from his chair.

"One song," he grunts.

Vicy grins and hands him a mic. "Promise. Only one song."

Taz and Vicy jump off the stage and take seats across from me at the table.

"You don't sing backup for him?" I ask.

They both shake their head, and Vicy says, "You'll understand why in a minute."

When the song starts, my eyes are jerked to the stage. It's not a song I would have picked for Lewi. Ghosts by Nathan Wagner begins, and my jaw drops when he opens his mouth to sing. His voice is smoky and deep. His eyes meet mine and, in that moment, it's like he's singing this song directly to me.

Chapter Sixteen

Dean 'Lewi' Lewis

Ten minutes earlier...

She looks like she's having a blast up there with Vicy and Taz. Not gonna lie, I'm a bit envious of how easy it has been for them to bond with her. They don't seem to care what she thinks of them as long as she's having fun and laughing.

They tell her it's her turn to sing now, and I see hesitation cross her face, but she eventually gives in. They have a way of breaking someone down until the person does as they ask. They are stubborn and determined. The song she chooses isn't one I would expect from her. I could see her picking a happy and upbeat pop song. But instead, she picks a country revenge song which makes me smirk.

I think she takes us all by surprise the moment she starts to sing. *Holy shit.* My jaw drops. The woman couldn't be any more perfect. She had me sold on her personality alone. Any man who tells you personality doesn't matter is a fucking liar. Her looks are a bonus, plus she skates. That's too many checkmarks for just one woman.

I can tell the moment she gets into the song because she sings from her heart. She's no longer worried about the audience. Instead, she puts everything into belting out the lyrics.

Mac bumps my shoulder. "Damn, she can sing."

All I can do is reply with a mumbled, "Yeah."

The moment the song ends, Taz and Vicy beg her to sing another one and end up picking one out for her. Her eyes widen, and I can tell she doesn't want to sing whatever it is they chose. But they don't give her a chance to argue before it begins.

The moment the lyrics of Dirty Thoughts by Chloe Adams slip through her lips, I'm a goner. I don't think it's normal to fall for someone this fast. My heart beats faster as dark thoughts of my past slither through my mind.

Memories of my father and mother start to overwhelm me. My chest tightens, and their toxic words ring through my head, slowly suffocating me. It's as if the words themselves are a noose around my neck, tightening their hold to prove each word true.

I jump when I feel someone nudge my knee.

The past begins to blur with the present, and whispered words slip past my lips. My throat tightens through the suffocating feeling as I speak to a ghost that still haunts me every day. "No...no..."

"Dean?" Mac's concerned voice briefly breaks through my panic and pulls me to the surface.

"Let me finish... Let me finish. I've got to prove it. I've got to prove myself." My whispered words don't reach anyone's ears except Mac's.

Leaning closer, Mac asks, "Prove what, brother?"

I turn so his dark eyes meet mine as I answer, "I'm not a mistake."

His eyes widen before he gives me a sad smile. "You're not a mistake. You have nothing to prove."

Before I can answer, Liz heads our direction and takes a seat one chair away. Oli squeezes my knee and leans over to whisper something to Liz. Taz clears his throat, and my eyes shift to his. I groan when I see the mischievous gleam in them, knowing he's going to ask me to sing.

Whoops and hollers erupt around us, and Liz turns to look at me. Well, what better way to show her how broken I am then by singing. I don't want to sing, but Taz won't let it go if I don't.

I huff a sigh and stand from my chair. *Fuck me.* "One song," I say as Vicy hands me the mic.

He nods. "Promise. One song."

I huff another sigh as they jump off the stage. I flip through the list of songs and find one that speaks to me. I'm sure it will show her the type of man I've become. Ghosts by Nathan Wagner begins to play, and my eyes meet hers as I sing. I feel a sliver of satisfaction when her eyes widen and her jaw drops.

Not many people know I can sing, and they often don't expect my voice to change the moment I do. I can't look away from her as I sing each line from the depths of my heart. Giving her a glimpse of my soul. Something I've never allowed anyone to see.

Her eyes never leave mine, and I can see them sparkle in the lights. Can she see how broken I am? How I've slowly killed myself, and there isn't anything left for her to like, let alone love. Why the fuck do I even want her to love me anyways?

The song ends, and I quickly drop the mic. I can't stand looking in her eyes anymore. I feel exposed. My eyes shift to Mac, and he gives me a sad nod. He knows what I need to get my mind right again. Without stopping to say goodbye, I head to the parking lot. The cool air hits me, and the past overwhelms me. I can't hold it back any longer. I race to the car and drive to the only place I've ever felt safe. *The ice rink.* Memories of my past swallow me whole.

10 years ago...

By now, you'd think I'd be used to the hours of lecturing I get from my parents after each game. It doesn't matter that I've been playing hockey since I could walk. The irony is a room filled with trophies, medals, and certificates proving I'm the top player on any team, don't matter.

We just won the final game of the season and claimed the top spot in the league. I even won MVP. But all my parents care about is that I could have done better. What more could I have possibly have done to prove that I'm the best. I don't have a single friend to call my own because everyone hates me.

They call me a kiss ass or goody-two-shoes. I hate it. I hate this house, this family, and worst of all, I hate myself.

I'm jerked from my reverie when my father yells, "Have you heard a single word we've said, Dean?"

I nod even though I blocked them out for the last thirty minutes. "I'll do better next time."

He glares at me before nodding. "Good. We can't have you tarnishing the Lewis name." He huffs before adding under his breath, "Your sister certainly wasn't this much work."

I flinch. No matter how many times he says that it finds a way to slice me each time. "May I leave now?" I ask quietly.

"Where are you going?" My mother asks in a huff.

I want out of this hellish house and to be left alone. I want to lick my wounds without them hovering over me like a starving pack of wolves. "The park across the street to think. The fresh air will help."

My father had already walked away having said what he wanted to get his point across. "Let him go. He deserves a reward for winning the game tonight at least."

I have to hold back an eye roll at that. Because allowing your son to go outside is considered an adequate reward for winning a hockey game and being named MVP. As if there would be no other reason to allow me out of this prison of a home.

My mother waves me off, and I don't need to be told twice, so I race toward the door. As soon as I'm outside, I take off running, not stopping until I reach the park swings across the street.

I sit on one of the swings and begin to slowly move. My fingers tighten around the chains as I stare down at my feet. There's a burn behind my eyes, and I bite my lip to keep the tears at bay. Crying won't fix anything. It's never fixed anything. The one time I cried in front of my parents, they sneered at me and demanded I stop acting like a child.

When the swing beside me squeaks, I'm jerked out of the memories. A gentle voice asks, "You okay?"

I quickly look up to see who it is before dropping my eyes again. It's the goalie on our team; I think his name is Mac. I grunt as I reply, "Fine. Fuck off."

"Well, that's not very nice." He chuckles from the swing beside me.

I envy him. He doesn't seem to have a problem talking to anyone. There are always people surrounding him. Friends everywhere he looks. "Haven't you heard, I'm the asshole on the team. I'm not nice."

He hums before bumping his shoulder into mine. "I don't think you're an asshole." We are quiet for a moment before he asks, "Shouldn't you be at home celebrating? We won, and you were named MVP! That's pretty awesome."

I snort. "My parents are more worried about how I could have done better than praising my accomplishment."

His feet hit the ground with a thump, and I look up when his feet stop in front of me. With a wide grin, he holds out a hand. "Well, my mom made cake. You should come to my house."

I look at his hand before looking up at him with a glare. "Are you trying to punk me or something? Do you have brain damage?"

His head tilts as he asks, "Punk? What's that mean? And no, I do not have brain damage as far as I know."

That's when I notice his accent. It's the first time I've actually listened to him speak. He's not from around here. "Where did you move from?"

"Canada. My mom wanted me to join a team here."

"Punk means that you're fucking with me. You're trying to play a trick on me," I explain.

His eyes widen as he says, "My mom would have my butt if I was mean to anyone, let alone one of my friends."

"One of your friends?"

He rubs the back of his neck, but he's still holding out his hand to me. "I mean. I think we are friends. Are we not friends?"

I can't help but laugh; he looks concerned that we wouldn't be considered friends. Looking at his hand one last time, I put mine in his. "Yeah... yeah, we're friends."

He gives my hand a squeeze and drags me to his house. "Good. I was a little worried there for a moment that you hated me."

Emotion clogs my throat as I manage to say, "Not a chance." How could I hate a guy who's this genuine. To be honest, I don't really hate people, I'm just envious of them. I've always wanted to be part of a group. To have a friend who won't leave me behind. But they always do. Everyone leaves eventually.

He smirks at me over his shoulder. "Congratulations on getting named MVP. I'm proud of you. You worked really hard for that."

He either ignores the tears sliding down my face or doesn't notice them. "Thank you." My chest aches, but it feels good. I never realized how much I wanted someone, anyone, to say that they were proud of me. Proud of what I've accomplished and worked so hard for. That I was more than just a waste of space or a pawn for my parents to use.

He gives my hand a squeeze as he leads me to his house. "Don't worry. My mom will gush all over you too."

I'd never met a woman quite like Nora Oliver. After that day, she became my adopted mother, and I never felt a lack of love when I was around her. She'd truly become my mother. Mère was a godsend for the years I had her. She was the one person other than Mac who I could rely on. They were my family.

She died while Oli and I were in college. I'd never cried as hard as I did at her funeral, and I didn't care who saw. My chest ached for weeks after, and I hid in our dorm room, bawling. I wanted my mother back. Oli wasn't the only one who lost a mom that day. I did, too, and he didn't fault me for it.

We clawed and fought our way into the NHL for her. Her one wish for us was that we played together in the NHL. And we did it. We did it for her. But, at some point in life, you have to do something for yourself. The only problem was... I didn't ever want to feel the pain of losing someone else I loved.

Chapter Seventeen

Elizabeth 'Liz' Monroe

L ewi leaves in a hurry, and it shocks me. Is something wrong? I turn in the direction he ran off before looking to Oli. He has a sad look on his face, but he gives me a small smile. "He needs a moment."

"Was it something I did?" I ask, biting my lip with worry.

He shakes his head. "Old demons coming out to play. He just needs a moment, and then he'll be alright."

I look toward the door again before gathering up my stuff. Oli grasps my forearm and asks, "Where are you going?"

I point to the door. "After him."

He shakes his head. "That's not a good idea. He often says things he doesn't mean when he's in one of these moods."

I tug out of his grasp and smirk. "Someone has to drag him out of his head. Who better than me?"

"Liz it isn't smart. He's going to say something and later regret his words. He can't help but lash out when he's like this," he pleads for me to understand.

With a soft smile, I say, "I promise I have thick skin, Mac. I will keep your words in mind when he lashes out."

After a moment, he deflates and lets out a heavy sigh. "Fine. Just... be careful with him. He acts tough, but he's more broken than he lets on."

I can't help but lean forward and press a kiss to the top of his head before backing away. "It's a good thing I'm familiar with handling broken things."

He shakes his head with a laugh. "He'll be at the rink. Most likely on the ice."

I nod and hustle out of the building, toward my car. It's not long before I'm pulling up to the hockey rink. I use my badge to get in since it's locked up for the night. This place is a little creepy when all the lights are off. Using the flashlight on my phone, I make my way to the ice.

The moment I step through the doors, I hear the scrape of his skates across the ice. It doesn't sound like he's doing anything hockey related though. As I get closer, I see him skate across the ice in no specific way, but then I hear him singing.

Keeping myself out of sight, I take him in. He's wearing head-phones while he skates, slicing his feelings into the ice. The longer I listen to him sing, I realize it's Lonely by Nathan Wagner. His voice echoes around the empty rink as he sings the hauntingly beautiful melody.

I watch, enraptured by both his skating and his voice. When the song ends, I'm about to make myself known, but then he jumps straight into another song. The lyrics to Tattoo by Loreen slip between his lips, and it reminds me of a guy I once watched sing this on TikTok. Deep and melodic but also extremely sad.

This man has more scars and demons than I thought. It's like he's fighting between the man he wants to be and the man he believes he ought to be. I'm not sure whose standards he is trying to meet. His own or another's.

I can't stay hidden in the shadows anymore. Not when he's this distraught over something I don't know how to help or fix. It's a moment before he sees me, and he does a double take, almost tripping over his skates.

"Liz?" he chokes out.

I give him a shy wave. "Hey."

He looks around for a moment before back at me. "Did... did anyone else come with you?"

I shake my head. "No."

He doesn't move from his spot as he asks quietly, "How long have you been there?"

I shrug, trying to play it off like I haven't been here long, but his eyes narrow, and he asks again, "How long have you been there, Elizabeth?"

Ouch... using full names now. "About halfway through Lonely, I think."

"You think?" he asks with a raised brow.

I shrug again as I reply, "I mean... I don't know the exact halfway point between the beginning and end of the song. It's a rough guess." Something flickers in his eyes, and I realize that he's about to do exactly what Mac warned me he would.

"You don't belong here," he grunts.

I don't back down. "I have every right to be here just as much as you."

His eyes narrow. "I didn't say you *couldn't* be here. I said you don't belong. Fuck off, Elizabeth."

Squaring my shoulders, I stand a bit taller. "No."

He throws his hands in the air. "Fine! I'll fuckin leave then." He growls and turns to skate away.

I point at him, not that he can see it, as I shout, "Don't you dare skate off! We are not done here, Lewis."

"Yeah, we are." He huffs and moves to skate away.

"Lewi!" I yell.

"FUCK OFF, ELIZABETH!" he bellows.

Oh hell no. He did not just do that. No one uses that tone with me. I spent far too many years letting a boy disrespect me. It will be a cold day in hell before I let this man do the same. "Dean Lewis, you better stop right now!" I command loudly.

"Or what?!"

"Don't make me get on this ice."

He continues to skate the other direction, but at least he's moving slower than before. "Just go away! You don't actually care; all you want is Oli's dick and maybe even mine! You don't care. All you're going to do is use us, then walk away. So fuck off!" he roars; his chest heaving.

I jerk back as if he'd slapped me with those words. Use them? When have I ever given them that impression. I'm about to say 'fuck it' and 'fuck all the way off' when Mac's words reply in my brain. *He's going to say things he doesn't mean. He's going to regret his words while trying to push you away.* Yeah, his words hurt, and they do make me want to walk away. But... that's exactly what he wants, isn't it?

Swallowing down the hurt I feel, I march toward him. Walking on ice in tennis shoes takes skill and practice and isn't altogether the smartest idea, but that doesn't matter to me right now. I need to knock some sense into the hockey player before me. "I'm going to kick your ass for that."

He looks over his shoulder and slides to a stop. He looks confused when he turns to skate in my direction. "What the hell are you doing?"

I'm trying to focus on my footing, so I don't eat shit and bruise my ass. "Apparently, being a woman of action and refusing to take your shit." The moment he's close enough, I slap him across the face before cupping his cheeks with my hands. It's a bit difficult and a little awkward, considering he's tall to begin with, and now he's got the added height from his skates.

His gaze meets mine and he asks again, "What are you doing?"

"Being your friend." I sigh. "Stop pushing me away. I'm not going to do this hot and cold with you. Either you want to be my friend or not."

He looks lost as his eyes flick over my face before he whispers, "I'm scared."

"Of what?" I ask softly.

"You seeing how much of a fuck up I am."

My brows knit as I argue, "You're not a fuck up, Dean."

"I am... I have to prove to you that I'm not."

I pull his face down to my own, so we are now eye level. I put every bit of conviction I feel into my voice. "You have *nothing* to prove to me. Nothing at all. You are not a fuck up, and there is nothing wrong with you. No one is perfect, and if anyone says they are, they're lying."

He takes a few breaths before asking in a hushed tone, "Can I hug you?"

The question catches me off guard, but I nod. "Yeah... Of course." I feel tiny when he wraps his arms around me, holding on tightly.

"I'm sorry," he whispers into my neck.

His body is shaking in my arms, and I give him a squeeze as I reply, "I'll forgive you, as long as you never full-name me again. It was really weird hearing you call me Elizabeth."

His body relaxes slightly, and he chuckles softly. "Done."

"Also, if you ever talk to me like that again, know that I'll do worse than slap you across the face." I threaten with a snort.

"I would deserve it."

"Do you want to skate a little longer?" I ask.

He shakes his head and pulls away. "Let's go home."

"Movie night?" I ask in a hopeful tone. I know we have work in the morning, but I could really use a good movie and popcorn night.

He chuckles and nods, then skates over to the edge of the ice. He goes slow as I walk beside him in my tennis shoes. "What movie do you have in mind? I'm not sure all the guys will stay up to watch. Most of them have already gone to bed."

I huff in disappointment. That's true. "We don't have to do a movie night. I just thought it may be a nice way to wind down."

He bumps my shoulder before stepping off the ice to remove his skates. "Mac is still awake, I'm sure. He's a mother hen when it comes to me and my moods. We can stay up and watch a movie with you, if you'd like."

I bite my lip; I don't want to be an inconvenience. "It's fine. I can watch it in my room, so all of you can sleep."

He chuckles, shaking his head as he looks up at me from the bench. For the moment his chocolate brown eyes are filled with mirth and laughter, which takes me aback. They held so much pain when I first walked in. I've never seen Dean's eyes so light and airy. "We will be awake anyways, Ice Princess. Mac won't mind staying up to watch a movie with you."

Ignoring the new nickname for now, I arch a brow. "And you?"

He shrugs, packing up his skates before he says, "I owe you for treating you like shit." He rubs the back of his neck as he continues, "I'm not good with new people, let alone with them seeing my short-comings."

Without thought, I step forward, wrapping my arm around his forearm that holds his skates. I give him a gentle tug to head toward the exit. "Everyone has flaws and shortcomings, Dean."

He hums and follows my insistent tugging. His voice is so quiet, I'm not sure I'm supposed to hear him say, "You seem pretty perfect to me."

I pretend to not hear it as I look over my shoulder with an arched brow. "What?"

His eyes widen, and he shakes his head. "Nothing. You never said what movie you wanted to watch."

"Have you seen *Howl's Moving Castle*?" I ask as we step outside the building.

"Can't say that I have," he answers.

I release my grip on his arm, but he quickly takes my hand. When I look back, his cheeks are lightly dusted pink. He nods toward his car. "I can give you a ride home, and one of us can give you a ride to work in the morning."

I look at my car before shrugging my shoulders. This is probably a horrible idea, but something about the look in his eyes makes me want to go with him. He looks like he wants a bit more one-on-one time with me. Only me.

I know this is a bad idea. These guys are finding ways to melt the ice around my heart. I need to stay strong and not give into the temptation of these two men. But... a car ride won't hurt anyone. Will it?

Chapter Eighteen

Today is a surprisingly sunny day, which I am thankful for. It sounds like the team always throws a Fourth of July cook out, and I am required to attend. Mac and Dean stayed behind with me while the others left for the party already. It's started to feel weird calling them Oli and Lewi in my head, let alone out loud. They don't feel like Oli and Lewi when we aren't at work. To be honest, it's beginning to feel weird calling any of the guys by their nicknames, now that I've built a friendship with them.

I'm not exactly nervous about the cookout but, at the same time, I am. I'm about to meet the whole team's significant others, not just the guys I'm in charge of. Who am I kidding. I'm beyond nervous about meeting my guys' wives.

A knock sounds on the bathroom door, and I'm jerked out of my thoughts. "Yes?"

Mac laughs and asks, "Are you almost ready? We got back from the rink three hours ago."

I snort a laugh and open the bathroom door. I went light on the make-up, but I'm wearing a soft blue sundress, considering how warm it is. Washington doesn't get hot often, but today is one of those rare days that gets above eighty degrees and sunny.

My gaze collides with Mac's wide eyes as he takes in my outfit. I run my fingers through my loose waves as my nerves take over. Does he like the dress?

When his eyes finally meet mine, he's grinning. *"Tu es rayonnante."*

My cheeks heat as I reply, "Thank you."

Dean darts around the corner from the living room. "Is she ready yet? We need to..." his words die off when he sees me.

I twist my hips to let my dress swish around me. "I'm ready."

After another moment or two of staring, he shakes his head. "Yeah—um—you—"

Watching him trip over his words has a smirk pulling at my lips. "Yes?"

Mac chuckles. "It seems you have shocked my brother speechless, Chérie."

Dean grunts and growls at him. "Fuck off. I'm just trying to find the right words."

I slowly walk over to him before peering up at him with a smile. "And what words are those?"

He jerks his eyes from Mac to land back on me. There's a tinge of pink on his cheeks as he says, "Still haven't quite found them yet."

I chuckle as I rise on my tiptoes to place a chaste kiss on his cheek. I couldn't help myself. These two make me feel more beautiful and cherished than anyone else I've encountered. Which is a shame, considering I'm not allowed to date them. But maybe a little flirting when no one else is around is okay. "I look forward to hearing them when you do," I whisper before brushing against him as I walk around him toward the front door. I look over my shoulder with a smirk. "We are going to be late if we don't leave now."

Mac follows, hooking an arm around Dean's shoulder and tugging him along. "Let's go have some fun and make sure our girl has an amazing night."

I snort as they pass me. "Your girl?"

"Amuse us for the night, Chérie," he says as he opens the passenger side door for me.

I slide in with a smirk. "How exactly am I your girl if no one is supposed to know? We could get in serious trouble if anyone on the team even thinks are together."

He rolls his eyes playfully as Dean gets into the backseat. Mac closes the door before rushing around the vehicle to slip into the driver's seat. Dean leans forward to say, "No one on the team will care if we are together."

I arch a brow. "I'm pretty sure the documents I signed when I was hired say otherwise."

Mac blows out a raspberry. "Upper management is who makes you sign that shit. No one from upper management will be there."

"It's still such a bad idea," I argue with a huff.

"What if we are subtle about it?" Dean asks from the backseat.

I can't help but laugh. "Subtle? I don't think you know what subtle is, Dean."

His brow knits, and he pouts. "I can be subtle."

I hold out a hand in his direction. "Bet?"

His eyes sparkle with mischief as he smirks and slaps his hand into mine. "Bet. What do I get when I win?"

"So sure of yourself?" I snicker.

He nods, releasing my hand. "I'll be the best subtle boyfriend ever."

My body heats at that, and Mac chuckles. "I want in on this bet too."

I roll my eyes, but the flush of my body betrays my nonchalance. "Fine. What do you both want?"

Mac hums. "Oh no, Chérie. This is a separate bet. We are lumped together. I get a separate prize if I win."

I shift in my seat as I grow flustered. Good lord. I sigh and say, "Fine. Dean what do you want as your prize?"

He leans forward, so his lips are next to my ear. "I want a kiss. A *real* kiss."

Mac groans. "Yes. I want that too! That's my prize too."

"You both want a kiss?"

They agree and Dean falls back into the seat. "What do you want if you win?" he asks casually.

I nibble my lip as I try to think of something I want. At this point, I'm not sure if I want to win or lose. If I'm kissing them for a bet, then it doesn't count right? What do I want? I can't think of anything else now that they mentioned a kiss. "I'll let you know what I want when I win," I say mischievously.

"Spoil sport," Dean pipes up from the back.

"Well, she has me curious now," Mac adds as he parks the car.

Dean climbs out and opens my door. He offers me a hand to help me out. I smirk as I slide my hand into his, allowing him to help me. He looks around briefly before leaning in to press a kiss on my cheek.

With a wink, he pulls back and whispers, "I'm going to win this bet, Ice Princess."

His hand slips out of mine, and he begins to walk toward the crowded park. I can feel my cheeks heat as I catch Mac out of the corner of my eye. Our eyes meet, and he shoots me a teasing smirk and wink. "Good luck, Chérie. We plan to win that kiss."

Like a proper gentlemen, he offers his elbow, and I slide my hand around his forearm. "I didn't know a kiss was worth that much," I whisper.

He chuckles softly as we head in the direction Dean went. "You have no idea what we'll do to get a few moments with you, let alone a kiss, Chérie."

"Noted," I say, trying to get my flustered face back to normal before someone notices.

As we get closer, a wolf whistle rings out, and I look around to find Taz and Vicy making their way toward us. I can't stop the giggle that bubbles up in my chest when they give me dramatically wide eyes and gesture wildly to me.

"Damn, Roe Roe! Who knew our favorite AT was so drop dead gorgeous," Vicy says teases.

I shake my head with a laugh. "What does AT mean?"

"Athletic therapist. Much easier to say," Taz answers for him.

I hum as Dean comes over to us, holding three beers. He hands one to Mac, who opens it before handing it to me. I smirk and accept it with nod to them both in thanks. Dean smirks before taking a swig.

"Elizabeth!"

I jerk around, looking for whoever said my name. When I see Perri, Merc, Gilly, and Fenni walking our way, I smile. Slipping my hand from Mac's, I wave. "Hey guys!"

Perri is the first to greet me, and he leans in to give me a hug. Just a quick squeeze before pulling away. He gestures to his left and says, "This is my wife, Karen."

I hold out a hand. "It's a pleasure to meet you."

She waves a hand in the air but pulls me in for a hug. "There is no handshaking here, girl. We give hugs."

I chuckle and hug her back, then she pulls away, allowing the others to greet me. Merc is next, giving me a quick hug before shuffling the two wiggling children out of his wife's arms. "These are my kids, Sebastian and Savannah"—he then turns a wide smile toward the woman beside him—"and this is my stunning wife, Cheryl."

I wiggle my fingers at the kiddos, then hold my hand out to Cheryl. "It's wonderful to meet you."

She chuckles and grasps my hand before also pulling me in for a hug. "Karen did say we are huggers, right?"

I laugh but hug her back. "I wasn't sure if that meant everyone."

She pulls back with a grin. "We're a family, so that means we hug. If you are part of the Wraiths, then you are part of the family."

My cheeks hurt from smiling so much as Gilly and Fenni greet me together. They each lean in to press a kiss to my cheek before pulling away. "Hope the guys aren't driving you too crazy at the house," Gilly says with a laugh.

"You know just how crazy they are, Maxy," I say with a wink.

He grins and takes a step back for his wife to slip under his arm. "Liz this is my wife, Dannielle."

I smile as I take in her *very* pregnant belly. "Congratulations! I'm not sure if you want a hug, but considering I was just told everyone is a hugger..."

She laughs and shakes her head. "Hugging a pregnant woman is always awkward." She holds out a hand, and I take it with a smile. "It's a pleasure to meet you, Elizabeth."

"Liz is fine," I say as I release her hand. Next, I turn to the woman under Fenni's arm. I point to her. "And that must make you Samantha."

She nods and holds out a hand. "It's a pleasure to meet you, Liz."

A clap sounds from behind me. Releasing Samantha's hand, I look over my shoulder to see Vicy cupping his hands around his mouth. "Let's get this party started!"

Samantha laughs. "I'm not sure how you handle all of them."

I shrug and watch Vicy and Taz rush toward the table that holds hundreds of fireworks. "I've been teaching kids how to skate for several years. It's pretty similar to that."

"So you're saying they are like children," Dannielle says with a laugh.

There's an explosion in the distance, and the guys around me groan but rush in Taz and Vicy direction. I snort and reply, "No. They are much, much worse."

Karen and Cheryl link arms with me, Dannielle and Samantha following behind as we slowly walk in the direction of the others. Cheryl leans in with a soft laugh and says, "I'm not sure I should have let Corin run off with the kids."

My eyes widen when I see Corin, his twins in tow. They look about three, which I have to admit is an adorable stage. They walk next to their dad, each holding on to his pointer finger. He tugs his son along and veers to the left, which is where the other children and parents are. His little girl squeals in excitement as she tries to pull him to walk faster. "Seems he knew only trouble would be in the direction the others went."

"Smart man," she says with a chuckle. "Though, I'm sure the twins will cause him just as much trouble as Vicy and Taz."

I laugh. "No argument there."

The night quickly flies by as I enjoy my time with the team and their wives. I didn't meet a single girlfriend for the other players, and when I asked, Perri sat on the ground in front of his wife and looked up with a smirk. "They don't want puck bunnies anymore. Seems you've made them all want wifey material."

I snort out a laugh. "Wifey material? I don't think I'm much of an example of wifey material."

He points to Vicy and Taz in the distance as he says, "Those two were the worst with puck bunnies. I haven't seen the guys give them the light of day once over the last few months." He chuckles. "Though, that may have something to do with a certain single mother they met at the rink during one of your ice-skating classes."

I sit up in my chair, interested in this new information. "They have eyes for one of the moms?"

He nods as he replies, "I think it's the mom that you've been talking to. The one who will be your assistant for now, so she can take over when the season starts."

I furrow my brows before the realization hits. "Daisy?"

He nods. "She's the one with the little girl who always has pigtails, right?"

I nod with a grin. "Aspyn is the little girl's name. Daisy used to skate professionally until she got pregnant. She loves the ice, so I'm excited for her to take over for me. I know she'll do a great job."

Merc plops his daughter in Cheryl's lap beside me and joins in on the conversation. "Didn't she recently get divorced?"

I laugh. "How did you guys find out this information?"

Merc grins as he joins Perri on the ground with his son. "You do realize the moms there are full of gossip."

I roll my eyes. "Well, if you must know, her and her husband have been separated for a few years now. But the divorce wasn't finalized until a few months ago." A bottle of beer is suddenly in front of my face, making me jerk back in surprise. Looking up, I find Mac hovering behind me, a smile on his face.

"Figured you were short on refreshments," he says with a smirk.

"Thanks, Mac." Our fingers brush as he hands it over with a wink, and I try to keep the butterflies from flying away with my stomach. Damn, I forgot about our bet.

Mac nods as he leans back onto his elbows between Cheryl and me. She arches a brow before looking between him and me. I must not have kept my blush at bay because she sends me a knowing smirk before miming that her lips are zipped.

My blush is made worse when Dean plops down in the grass between my legs. He looks around before asking, "What are we talking about?"

Perri grins when he sees the others closing in on us. As Taz and Vicy get closer, he says loudly, "We were talking about Daisy and her daughter."

Vicy and Taz look up when the names are mentioned, somewhat startled. Fenni and Gilly smirk to themselves as they find spots near their wives. Tuck and Ozzy join the circle on the grass as Vicy and Taz ask in unison, "What about them?"

I can't hold back my laugh when I see their eyes, hungry for information. "We were just talking about Daisy replacing me once the season starts." Their shoulders drop, and I can't help but give them a little hope. "I may have also mentioned that she may need some help with a few of the classes when I'm not available. You know how that group of kids can be."

They share a look between them before giving me a hopeful look. "We can help," they say at the same time again.

I nod. "Sure. I'll mention it to her."

They give each other a fist bump before joining the others on the grass. Bonfires are lit around us as the sun sets, and the show begins. I gaze above me as explosions of color spread through the sky. A finger slowly caresses my shoulder, and when I look, I find Mac staring at me instead of the sky.

I jerk my gaze back to the sky when I feel another hand caress the bare skin on my calf. My cheeks heat, but I don't look down because I know it's Dean. They are doing this because no one will be looking at them. All eyes will be on the sky, which gives them free rein to look at me.

I suppose this means they won the bet. But I can't say I'm upset with losing. I've never looked forward to a kiss, but with them? It seems my heart won't stop beating in anticipation for this night to end. I won't admit I'm hungering for a kiss with the two of them. Not out loud anyway.

CHAPTER NINETEEN

A few weeks have passed since the Fourth of July party. Mac and Dean did call in their prize, but certainly didn't do it at the same time. Mac didn't wait long just a few days later and we're in his room as he slowly kisses me. Not going to lie, I whined a little when he pulled away, and he only smirked as he backed away and out of the room. Dean had waited a week to press me against the wall and ravage me with a single kiss. We had found ourselves alone at the house and it'd only taken him moments to press his body to mine. Where Mac's kiss had been sweet and sensual, Dean's was dark and hungry.

I wanted more kisses. But that would mean admitting I wanted more in this odd thing between us, and I couldn't do that just yet. I'd expected it to be awkward, but Dean's been more talkative lately, and Mac has upped his flirting game. The guys have been trying to help me search for an apartment, and I finally found one. They even helped me move, and I've found the best way to do it.

They love home cooked meals, and they told me they haven't had homemade fried chicken with mashed potatoes. So, since today is my day off, I've managed to gather all the ingredients to make it.

Spotify is playing on shuffle, though most are country songs. The boys have me on a country music listening spree. The next song that pops on is Yeah Boy by Kelsea Ballerini. I smirk and sway my hips to the beat.

I'm in the middle of whisking the gravy and flipping the chicken while singing along when I hear Dean's voice behind me, and I let out a loud squeal. "Whatcha cooking there, Liz?"

In a flurry of gravy and hair, I spin around, and the tongs go flying out of my hand. Dean yells, "Oh shit!" but he ducks fast enough that the tongs hit Vicy in the chest.

"Ouch!" he yelps and rubs his chest.

"You scared the shit out of me!" I screech. Then I throw the gravy-covered whisk at Dean, who ducks again, which means Vicy gets hit by the whisk as well.

He throws his hands up in defeat. "What did I do?"

Dean looks over his shoulder and chuckles. "Bad reflexes."

"How was I supposed to know she was going to start throwing things? I'm not the one who scared her!" Vicy whines.

Turning off the heat for the gravy and grabbing a new pair of tongs, I pull out the chicken. Once done, I take my handmade cookies from the oven that has been keeping them warm. With a chocolate-chip cookie in hand, I turn and ask Vicy, "Will a cookie make it better?"

His eyes fill with excitement as he bounces over to the kitchen. "Yes!" He grins as he takes the cookie and immediately takes a bite. He groans and mumbles, "This is so good."

Dean goes to grab one, and I swat his hand. "You scared me; you don't deserve cookies."

He pouts and asks, "What can I do to get one of those cookies?"

I ponder the question for a moment before giving him a mischievous grin. "You have to come to my ice-skating class and participate for a month."

His eyes widen, then narrow. "Seriously? For a cookie?"

I chuckle as I wave the smell of the warm cookies toward him. "For a cookie and an apology for scaring me. You could have ruined dinner."

He huffs as he holds out a hand. "Fine. Can I have a cookie?"

Instead of handing him one, I put my hand in his and give it a shake. "You shook on it."

"This seems like a deal made under duress," he grumbles.

With a chuckle I replace my hand with a warm cookie. "Let me know if it's worth it."

He stares at me with narrowed eyes as he takes a bite. It only takes seconds before his eyes flutter closed, and he hums in satisfaction. I smirk as he opens his eyes and narrows them on me again.

With a knowing look, I ask, "So?"

"I plead the fifth," he mumbles through another bite.

Laughing, I wave the guys out of the kitchen. "Out. Out, so I can finish making dinner."

Vicy plants a kiss on my cheek as he steals another cookie before running off. "Thanks, Roe Roe!"

I chuckle, shaking my head. The others walk out of the kitchen, and I assume they're heading for the couches in the living room. Mac and Dean stay behind, silently leaning on the counter on either side of me.

I arch a brow as I fry more chicken. "Yes?"

"Do you need help?" Mac asks.

I shake my head as I begin to bop to the new song playing. "I'm good. You guys relax. This is my thank you for helping me."

Mac chuckles. "You wouldn't have been able to move all your stuff by yourself. Plus, do you think we would make our favorite athletic therapist move everything by herself?"

"I suppose you're right." It's quiet for a moment, and it's becoming awkward as they stand there and watch me cook. When I look up, Mac is looking at Dean with a concerned expression.

Switching my gaze to Dean, I see him staring down at his hands while he rolls a beaded bracelet with his thumb. Mac and I exchange a quick glance, his eyes pleading for me to do something.

With a deep sigh, I bump Dean with my shoulder. "I like your bracelet."

He hums but continues to fiddle with it. I turn to Mac, whose eyes are flicking his eyes between me and Dean. What does he expect me to do? He leans forward and whispers in my ear, "He got a call from his dad today. He's been down all day. Help him, please."

As he pulls away, I arch a brow and ask with my eyes, *how am I supposed to do that?*

He smiles softly as he whispers, "You helped last night."

Huffing a sigh, I hand him the tongs. "Don't ruin my chicken."

"Yes, ma'am," he says with a mock salute.

I take a deep breath and turn my focus on Dean. I brush my fingers over the bracelet as I say, "It's really pretty." The bracelet holds all his focus right now. Maybe if I can get him to talk about it, he will open up about what's on his mind.

He answers, but he sounds far away. "Mère gave it to me."

If I remember correctly, that means mother in French. I'm not sure what his relationship with his parents is like, but considering his attitude right now, I'd guess he's not close to his dad. Is he close to his mom, though?

"So, your mom gave that to you?"

He shakes his head and finally looks up at me. "No, my mère. She was Mac's mom."

I hadn't realized Mac and Dean were so close that he would call Mac's mom an endearment like that. Trying to keep the conversation light, I comment, "That was nice of her."

He nods as he looks back down at the bracelet. "She would know what to do. She always knew how to handle my parents." He lets out a bitter laugh as he continues, "A quality I was envious of. Still am."

When I turn to look at Mac, I see him staring down at a matching bracelet on his wrist. He must feel my eyes because he sends me a sad smile. He mouths the words, *she died.*

Well. This conversation just turned heavy. I bite my lip, not entirely sure how to go about helping. Should I give him a hug or talk him through his thoughts? I inwardly sigh but ask, "What would she do first in this situation?"

He shrugs as if it's no big deal before saying, "I guess she would give me a hug and say, *je suis fier.*"

"That's pretty. What does it mean?" I ask softly.

"It means, *I am proud,*" he whispers.

He's still fiddling with the bracelet, so I cover his hand with my own and ask, "What did your dad say?"

His shoulders drop. "Same thing he always does. That I need to be better. Don't sully the Lewis name. Make sure I do better than my best in the first game of the season."

My heart aches at the words spilling out of his mouth. *Do better than his best?* I've never seen him do less than his best. He's his own worst critic and often pushes himself too hard. I have a feeling those are words his father says often and have been drilled into his head, over and over, for years. I can see why he turned to Mac's mother when it came to comfort.

I push into the space between his arms and wrap my own around his torso. I didn't realize how small I was until this moment, but if a hug is what he needs, then a hug is what he'll get. His body stiffens for a moment before he seemingly melts in my arms. He wraps his own around me and pulls me in closer.

"I'm proud of you," I mumble into his chest.

His chuckle sounds hollow. "You don't know me well enough to say that."

My arms tighten around him as I say with force, "I bet I know you better than you think. I have those notebooks for a reason."

He lowers his head to rest it on my shoulder as he grumbles, "Enlighten me then."

I smirk. "Well, let's start with the easy stuff. You are twenty-seven years old and grew up in Bellevue. Your birthday is March 27th, which may explain why you are so hotheaded."

He snorts and huffs. "Alright. You said that was the easy stuff, and I agree. Anyone can find that information. What's the hard stuff?"

Squeezing him tight, I say, "You are loyal and extremely protective of those you consider family. Your favorite ice cream flavor is vanilla, but you will argue otherwise because you don't want people to think you're ordinary. You hate chocolate and chewy candies because you don't like the way they stick in your teeth. Your favorite color is blue."

"Blue is so not my favorite color." He chuckles softly.

I roll my eyes. "Blue is the generalized color, you dork. Your favorite blue is sky blue. When there aren't any clouds in the sky."

His arms tighten around me as he whispers, "All that is in your notebook?"

I nod and whisper, "Yes. There's other stuff not in my notebooks though."

"And what's not in your notes?"

Swallowing my nerves, I reply, "You are your own hardest critic. You stay for hours after practice if you feel like you could have done better. Your caliber of skating is higher than most hockey players I've worked with previously. And playing both offense and defense positions are no issue for you."

I pull away just enough so I can look into his eyes. His head is lowered as if still resting on my shoulder. I want to make sure he can see the truth in my eyes. "When I say I'm proud of you, know that it's the truth. I'm proud of all my guys, but I see how hard you work to always be your best."

He looks away from me as if my words are too hard to hear. I reach up to press my fingers to the side of his jaw to pull his eyes back to mine. "Stop being so hard on yourself. You are amazing the way you are. Sure, you can always grow and become better. But don't make it seem like there NEEDS to be improvement. You are enough just the way you are."

There's a gleam in his eyes when he lowers his head to my shoulder and pulls me into a crushing hug. "You are too perfect, you know that?"

I laugh as I pat his back. "I'm far from perfect. But I appreciate the sentiment." I give him one last squeeze before saying, "Now, I need to get back to my chicken before Mac ruins dinner."

There's a mock scoff beside me, and Dean allows me to pull away. "I'm offended you think I would ruin your chicken!" Mac says, his tone dripping with fake hurt.

Laughing, I pull away from Dean and dart toward Mac to snatch the tongs. I snap them at him. "Get out of the kitchen, so I can finish."

His smile is wide as he leans in, pressing a kiss to my cheek before jumping away. "As the boss commands." He then mouths 'thank you' before leaving to join the others in the living room.

Dean chuckles and kisses my other cheek. "Thanks, Ice Princess."

I roll my eyes. "You've been calling me that lately. I'm not a princess. Plus, calling me ice princess makes me sound cold and heartless."

He tugs on my ponytail. "You are a princess on the ice. That's why I call you that. You're confident and passionate when you are near or on the ice."

My cheeks heat. "So that makes me an ice princess?"

I see him shrug from the corner of my eye. "You are too me. That's a nickname only I can use, though."

I smirk. "Only for you?"

With a mischievous smile, he lifts a hand to brush his thumb across my bottom lip. "Mac isn't the only one interested in you."

I swallow down the squeal my inner, love-sick self wants to release and stutter, "Y-yeah?"

He leans in to bump his forehead against mine. "Be careful with my heart, Ice Princess. You'll find it's as delicate as the ice we skate on." He pulls away, leaving me speechless. I let out a squeak when hot grease splatters on my hand. I quickly pull the fried chicken out of the pan.

Leaning back against the counter, I take a few deep breaths. *Good lord, these boys are going to test my will to keep them at a distance. Friend zone is a safe zone. Though, I'm not sure how much longer I want them to stay in the friend zone. I want more; I hunger for something forbidden.*

CHAPTER TWENTY

To my utter amusement—and Dean's embarrassment—he participates in my Saturday ice-skating class. I have never seen a man look so awkward in a pair of yoga pants and an athletic long-sleeve shirt. You'd think he was in his birthday suit.

"I feel too exposed," he grunts.

I chuckle. "I promise you look fine."

A little boy—the only boy in my class—stands beside him. His tiny elbow bumps Dean's hip, and he says, "Stop being so weird. Miss Lizzy is teaching, and you're interrupting. That's rude."

I bite my lip to stifle the giggle that wants to burst free. Dean looks down at him, slightly shocked, before his gaze flicks to me. When he sees me trying to hold back laughter, he rolls his eyes. "Fine. Sorry, Miss Lizzy, for interrupting the class."

"It's alright Dean. We are close to the end of class which means..."

"Free time!" the kids yell excitedly.

I clap my hands to get their attention again. "Correct! Alright, my little snowflakes, let's get the cones and equipment cleaned up. The rest of class is time to have fun."

The kids quickly skate around the rink to gather everything up, which makes it easier for me to put things away. I turn to find Dean looking at me with a pleading expression. "What now?"

"Can I PLEASE go change?"

I snort a laugh as I shake my head. "Go change, you diva."

He points a finger at me and glares. "I am *not* a diva. I don't like tight clothes! I am a hockey player not an ice skater. This"—he gestures wildly at himself—"is not me."

Laughing, I wave him off. "Go change."

He sighs in relief. "Thank you. Oh, glorious sweatpants and hoodie, here I come!"

After I finish helping the kids clean up, I wave goodbye. I make a few laps around as Dean makes his way out of the changing room.

He cups his hands around his mouth and yells, "Are you going to skate tonight?"

I give him a nod and skate over to my phone. Dean meets me at the edge of the ice, where the concrete walls divide the inside from the outside of the ice. Scrolling through Spotify, I find the song I've been practicing to.

As I hand him my phone, I hear the doors to the rink open. In walks Mac, quickly followed by the rest of my team. My jaw drops when all ten guys stroll in.

"What are you all doing here?" I squeak out.

Taz points to Dean. "Lewi texted that you were gonna skate, and we want to see what the amazing Elizabeth Monroe can do."

I send Dean a glare, but he just gives me a mischievous smirk. "You made me participate in class today. This is only fair."

I throw my hands up and huff. "How is this fair? You are taking the classes for scaring me!"

He shrugs. "You made me wear that weird outfit."

"It's normal attire for ice skaters," I mutter.

"And I'm not an ice skater," he counters.

These guys are going to drive me crazy! "Fine, whatever. Hit play on the music once I'm in the center," I grumble, then make my way to the center of the ice. "Got it!" he shouts.

I wasn't expecting an audience this big to watch me skate. It's a bit intimidating, to be honest. It's been years since I've had this many eyes on me while I skate. This isn't going to be an impressive routine, considering I'm not doing any jumps. I don't want to ruin the progress when my ankle is still healing after my last skate.

The first notes of Are You With Me by Nilu play through the Bluetooth system. I start with my head bowed, but as the music starts, I spin out of the center while one arm flares up, and the other flares down. I pick up speed as the first lines fill the room. I bring my hands up with my fingers flared out over my face, continuing up and over my head.

I go into a scratch spin with my hands above my head, then slowly bring my hands over my heart as I spin faster. Digging into the ice with my toe pick to stop my spin, I point to the audience. Oddly, Mac and Dean are standing where I point as the words echo around us, *I need you here.*

I skate toward them, then cut to the right as I pick up speed again. This routine is more about having fun rather than how many points I would get in a competition. I'm skating from my heart instead of worrying what the judges would think of my choreographed routine. It's a freeing feeling.

I add in a few spirals that feel right in the moment and point to the others as the chorus begins. The vibration and emotion in the lyrics fill the room as I spin. As the beat drops at the end of the chorus, I go into a low back spin.

I lunge out of the spin before lowering both knees to the ice, just as the second verse starts. I lower my back as my hair slides across the ice. My fingers gliding across the smooth surface before I rise. I kick out my right leg to spin and rise from the position. I pick up speed as I do a spread eagle, then end on a camel spin. Bringing my leg back in, I do another scratch spin before stabbing my toe pick into the ice to lift one arm toward the stands as the song draws to the end.

When the song ends, I find myself looking at Mac and Dean. My breaths are more like heavy pants as I stare at the guys, unable to take my eyes off them. Their expressions vary but most have wide eyes, filled with a mix of shock and awe. Dean's eyes appear have a sheen to them.

A sudden roar of applause makes me jump. I finally break eye contact to look around at everyone else. Vic and Taz are jumping up and down like little kids while whistling. I can't stop the laugh that bubbles up as I give them a bow. My hands come together in prayer position as I bring them to my lips. It's been so long since I had this type of attention, and I feel my eyes burn. I'm not sure if it's from excitement or the longing to be seen by others I feel as I skate. It could be both.

I skate over to where you enter and exit the ice, and before I can step off, I'm swung up into Vicy's arms. I squeal as I do my best to keep my legs from flying, so my skates don't hurt anyone. He gives me a tight hug before releasing me. "That was amazing!"

My cheeks heat. "Thank you."

Taz throws an arm around my shoulders and tugs me in for a hug. "Absolutely breathtaking."

My smile widens. "Thanks."

Each of the guys give me a hug and tell me how amazing I looked on the ice. Dean and Mac are last, both greeting me with wide grins.

Mac leans forward and presses a soft kiss to my forehead. "You are beautiful on the ice, Lizzy."

My cheeks brighten as I shrug off the praise. "I didn't do any impressive jumps."

Before Mac has a chance to reply, Dean softly nudges me and rolls his eyes. "You don't have to do impressive jumps to be beautiful on the ice, Ice Princess."

Their words make me giddy, but I try to hide it by giving them a dramatic eye roll. "If you say so. Are you guys going to wait for me to change?"

They nod, and Dean points to the others. "We're planning to head back and chill at the common house for a bit."

I nod as I slide my blade covers on and make my way to the locker room. "I shouldn't be long." They nod as I leave to change.

The moment I step into locker, someone snatches me from the doorway. I scream before it's muffled by a cloth is placed over my mouth and nose. In my panic, I take a deep breath, but my mind becomes hazy.

I hear a warped voice coming from somewhere behind me say, "Not too much. Don't want you out too long. Just long enough, so you won't fight me."

The last thought I have before the haze completely fills my mind is that my stalker must have found me. I'd grown too comfortable and blind with the safety the guys provided. I should have been paying more attention, now that I have my own place again. *Please... please, find me.*

Dean 'Lewi' Lewis

Liz is taking longer than normal to change. I scan the rink to see if maybe we missed her coming out of the locker room, but I don't see her anywhere. A blood-curdling scream echoes around the rink, and my blood turns to ice. Mac, and I exchange a look, his eyes filled with just as much panic as mine.

"Liz," he grunts before taking off for the locker room.

Suddenly, the rink's sound system is filled with a distorted voice repeating, "Mine. Mine. Mine."

"Fuck!" I shout, looking at the others. "Search the entire building. Liz's stalker must have come back."

Their eyes, wide with worry, meet mine before everyone takes off running. I hear them scream her name as Mac and I race to the locker room. We slam through the door, looking around. The lights in the room are off, which makes no sense. After we've searched every inch of the room, we are forced to accept that she's nowhere to be found.

"How the fuck did they take her without us seeing?" Mac asks with a deep growl.

I have no fucking idea. This rink isn't as big as the hockey one, but it isn't exactly small either. There are so many places she could be hidden. What if she isn't even in the rink anymore? Panic builds in my chest as I pull out my phone with shaky hands.

"What are you doing?"

I don't answer as I pull up Liz's number and press call. When she went to change, I'd handed her phone. Holding my cell up to my ear, I frantically look around, waiting for it to start ringing.

I hear the faintest sound of Ghosts by Nathan Wagner, and I rush out of the locker room, pausing to figure which direction I need to go. Running to the right, I hear the song getting louder in the direction of the storage closets.

Loud footsteps sound behind me, and I look over my shoulder to see Mac trailing after me. I focus back on my mission, pressing the call button again when it goes to voicemail. I slow when we step into the hallway, listening to find where the music is coming from.

I stop in front of the door where I hear the music coming from. Wiggling the handle, I find it locked. So without hesitation, I take a few steps back before throwing the weight of my body into the door.

The moment it slams open, I'm bombarded by the scent of citrus. It's overpowering, but I try to ignore it. There's a shivering body in the corner, and I rush in but freeze once I'm closer. Her stalker blindfolded her and covered her ears with headphones. Her hands are tied behind her, and there's a gag in her mouth. The blindfold is soaked with her tears.

I tentatively reach out and pull the gag out of her mouth first. She begins to scream, and I wince as I quickly pull off the headphones and blindfold.

She looks around wildly, and I try to soothe her by holding up my hands in surrender. I don't mean to sound like I'm talking to a wild animal as I say softly, "We're here now. We've got you, Ice Princess."

Her eyes shoot up to mine, and I have to stifle a gasp. She looks like a ghost of her former self. Her skin is pale and clammy, and her body shakes with uncontrollable tremors. Her eyes are wide as she stutters, "D-dean?"

I bite my lip as emotions overwhelm me. What do I do? How can I help? I lower myself to the floor, so I'm more at her level. "Yeah... yeah it's me." I slowly reach out and untie her hands.

When she shoots up from her crouched position, I jerk and almost fall backward by the force of her jumping at me. I barely catch her as she wraps herself around me. Her hold is almost too tight as she chants in a hushed tone. "You're real. You're real."

I glance at the headphones and wonder what she was forced to listen to while we searched for her. My grip on her tightens as I say softly, "I'm real, Ice Princess."

Mac follows my gaze to the headphones and slowly makes his way over. He bends to pick them up before holding them next to his ear. His eyes widen before darkening with rage. When his eyes meet mine again, I almost shrink back from the hatre I see there. I've never seen my fun-loving friend look like he wants to kill someone before.

Her fingers tangle in my hair as she tries to snuggle closer. "Don't let go, Dean. Don't let go."

I manage to stand, and her legs wrap around me like a boa constrictor. Coiling around me as tightly as she can. I'm not entirely sure the best way to hold her so she doesn't drop. I slide my hands to the edge of her butt, and when she doesn't shy away, I get a better grip on her.

Whatever Mac heard on the headphones makes him throw them against the wall before turning to me. "Let's get the fuck out of here." He points to Liz. "She's coming home with us."

I nod, no point in arguing. I had already planned to bring her home with us or stay at her place. There's no chance of us letting her out of our sight again.

As we head for the door, we find a note stuck to it. Without even needing to read it, my stomach angrily churns.

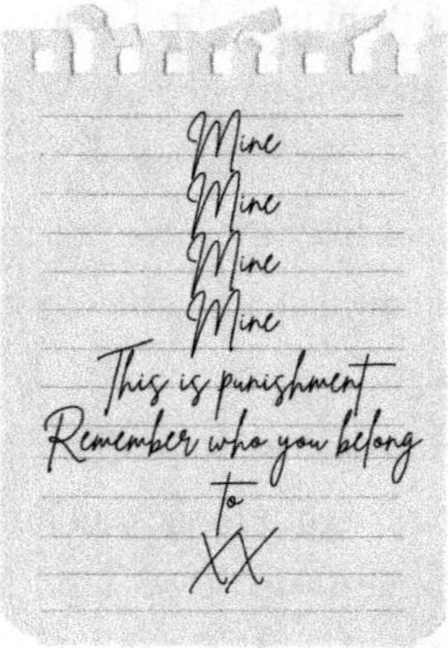

Mine
Mine
Mine
Mine
This is punishment
Remember who you belong
to
XX

Chapter Twenty-One

A few weeks have passed since the incident at the rink, and the guys haven't left me alone once. I'm either at the common house or my apartment with guards posted outside. Though, I don't mind having Dean and Mac all to myself, which is probably a bad thing, considering we shouldn't be flirting with the idea of a relationship.

I haven't seen a note from my stalker since, which probably means they are no longer being sent or the guys find them before I do. Either way, I'm glad. The stress of what happened still hasn't left my body, and it has me lashing out.

I throw my hands in the air as desperation, stress, and the general feeling of being overwhelmed consume me, and I yell, "I can't take this!"

Mac and Dean jump up from their seats on the couch in my living room with worry in their eyes. Mac holds his hands up in a placating gesture as he says softly, "What's wrong?"

My eyes burn as tears build, and I gesture around me wildly. "I feel confined and claustrophobic!"

Dean looks to Mac before walking around the couch to me. "What can we do to help?"

"I don't know!" I scream.

He instantly wraps me in his arms, locking me in tight. I go to fight, but a sense of calm washes over my body as I'm wrapped in his warm scent. I melt in his arms as I continue to cry. "I'm sorry."

He holds me close as he whispers, "Nothing to be sorry about, Ice Princess."

I feel another warm body behind me, enveloping me in the smells of Mac and Dean. Like a campfire on a snowy night.

"Breath with me, Chérie. In. Out," Mac says from behind me.

I do as he says, inhaling fire and ice. It's a few minutes before my tears dry, and Dean loosens his hold on me, so I can wrap my arms around him. My grip tightens in his hoodie as I continue to take in deep breaths.

"Bien?" Mac whispers.

"Yes," I whisper back, refusing to let go of Dean.

Dean's chest rumbles as he asks, "Why don't we go out for a bit?"

I groan. "We can't go out just the two of us."

Mac chuckles. "No date then?"

I twist enough to see Mac. "You know we can't be seen together like that. We aren't dating, and I don't want rumors to start."

Dean gives me a squeeze before releasing me. "Well, it can be a date to us. No one else needs to know."

I go to argue, but he holds up a finger and pulls out his phone. He looks down, scrolling, before pressing a button and putting the phone to his ear. I arch a brow in question, and he smirks. "Hey. Do you and Taz want to come hang out with the three of us? Liz needs to get out of the house."

I can't hear what's happening on the other side but Dean chuckles. "Yeah. She doesn't want people to think we are dating." My cheeks heat as he laughs at whatever Vicy, I assume, says.

"I know. Mac and I are trying, but you know how stubborn she is. Do you want to meet up at the plaza, and we can grab lunch?" He hums. "Sounds good. See you in thirty."

He hangs up with a grin before leaning forward to steal a kiss. I yelp in surprise when he jumps up and heads down the hall. "Let's get ready, Ice Princess. We have places to be."

Mac leans in behind me to press a kiss to my cheek. His lips caress my ear as he whispers, "We are yours whether you want us or not. We will wait for you to be ours, Chérie."

He pulls away and follows Dean to get ready, leaving me speechless. I press my finger to my cheek before moving it to my lips. A small smile pulls at my lips. Little do they know, I want to be theirs more than anything else, but the rational side of me remembers I need to protect my job before I fall down that rabbit hole. So I will cherish this time with them for as long as I can.

Reality is always harsher than the dreams we fight to bring to life. These guys are slowly slipping into my dreams for my future. The question is, will I fight for them as hard as I fought to get back out on the ice?

When we meet up with Taz and Vicy, they waste no time wrapping me in hugs. I laugh as they squish me between them in greeting. "Guys, you're going to smash me."

Taz smirks as he pulls away. "Like we could do that to you," he says with a wink.

I swat him with a huff of laughter. "Not what I meant, and you know it."

Vicy releases me before throwing an arm over my shoulder. "Well, where are we headed?"

Since this is a spur of the moment thing, I shrug. "Didn't have a plan in mind."

Taz looks around before nodding. "Are you hungry yet?"

I shake my head. "Not really."

He nods and grabs my hand to drag me along the sidewalk. "The bookstore it is."

"Bookstore?" I ask with a smirk.

He nods, looking over his shoulder. "You and Vicy can look at the manga section. Then I figure you can get a few of those romance books I've seen you try to hide," he teases with a wink.

I roll my eyes, but the blush creeping across my cheeks doesn't hide the embarrassment I feel, knowing he found my guilty pleasure. My attention is jerked to a few girls giggling as they stare at our group. My brows furrow when one of them points at me, then whispers to her friends.

As we pass them, I hear her whisper loudly, "Puck bunny incoming."

Vicy and Taz both stiffen at her words and jerk to a stop. I give Taz's hand a squeeze. "It's fine."

Vicy moves his arm from around my shoulder, and I look up to find his eyes narrowed on the girls. "Do you have something to share?" he asks coolly.

The girl who made the comment shakes her head with wide eyes. "No, not at all."

Taz releases my hand and crosses his arms. "I believe she does, brother. If I heard her correctly, she said 'puck bunny incoming'. Which is a bit forward considering she has no idea who this woman is."

"Guys, it's fine," I say, trying to de-escalate the situation.

Vicy keeps talking, pretending he didn't hear me. "You're right, they don't know who she is. Maybe we should do introductions?"

Taz and Vicy wrap an arm around my shoulders in sync as they say together, "She's our sister."

Vicy arches a brow at the girls. "So maybe you should apologize?"

The girls nod furiously as they stammer, "Sorry, sorry."

"Now, move along," Taz says, waving a hand to shoo them off.

They waste no time and rush off. I bite my lip to keep my laugh at bay, but it bubbles out of me anyways. "Was that really necessary?"

Vicy shrugs as he moves his arm from my shoulders, taking my hand instead. "People should mind their own business."

I have to agree, though, as eyes follow us when Taz grabs my other hand. I know I should probably pull my hands from theirs, but they seem to enjoy dragging me everywhere. They are touchy-feely guys; maybe that's how they show they care.

The moment we walk into the sports section of the store, I know I've lost them. Hockey season is upon us, so the section is mainly filled with hockey gear. They release my hands and rush to the helmets and sticks.

They immediately slap on a helmet and grab the closest stick, and I can't help but laugh. Boys and their toys.

"Prepare yourself, brother!" Vicy says in a posh tone.

Taz grins as he holds his stick out as if it were a sword. "You will be the only one falling this day."

I cover my mouth to quiet the giggles that bubble out of me. Mac and Dean stand beside me with smirks. Mac bumps my shoulder as he whispers, "It's good to see you laugh and smile."

I turn to look up at him with a grin. "Thank you."

He bends, pressing a kiss to my forehead. "Anything for you, Chérie."

When I hear Vicy yelp and Taz laugh manically, I jerk around to find Vicy on the floor, Taz's hockey stick held to his throat. Taz grins as he looks over at me. "Did you see? Did you see me win?"

I snort at his excitement. "I saw, Taz."

He puffs out his chest and announces, "I have won this battle for thy lady's honor."

"I didn't realize my honor was in question," I say with a smirk.

He shrugs as Vicy swats the stick away from his neck. "It sounded cool to say."

I hear giggling girls behind me and huff out a sigh, trying to ignore the whispers. I'm successful until I hear, "Guess they are only good for hockey. Doesn't look like they have brain cells for anything else."

That makes my hackles rise, and Dean and Mac each grab one of my hands. Dean squeeze and grunts, "Ignore them, Ice Princess."

I take a deep breath before nodding. It's not worth it. Though my composure falls when I hear another girl snicker. "It's possible they only have one brain cell to share between the two of them."

That's it! No one fucks with my boys. I rip my hands out of Mac and Dean's as I spin to face the girls. They look posh and are wearing *way* too much makeup to appear natural. I arch a brow, pointing between them as I say, "And I suppose you have more than one brain cell between the four of you?"

Their eyes widen before narrowing on me, mean girl style. One of the girls—who I just know is going to respond with a horrible comeback—opens her mouth, but I interrupt. "Don't FUCK with my boys, or I'll show you how bloody hockey can really be."

They gasp in horror as one of the fake blonde bimbo's squeals, "Bitch!"

I'm sure my grin is deadly as I say, "Proud president of the bitch squad, now move along." Miming a shooing motion, I continue, "Wouldn't want to kill off that one brain cell you share with our company."

The girls rush off, bickering and hissing insults, but I don't care. They don't faze me. I'm suddenly lifted into the air, and I look down to see Taz with a grin on his face. "Damn, Liz!"

Vicy snorts and smirks. "Seems she's fought and won the battle for our honor."

Taz shifts me, so I'm on his shoulder as he chants, "Liz! Liz! Liz!"

I can't help but laugh as the others pick up the chant. Today started out shitty, but it's definitely turned into one of my favorite memories.

Chapter Twenty-Two

We're a month away from the season opener, and I can tell the guys are getting jittery. Nerves are running high, and I can tell in practice that they've been running themselves into the ground to make sure the first game goes well. They may only be exhibition games, but those games set the tone for the season.

Maybe we should have a fun, chill night instead of going out and getting into trouble since it's the weekend. I'm still staying at the common house most nights, so it shouldn't be a problem.

We're sitting in the living room as the guys discuss plans for the night to blow off steam. I clear my throat as I throw out the idea. "Would you guys mind staying in for the night, and we can do movies and popcorn?"

Vicy tilts his head in question. "You want to stay in?"

I shrug. "I think it's better than going out and causing trouble. The media is going to be focused on you guys for the next few weeks since the season is about to start. They are going to look for anything and everything they can post about you guys."

Taz groans. "She has a point. We don't want a repeat of what happened last year."

Consider my interest officially peaked. "Last year?"

Ozzy face-palms and groans. "Did you seriously have to bring that up?"

A grin spreads across my face. "What happened last year? Now you have to tell me."

There's a chuckle behind me as Mac leans over the back of the couch. He smirks and points at Ozzy. "Our defenseman over there drank a bit too much at a club one night."

"We told him going clubbing was a bad idea," Dean adds before shrugging. "But he didn't listen."

Ozzy winces. "It wasn't my fault."

Mac hops over the couch to sit beside me. "You were the one who kept taking shots."

Ozzy throws up his arms and grunts. "How was I supposed to say no to a bunch of pretty ladies buying me shots?"

I snort a laugh. "Um... you say 'no thank you'."

"They were puck bunnies. He wouldn't have said no," Tuck adds.

"Would you have said no, Bobby?" I ask, smirking.

He grins and replies, "I would have if you gave me that look and said my name like that." He shivers. "It's like my sister scolding me."

I hold up my hands in a placating gesture. "Alright. Alright. No going out and taking shots. So... movie night?"

Vicy jumps up from the floor and heads toward the kitchen. "I'll get the popcorn."

Taz rolls onto his stomach to push himself off the floor. "I'll get the beer."

I grin as I look at the others. "What movie do you want to watch?"

Tuck shrugs. "I don't care. As long as it's not one of those sappy romantic movies."

I snort. "Fine no sappy romance. Any other requests?"

Dean and Mac shrug as Ozzy says, "You pick."

"Me? You want me to pick?"

Tuck hums. "Why not?"

I tap my lip as I try to come up with a movie everyone will enjoy. Dean bumps my shoulder and whispers, "We could watch *Howl's Moving Castle.*"

I arch a brow. "Really?"

He shrugs. "We could have a Hayao Miyazaki marathon."

I can't help but squeal in excitement. He's favorite Japanese animator, and I love all his movies. I want nothing more than to share that with them. I'm a Studio Ghibli girl for life!

Vicy comes out of the kitchen with two large bowls of popcorn, followed by Taz carrying several bottles of beer. Vicy plops down between my legs as he hands me a bowl. "What's the plan?"

"A Hayao Miyazaki marathon."

He chuckles and hands me the remote. "Nice. What are we watching first, boss lady?"

My eyes are glued to the TV as I search for the movie first on the list. When I finally find it, I click on it and Vicy hums. "Good choice. We should watch *Spirited Away* next."

"Good choice," I say in approval. "But first, the adventures of Sophi and Howl." I settle into the couch between Mac and Dean. They've become touchier when we're here at the common house. The others don't seem to mind though. And I see their grins when they catch Mac and Dean pressing quick kisses to my cheeks randomly.

Even if the others don't seem to mind, I know it would be bad if upper management found out that I am even entertaining the idea of a relationship with my players. Which is why I've been holding back when around the others. It's one thing at the apartment when no one but us knows what is going on. It's an entirely different scenario when it's around the other teammates.

Deep down I know none of the guys will say anything. It honestly feels like they are trying to encourage it. Maybe I need to stop worrying about things and learn to just live in the moment. My whole life has been spent worrying about things and playing by the rules. Maybe a little fire and ice would be good for me.

Tossing a handful of popcorn into my mouth, I look to Mac on my right. He's watching the movie, but his arm is resting on the back of the couch. I have been so consumed with my thoughts that I didn't notice that his fingers are tangled in my ponytail. He slowly twirls my hair around his fingers without thought.

Fingers slip into mine, and I look down to Dean's fingers intertwined with mine. I look up to see if he's watching me, but he's not. He's completely entranced by the movie, as his thumb slowly caresses the top of my hand.

I turn back to the movie and try to pay attention, but it's a bit hard when I think about these two men showing me affection in the smallest of ways. And I love it. I love that they give me their attention. That I mean something to someone. Two someone's.

As the movie nears the end, I hear Dean's whispered words beside me. He repeats what Sophi says to Howl. "A heart is a heavy burden."

I turn to him, and I see his eyes shining as he worries his bottom lip. I realize then that this movie hits differently for him. The relationship with his parents was difficult, and the relationship he had with Mac's mom was the only one to show him love.

I give his hand a soft squeeze as I lay my head on his shoulder. My words are soft and quiet as I say, "Your heart may be heavy, but we're here to help carry the weight of your burden if it becomes too much."

His breath hitches and gives my hand a squeeze. "Thank you," he whispers.

A tug on my ponytail has me turning toward Mac. He gives me a smile before pulling my head toward his. I don't even get a protest out before his lips are on mine. It's a quick kiss before he pulls away just enough that his lips caress mine as he whispers, "Thank you."

I didn't realize my eyes had closed. They flutter open, and I pull back enough to glance up at him. He's looking down at me with affection. My words sound a bit breathless as I ask, "For what?"

Dean's eyes flick over my face before he answers. "For caring and for taking care of us."

My eyes widen for a moment before I smile. "Why wouldn't I? You do more than that for me."

He arches a brow, smirking softly. "Who's that, Chérie?"

I shrug, not entirely sure if I'm ready to reveal myself. I could probably word vomit everything that they do for me and then some. So I settle for the most important thing. "You... you make me feel safe."

His smirk grows into a grin, then he leans to press a quick kiss to the tip of my nose. "Good."

I jump away from Mac when Vicy asks loudly, "*Spirited Away* is next, right?"

I turn and find Vicy smirking up at me from his spot on the floor. My cheeks flush as I've been caught again under his unintentional watchful gaze. Clearing my throat, I nod. "Yeah. If you guys are up for another movie."

Taz snickers. "We'll turn the lights down low this time, so you guys have more privacy."

I kick my leg out toward him, but he just chuckles and moves out of reach. My eyes narrow on him as I grunt, "Asshole."

"So you want us to turn the lights down?" he teases.

Before I can reply we are bathed in darkness, the TV the only thing illuminating the room. Ozzy huffs as he plops back down on the love seat. "Stop fucking with her or she'll never date them."

My mouth drops open. They don't have a problem with me dating the two guys beside me? Vicy hums before saying, "He does have a point. It's taken her this long to be okay with us even catching a glimpse at the fact that she likes them."

Taz groans. "Fine."

The room falls quiet as Vicy starts the next movie. I look around the room at the men and can't help but huff out a laugh. I really have found a little family of my own.

Chapter Twenty-Three

Pre-season is upon us, and this is our last week of exhibition games. Everything has been off-the-record but, so far, the guys have been kicking ass. We need to keep up this energy for the season. I clap my hands. "Alright boys! Game time in a few hours. Everyone good to go?" I've ensured each of my boys are taped up like always. At some point, it became part of their pre-game ritual for them to meet me in the training room. I hope that carries over into the regular season.

"Yes Mom!" eight of my boys' groan in unison at the same time Mac and Dean yell, "Yes boss!"

I laugh. I know not all of them will play, but I still made sure they were all stretched well, in case the worst-case scenario happened. It's my job to make sure these men are ready for each game. Substitutions will happen, and so will fights. It comes with the game. Perri comes up beside me with a smirk.

"You do realize we are all capable of taking care of ourselves. You don't have to worry about us so much."

Perri is the oldest in my group, though, I don't feel like thirty-three should be considered old. But he has a family, which means he doesn't have to deal with the six guys who live in the common house. I, on the other hand, did, but I'm beginning to think of them as extended family. Plus, I don't mind being at the common house. It's better than my apartment. If I didn't want to stay at the common house, Dean and Mac stayed at the apartment with me. I groan thinking about my stalker. He has put a major damper on my personal life.

Shaking myself out of my thoughts, I bring my focus back to Perri. He is one of the centers playing tonight, and I finished taping him up a few minutes ago. He's managed to pull on most of his padding but still needs to suit up. I pat one of his shoulder pads. "I know, but there are only four of you who live on your own. Have you seen how those boys live in the common house? Plus, it's my job to worry. Part of the job description."

He shivers at the thought. "Point taken, Roe Roe."

I'm about to tell the boys it's time to head to the locker room when a voice rings out behind me. "Is that you Izzy?"

My whole body freezes, and I can tell Perri notices. He looks at the male behind me, then back at my face. "Who the fuck are you? Unless you're part of the team, you need to leave," Perri loudly snaps.

There's a ring of privilege in Emmitt's voice as he says, "My father knows the general manager. Nick and he go way back. Sorta like how Izzy and I go way back. Don't we Izzy?"

No...no, no, no! You cannot be fucking serious right now? My luck in life cannot possibly be this bad. There's no fucking way. It's bad enough that I have to deal with a stalker; now I have to face Emmitt? I glance around to find all my boys looking at me. My eyes flick to Mac and then Dean. I watch as Dean's eyes narrow dangerously on the man behind me, and it clicks who this is. He starts forward but Mac grabs his shoulder. His eyes are still on me as he mouths 'We're here. You got this' and gives me a wink.

Taking a deep breath, I put on a fake smile and turn around. "Right. Though, we haven't talked in over ten years."

His smile is sickening. "Now, Now, Izzy. I've come all this way to see you. You look so good."

I try to hide the shiver that runs down my spine. Hearing him call me that nickname makes it feel like fire ants are crawling across my skin. I *hate* that nickname. Composure still in place, I arch a brow. "Yeah. Sure. Am I supposed to be grateful or something? That after ten years you've finally graced me with your presence."

"Oh, come now. We were such close friends," he says with a wink.

I have to hold back the urge to vomit in my mouth. How the fuck did I ever think this guy was attractive. I'm about to say something when I feel an arm settle around my shoulders. I look over to find Vicy. Of course, he would be the one to step up and say something.

I have to hold back a laugh at the look of disgust on Vicy's face as he stares at Emmitt. "Wait. Wait. Wait. My beautiful and glorious, Roe Roe, please tell me you were not with this troll ass-licker."

I can't stop the giggles. *Troll ass licker? Where the fuck did he come up with that?* The look of offense on Emmitt's face makes it even better.

Emmitt clears his throat and glares as he asks, "What's that supposed to mean?"

Vicy's eyes meet mine, and he asks in utter horror, "Oh, sweet, Roe Roe! Please tell me you haven't been with him!"

Thank god for these men. I'm not sure what I'd do without them. I'm still giggling at his dramatics. "Does knowing him since I was six years old, being his figure-skating partner, and being his girlfriend for two years count?"

Taz doesn't give Vicy a chance to reply as he leans a forearm on my shoulder. "Fucking hell, Roe Roe. Did you kiss him?"

Good god these boys are acting more like little brothers than any-thing else. But I am living for it. I should have known he would play along. When Vicy wants to cause trouble, Taz is never too far behind. I ponder his question for a moment, but I really have to think about it. *Did I ever kiss him? Shit?* "Um... to be honest, I can't remember."

Emmitt bristles. "Of course, we've kissed!"

Taz and Vicy both snort. Taz shakes his head dramatically and says, "Well, obviously it wasn't a good kiss. She would have remembered otherwise."

Emmitt huffs. "Like you brats could do any better."

Without thinking, I say, "Oh, they can." It is true. I've seen them kiss girls at the house, and the girls seem pleasured out of their minds. But I hadn't meant to say that out loud. I feel my face grow hot as the two snicker beside me.

Vicy lays a hand on my shoulder as he says, "Now, Roe Roe, don't give away all our secrets."

Taz boops me on the nose and laughs. "He's right. Don't spread our secrets around."

God, I love these two. Emmitt's face is beginning to turn purple, and I'm having a hard time suppressing laughter.

"You're with these children?" Emmitt screeches.

My brows furrow. Why the fuck would he care? I mean, I would never date Taz or Vicy, they are family. I love them like little brothers. Nothing more. I know they feel the same way. But the way Emmitt sounded so offended at the thought of me dating them makes me bristle.

Ozzy speaks before any of us can say a thing. "Considering they are over the age of eighteen, that makes them adults." I look over my shoulder to find him walking in our direction. My eyes follow as he passes us, stopping right in front of Emmitt. "Also, I feel like Lizzy's relationships are none of your business, let alone her sex life."

Emmitt's about to say something when one of my other boys interrupts. "And considering her reaction when you called her Izzy, which isn't her name by the way, you should probably leave."

Tuck. I love calling him Bobby though. He told me, "You sound like my big sister when you say my name." So I try to throw it in when he is doing great in practice. He makes his way over to stand shoulder-to-shoulder with Ozzy.

I'm about to tell the boys to chill when I notice that Emmitt looks like he's about to pee his pants. With the look on his face, there could be a debate between that and shitting his pants. But I'm interrupted yet again.

Gilly walks past me as he says, "Yeah. You've got this strange smell about you. Like lies and betrayal."

"Maxy," I say with a laugh. He looks over at me and winks. I am the only one allowed to call him that. He told me little sisters are allowed to give their big brothers nicknames. That's how he treats me too. Like a little sister. I love and hate it.

Merc and Fenni are right below Perri in age. Both live outside of the common house. I don't have as close a relationship with the three of them because of that. But that doesn't matter right now.

Merc and Fenni flank Vicy and Taz. The former stand with their arms crossed over their chests, looking admittingly scary. "Seems you should get a scurry on," Merc says with a scowl.

"I'd advise you not to come around again," Fenni growls.

Emmitt surprisingly seems to debate whether or not to run. I'm not sure if it's pride or pure stupidity, but he straightens his spine and looks around Ozzy, to me. "Guess this was a bad time. Maybe we can catch up another time, Izzy."

"Not her fucking name," Tuck growls.

He looks to Tuck before bending in an odd-looking bow. "Right. Well, next time." He turns and briskly walks away. And when I say briskly, I mean walks fast enough that it's just below a jog.

There are a few moments of quiet before I burst into peals of laughter. The boys all turn to watch me as I hold my stomach from laughing so hard. Tears are streaming down my face, and I try to pull myself together. I'm not sure when the laughter turns to sobs, but Vicy and Taz are right there to wrap me in a hug.

"We've got you, Roe Roe," Vicy says softly.

"It's okay. It's okay," Taz tries to soothe.

My arms tighten around Vicy. "Thank you, guys."

Vicy clicks his tongue. "No reason to thank us."

"We will always have your back, Liz," Perri says from beside me.

"Like you'll always have ours," Gilly chimes in.

Sniffing, I say, "Fucking hell. I love you guys."

There's a unison of, "Love you too."

I pull away as I wipe my face. *God, I hate crying.* "Ugh! Okay, boys let's go get ready!" I make a shooing motion. "Go! Go!"

They snort and file out. Everyone except Mac and Dean. "I'll be fine," I say with a smile.

They exchange a look before turning back to me. They begin walking briskly in my direction, and I arch a brow. "What are you two up to?"

"Gonna make sure that smile stays on your face the rest of the night," Oli says before turning to Dean. "You locked the door?"

"Yep," Dean says with a grin.

I begin backing up. "What are you two up to? The game starts in a few hours. You need to get ready. Coach will want to meet you guys in ten minutes."

Oli hums. "You hear that, Dean? Ten minutes. Think that's long enough to make her scream?"

"Wait, what?" I screech.

Dean darkly grins. "Oh, I can make her scream. The question is, can you make sure she's quiet enough that we don't get caught?"

Oli smirks. "A challenge has been made. Challenge accepted."

I stare wide-eyed as Dean kneels in front of me. "Then let the game begin. Are you ready for us, Lizzy?"

Chapter Twenty-Four

"What are you two doing?!"

Mac cups my cheek, looking into my eyes. His almond-colored eyes stare intensely into mine as he smiles. "You can fight this all you want, but it's our turn to take care of you."

"What... what do you mean?" My voice sounds more breathless than I mean for it to be.

My eyes shift to Dean as he says, "We are going to take such good care of you, Lizzy." His face is so close that I can feel his breath through the material of my pants. My eyes widen when the heat of each breath pulses across my center.

Before I can say anything, Mac's lips are pressed to mine. I moan as his lips caress mine softly. Lifting my hands up, I thread my fingers through his thick chestnut hair. I feel Dean's fingers softly caress the edge of my waistband, then slowly tug them down. I should protest, but I'm too engulfed in the kiss.

This is... this is a bad idea. We could get caught. Any other thoughts are dismissed when I feel Dean slip my panties down my thighs and stop at my knees. His hot breath brushes over my core, and I whimper.

"She's so needy, Oli. We should take care of her," Dean says with a laugh.

Mac pulls away and looks down at me through hooded eyes. "Will you let us take care of you?"

"We shouldn't. What if we get caught?"

Dean growls from his spot below me, and I can feel the vibrations against my core. "Don't worry about getting caught. Do you want this?"

A whimper slips through my lips. "Yes."

Mac gives me a heated grin. "Good girl. So proud of you for telling us what you need."

My fingers tighten in his hair as I moan from the praise. Dean shifts forward as my back hits the wall. *When did I move across the room?* He spreads my legs wide and presses his face to my core. The first brush of his tongue against my slit has my legs trembling. He hums as his hands brace under my thighs, lifting me up.

I wrap my legs around Dean's shoulders as Mac presses forward, bracing his hands against the wall under my armpits. His lips capture mine, swallowing my moans as Dean devours my cunt.

Each thrust of his tongue warms my core a little more, and I can't stop my hips from writhing against his face, trying to get him deeper. My fingers are gripping Mac's hair tight while my tongue spears between his lips. He growls into my mouth as his hand briefly caresses my cheek before threading into my hair.

I whimper, needing more from Dean. I need more. I am so close. Mac pulls away panting. "Fuck his face, baby. Take what you need. Such a good girl."

Dean growls again as he slips a single finger into my needy cunt while he moves his mouth to my clit. He sucks that little bundle of nerves hard, pumping his finger slowly through my wetness.

Whining, I try to get him to move faster, but he only chuckles and continues his slow pace. "Please... please I need more," I beg. The burn in my lower abdomen is becoming too much. My eyes burn as my need grows.

Mac stares down at me with soft eyes. "So fucking beautiful. You are so fucking stunning with your eyes glazed with pleasure and need. I bet your cunt is so tight around Dean's finger. Tell him what you want."

The tears slip down my cheeks as I whimper. "More."

"Use your words. Tell us what you want more of, baby," Mac says softly.

"Him. I want more of him." I pant and point to Dean.

He hums against my clit as he inserts another finger. I moan at the feeling of fullness, but it's not enough. "More," I say needily.

Dean waits a few moments but does as I request. Now pumping three fingers into my wet cunt in slow movements. He almost hits that perfect spot before retreating. Leaving me on the edge of release but not letting me fall over.

Mac brushes his lips across mine before whispering, "Say it. I can see you want to tell him you want something. Say it."

"Faster," I whisper.

Mac snickers. "He can't hear you with your legs wrapped around his head like that. You'll need to speak louder."

I slip a hand from Mac's hair to tangle my fingers in Dean's hair. With a tug, I demand, "Faster."

A rumbling laugh vibrates against my clit as he thrusts his fingers, hitting just the right spot. He does it over and over. My fingers grip his hair tightly as my hips grind against his face.

My climax slams into me, blinding me as I scream. Mac covers my mouth with his, devouring my scream of pleasure. He pulls away, allowing me to breathe. I'm panting heavily as Dean's fingers slow, and he pulls away enough to look up at me with a grin. He slips one hand over my thigh while he puts his fingers that were inside me between his lips.

His glazed eyes close as he sucks on his fingers. A few moments later, his eyes open and look up at me. "Fucking delicious."

My head thumps against the wall as I try to catch my breath. When my eyes meet Mac's, I can't help but smile. They seem darker than his normal almond color. "Doing okay there, big boy?"

He smiles wickedly as he hums and helps me off Dean's shoulders. Dean stands, then groans. He looks down, and I follow his gaze to a *very noticeable* bulge in his hockey pants. He presses down on the bulge while adjusting himself. "This is going to be a fucking bitch to play with. I hate playing with a hard-on."

I arch a brow with a laugh, pulling my underwear and pants up. "Do that often?"

He hums. "Not often, but it's uncomfortable as fuck when it happens."

"Need me to help you out?" I offer.

He shakes his head. "Fuck no. Not knowing what you feel like wrapped around my cock is bad enough. If I knew what you felt like, then I'd have a hard-on all game."

I snort as I look at Mac. I can't help but look down and notice he's also sporting an impressive bulge. "How bout you big boy?"

He shakes his head moving away. "I'll have to decline, Liz. This was for your pleasure. We were taking care of you."

"I'm offering."

His smile is devilish. "I have to agree with Dean on this. Playing with a hard-on is bad, but I feel like taking you up on that offer would only make it worse."

"If you say so." I stand on my tiptoes and tug on the neck of his shirt to pull him toward me. When I press my lips to his softly, he hums in satisfaction. Pulling away, I offer them a smile. "Good luck tonight."

Mac's smile is wide as he nods, then turns to head to the locker room. My eyes meet Dean's, and he looks a bit confused and unsure what he's supposed to do. Like he wants to give me a kiss but isn't sure if he should.

Walking slowly, I make my way over to him. "I'm not really sure what this is." I gesture between the two of us before pointing at Mac's retreating back. "But it doesn't have to mean anything if you don't want it to."

His eyes jerk to mine, widening before looking away. He rubs the back of his neck. "I've—I've never done the relationship thing before."

I nod. "This doesn't have to be a relationship. It can be for fun. No strings attached. It doesn't have to mean anything."

His gaze briefly flicks to mine before a hint of pink tinges his cheeks. "What if—what if I want it to mean something? What if you mean something—to me?"

I turn to face him, so his eyes meet mine, and caress his cheek. "Then it can mean something," I reply, with a soft smile on my face. Gathering some courage, I rise to press my lips softly to his. The deep keening sound he makes breaks my heart. It's as if he's never had someone care or want anything to mean more than a fling. His fingers flutter over my cheek as he cups it in his palm. He moves his lips against mine, as if he's savoring the brush of his lips across mine.

The kiss lasts longer than I meant for it to, so I pull away, but he whines, chasing after my lips. Kissing me a bit longer before my lips tilt into a smile. "You need to get ready for the game," I mumble between his kisses.

"Just a little longer," he murmurs.

"Dean," I scold.

He eventually pulls away, looking down at me. I've never seen his chocolate eyes melt the way they are right now. "Get a win tonight, and after, you can kiss me all you want."

Fucking hell, the smile he gives me. A damn puddle is what I am. "Promise?"

I smile, giving him a nod. "Promise."

He quickly presses his lips to mine before pulling away and backing up, his eyes still locked on me. "I'll hold you to that."

Lifting my pinky in the air, I laugh. "Pinky promise."

He curls his pinky around mine. "Done." He turns and rushes to the locker room. Once the door closes behind him, I shake my head with a huff of laughter.

What have I gotten myself into? Shaking my head to clear it, I rush to grab my belt with all my medical supplies. I shove a few pairs of gloves in one of the pockets and a few hair ties on my wrist before pulling my long hair back into a ponytail. Plucking my lanyard off the hook on the wall, I head out. I look down at my employee identification card attached to the lanyard. My smiling face looks back at me along with my name and title. It still catches me off guard every time I see that I am a part of the team. It feels surreal to have made it to the NHL. With one last deep breath, I open the door and head in the direction of the rink. Tonight will be the best night of my life.

Chapter Twenty-Five

It's the last weekend before hockey season officially starts, which means I won't be able to teach the kiddos anymore due to our busy schedule. But I have faith Daisy will be able to handle the class till we finish up the season. She seems really excited.

Clapping my hands, I try to get all the kids' attention. "Alright! This is my last week of teaching you all." There's a round of whines and huffs, and I can't stop my laugh as I try to wave them off. "I'll be back after hockey season ends. But that means you have a new teacher until then."

I gesture toward Daisy. "This is Ms. Daisy. She is going to help you. You may know her better as Aspyn's mom."

There's a hoot in the bleachers where the team hangs while I'm teaching on Saturday's. I'm not sure why the guys feel the need to be here each weekend, but without fail my boys are here.

I glance over to find Vicy and Taz pumping their arms in the air. I shake my head at the pair, then look at Daisy. Her cheeks are pink, but she's keeping her composure better than most would. She's trying to ignore them as she looks at me, so I smirk and give her a dramatic eye roll.

She grins as she gives a wave to the kids. "Hey everyone. I'll be your teacher while Ms. Liz is gone. Let's make sure we make her proud when she comes back!"

The kids yip before dispersing to their parents. I chuckle as I watch them fly off the ice. I turn to Daisy, smiling. "If you have any questions or issues just let me know. You have my number, right?"

She nods. "We shouldn't have any problems, but I promise I will take care of your little snowflakes."

I skate over to her and give her a brief hug. "Thank you for doing this. I feel so much better handing them over to someone I can trust."

"Of course!" She squeezes me back before leaving the ice as well. I look toward the bleachers and find most of the guys leaving as well, but two hockey players stay behind, busy with eyes trained on my new friend. I shake my head, laughing. I wish Taz and Vicy all the luck with her, but she won't be as easy to capture as a puck bunny.

Glancing around, I see Mac talking to Dean before looking my way and giving me a salute. I arch a brow as I watch him leave with the others. Odd. Dean spins in my direction and skates toward me.

As he gets closer, I see how nervous he looks. I give him a curious one in return. He surprised me by continuously showing up to the ice-skating classes. I hadn't expected him to keep coming; I thought he would have quit after the first few sessions.

He's gotten better with the moves, considering he's used to hockey skates. But he committed to wearing the ice skates instead. I wonder if I could talk him into doing a few lifts with me. I gesture to his face as he gets closer. "What's with the expression?"

A smirk tugs at the corner of his lips. "What do you mean? This is my face."

I shake my head as I begin to skate backward. "You look nervous."

He shrugs but continues to skate after me. "Why would I be nervous being completely alone with you?"

Gazing around the rink, I find that we are indeed all alone. My eyes bounce back to him, and I give him a shy smile. "You going to skate with me?"

"Do you want me to skate with you?"

I nod enthusiastically. "Yes."

He speeds so he's right in front of me as we continue our laps. "What do you want me to do then, Ice Princess?"

"Sing for me. I need music to skate to," I reply with a grin. I don't think for one moment he'll actually do it.

A flurry of emotions pass over his eyes before he begins to hum. It takes me a moment to realize it's Tattoo by Loreen. The melody has me drowning in memories of that night, and I think of the perfect nickname for him. It's only fair, right?

I hold my feet at an angle to slow down to a stop. Dean does the same. I smile as I look up at him. I slowly caress my fingers across his cheek as I whisper, "Sing for me, Ghost."

His eyes widen for a moment before he whispers back, "I don't feel like a ghost when I'm with you."

I grin as I fly across the ice, Dean not far behind me. I turn so I'm skating backward and reach for his hands to settle them on my hips. "Get a good grip. You're going to lift me into the air. You're going to help me fly."

The moment I finish speaking, I can see he's going to argue, so I interrupt him. "I trust you. Now lift me and sing, Ghost."

He chuckles but gives in. "As you wish, Ice Princess."

He lifts me into the air, and I can't stop the gasp that escapes me. I throw my arms out and close my eyes, enjoying the moment of freedom. He slowly lowers me back down, and we begin to spin. His arms encircle my waist, and I let myself fall backward. My heart stops for a moment, and I think I'm going to hit the ice, but Dean's hold on me tightens, allowing me to spin.

He pulls me back up as we slow to a stop in the middle of the rink. He's breathing hard, and so am I. Our breaths intermingle as he looks over me, a smile tugging at his lips.

"I thought I was going to fall for a moment," I say softly.

He lifts his hand slowly from around my back to brush his fingers across my cheek. His eyes bounce between mine as he whispers, "I'd never let you fall. Not when you trust me to catch you."

"I do," I whisper back.

He cups my cheek, and he leans forward to brush his lips against mine. The kiss is soft and sweet, which isn't what I expected from him. But I'm finding that my ghost man has more soul than he wants to admit.

My ghost? Fuck. I should... I should stop this kiss. But... mhm... he tastes so good. Fuck it.

I reach up to cup his cheek as I return the kiss. I want this man more than my next breath. It's about time I stopped cutting off my happiness to abide by the rules. It's time I live for myself.

Before the kiss turns into something more, he pulls away with panting breaths. He leans his forehead to mine as he chuckles. "Damn, Ice Princess. You're going to be the life of me."

I grin. "Life of you? Don't you mean death?"

He pulls away with a wide smile, his eyes filled with mirth as he shakes his head. "You're the first one to ever make me feel alive." His thumb caresses my cheek as he continues, "The one who makes me want to live rather than be a ghost."

Chapter Twenty-Six

W hat's a girl to do on her day off? I offered to work today, but Danni and Max told me to take the day off. Which leaves me at the common house by myself, well I suppose I shouldn't say by myself. The guys paid one of the team's security guards to follow me around today. It was a sweet gesture and actually makes me feel much better about being without the guys.

But I don't want to chill at the common house all day. I suppose I could do some shopping, but who wants to shop alone? Hum… I could skate, I suppose. I won't have a lot of time for it once the season starts.

Nodding to myself, I grab my bag with my skates and head out the door. I look around and find Robert sitting on the steps. His salt and pepper waves scattered on the top of his head. Hearing the door open, he turns to face me. His clean-cut beard is speckled with white, and his dark brown orbs find mine. With a smile, he nods. "Good morning, Ms. Elizabeth."

I grin. "I've said before; you can call me Liz."

He stands. "Of course, Ms. Liz."

I huff a laugh as I walk over to him. "Liz. Just Liz, Rob."

There's a twitch of his lips as he nods. "Where we off to, Liz?"

"I am thinking about going to the rink to skate for a bit."

He gestures to his car. "The one where you teach?"

I nod as I make my way to the passenger side. Opening the door, I slide in as he does the same on the driver's side. "I figure I won't get much time once the season starts."

He hums and starts the car, then we are on our way. The drive is quiet, but it's not an awkward quiet. I enjoy the silence as we cut through the streets.

We park, and Rob jumps out to open my door for me. I shake my head with a laugh as I slip out of my seat. "I can get the door, Rob."

He shrugs and ushers me toward the doors of the rink. "I'm here for your protection."

I snort as I reach for the door, but he beats me to it. I arch a brow. "And that means opening all doors?"

The tilt to his lip gives away his amusement as he shrugs again. "My mama taught me to be a gentleman."

I can't help but laugh. "Well, your mama should be proud." I make my way to the ice, not wanting to waste any time. I won't have much time to enjoy the ice once the season starts.

Sitting on the bench, I slip my shoes off and my skates on. I glide out onto the ice, and a smile creases my face. Closing my eyes, I inhale the cool, icy smell of the rink. My body relaxes the longer I skate. The sound of the blades cutting through the ice echoes around the rink.

A feeling of freedom surrounds me as I glide over the ice. I'm so lost in the feeling that I don't notice someone else is here until music echoes around the rink. My eyes shoot open, and I glance around till my eyes meet a figure standing at the edge of the ice.

I smirk when he skates in my direction. I wait until he's closer, then ask, "I thought you had practice today?"

Mac grins and skates around me in a circle. "Do you know how long you've been here?"

I shake my head as I watch him circle. He stops in front of me before holding out a hand. "Well, Chérie. May I have this dance?"

My eyes widen when I hear Can I Have This Dance playing over the speakers. It's the song that was playing when he found me after I had fallen on the ice. The day I pushed myself to the breaking point just to prove that I could still skate.

I slide my hand into his, and he smiles and tugs me closer. "How are we supposed to dance on the ice?" I whisper.

"Like this," he says, then pushes me away. He doesn't release my hand, though, instead he pulls me back, lifting his arm, so I spin under it. I'm brought back to his chest before he begins to skate backward.

It feels like we are slow dancing on ice as I let him drag me along before spinning us slowly. He lifts my hand to rest on his shoulder, and I use my other hand to twine my fingers behind his neck. The smile he gives me is blinding. I can't help but giggle as I lay my head against his chest, inhaling his peppermint and pine smell.

I feel him kiss the top of my head as we continue to skate around the rink at a leisurely pace, even when the song changes. Voice soft, he asks, "Did you have a good day?"

I nod against his chest. "Yeah. It's even better now."

His deep chuckle vibrates through his chest. "How so?"

"You're here," I whisper.

He hums as he tugs me closer. "My day is better now too."

Chapter Twenty-Seven

I'm standing on a bench as I clap my hands and announce, "Alright boys! This is the first official game of the season." Only a few of my boys are playing this first game, but that doesn't mean I didn't make sure they were fit to play, just in case.

Dean, Vicy, Taz, and Mac are my players in this first game, and I'm sure Danni made sure her boys were ready to go as well. Our little ritual carried over from our pre-games to today. This game is huge, considering we face off against the Tampa Tiger Sharks. That's the team my college bestie works for. I haven't messaged Jess much since arriving here, so she's pissed, but in my defense, I've been a bit distracted.

Shaking myself out of my thoughts, I focus on my guys. "Now, the roster has been finalized. Danni and I have done all we can to make sure the team is at its best today, so I need you guys to jump in and help Lewi, Vicy, and Taz." I point toward Merc and Ozzy. They are the first on the ice if need be. But I look at the others as well. Everyone will be geared up for the game, but Coach Fernandez has a plan, and we are going to stick to it as best as we can. All I can do is make sure my boys are ready to play.

"All of you have looked great on the ice. We've got this game in the bag if we stick to the plan." I point to each guy as I narrow my eyes. "Don't do anything stupid!"

They all chuckle and nod. I can't help but smirk as I yell, "Get your asses to the locker room!" I stay standing on the bench as each of them give me a fist bump before passing.

I watch Mac bump Dean's shoulder when they leave. And I see Dean give him a sad smile before lifting his cellphone to his ear. He veers off to the right as Mac turns to the left with a huff.

My brows pinch as I hear grumbled words out in the hallway. Stepping down from the bench, I hurriedly grab my stuff. Clipping my medical pouch around my waist and dropping my ID tag around my neck, I'm as ready as I'll ever be.

Pressing my ear to the door, I can barely hear Dean and whoever he's talking to. I slowly open the door before closing it behind me to be as quietly as possible. I walk in the direction I hear grumbling. The closer I get, the more I realize how upset he sounds.

I stop at the corner, listening in on a conversation I know I shouldn't, but I can't help myself.

"Dad. It's the first game of the season," he grunts into the phone.

There's a huff over the phone before a male's voice replies, "I am not stupid son. I know when the season starts." I definingly shouldn't be here if he has the conversation on speakerphone.

Dean sighs, and I peek around the corner to see him leaning against the wall. His head thumps against it as he explains, "I wasn't implying you were stupid, Dad. I am only stating that you and Mom have never missed the first game before. It's the most important one of the season."

The sound of mumbled words comes through the phone before the man's voice becomes clear again. "The way you play hasn't changed since you were a child. Our attendance at your first game versus your last will not make a difference."

"Dad…" he pleads. My heart clenches at the plea I hear in his voice as he looks down at the phone.

His father huffs. "Stop acting like a petulant child. We are attending the function your sister is hosting. This is her first benefit fundraiser, and you expect us to come cheer you on instead?"

Somehow, he made the word *cheer* sound like a dirty word. As if the last thing he wanted to do was show support for his son.

"No," Dean whispers.

"Good. Your sister will doing more for the Lewis name tonight than you will. Just because we are not in attendance doesn't give you the right to slack off. If I hear you have done anything to sully the Lewis name, our attendance tonight will be the last thing you blather on about. Do I make myself clear?"

Dean flinches with each word his father says before he nods. "Understood, sir."

"Very well. I believe your game starts soon. Do you not have somewhere to be?" Before Dean can reply, the line goes dead.

He looks down at the screen for a moment before he huffs out a sigh. He thumps his head against the wall and looks up at the ceiling. "No matter how many trophies or awards I get, I will never outshine her, will I?" His eyes close, and the devastation in his voice has me moving before I can stop myself.

I must have made a sound because his eyes snap open, and he looks in my direction. "Liz?"

The glimmer in his eyes has me wrapping my arms around him without hesitation. I hold him tight, thinking of all the horrible things I would like to do to his father. After a moment, he wraps his arms around me, hugging me back.

"Were you spying on me, Ice Princess?"

"I'm sorry," I mutter into his chest. I tighten my hold on him as I continue, "He's an asshole. An asshat. Nutter-butter-turd bucket."

He gives a watery chuckle. "Nutter-butter-turd bucket?"

I shrug. "I was trying to get creative."

He pulls away to give a cheeky smirk. "Don't quit your day job, Ice Princess."

Rising on my tiptoes, I press a quick kiss to his cheek before backing away. "I won't quit my day job as long as you don't let that man dampen your fight for a win tonight."

The cheeky smirk turns to a soft smile as he gives me a nod. "Deal."

I point a thumb over my shoulder as I bark, "Now get your ass in the locker room, Ghost."

He leans down to press a quick kiss to my cheek before he saunters past me. When I look over my shoulder, I see him walking with his shoulders held high. He no longer looks weighed down by his father's words, and I hope it stays that way.

As the players are announced, the crowd goes wild. It's the first game of the season, and I'm thrilled it's a home game. I'm down with the players on the bench.

I watch as the guys get ready for the puck drop, then the whistle is blown, and the first period of the season opener begins. I try to ignore the roar of the crowd and the commentators as I turn my focus to my guys and try to get into a work frame of mind. Dean and Mac are Lewi and Oli. I can't do anything to give away that I'm closer to those two than the other players. Friendships are normal, anything more than that is where things get questionable.

Lewi has the puck and is working his way up the ice, passing it to Ford at the blue line. I bite my lip as he banks it around the net to Vicy who then passes it to Taz while Lewi waits on the crease as the puck comes across the line for the Tampa Tiger Sharks. The Tiger Sharks center, Erickson, blocks the puck, sending it out of their half. Our left defenseman, Samy, chases it back before it is iced and catches it, sending the second line onto the ice.

I nervously bite my thumb as I watch Ozzy get slammed into the boards, and I make a mental note to check on him after the game. Merc winces as he cuts into the ice too quickly to get the puck from Taylor. I'll need to check his legs and make sure he didn't pull a muscle. If it's nothing serious, I can send him to Lorna for a massage and have Emma work on a few strength and conditioning exercises.

As I watching the game go back and forth where Oli gets some saves from the Tiger Sharks defensive line. I have to admit that they are really good. It took fifteen minutes in the first period to get a goal but, unfortunately, it was from the other team. Oli whacks each goal post before getting back into position. He's irritated that the puck got past him, but in his defense, it was a tip-in that he couldn't see due to the screen in front of the crease. As the first period wraps up, I can see the team's spirit dwindling, but this sport moves so fast, they can get this back in the game next period.

I love hockey. The second period begins, and right before the puck drops, Lewi sends me a wink, and I just know we are going to win this. That man wants to impress me too much to lose. Power Ride by Fred Couty echos through the rink as Taz mimics the exact same move that got the Tiger Sharks their first goal. I can't help but throw my hand in the air as Taz fist pumps with the crowd. I love that our guys are able to pick individual songs for home games. It hypes the players and the fans up, excited for each goal scored.

I can tell the guys are pumped as we wait for intermission to end. They guys don't hesitate to hop back onto the ice for the last period. This is it! It's fucking brutal to watch as the Tiger Sharks fight to get a goal, but Oli blocks each one. Minutes are left in the game, and I'm biting my thumb practically raw as I watch Lewi race down the ice. Erickson is right behind him, trying to steal the puck. They are against the boards, and I gasp when I see Lewi jerk and lose the puck. A whistle screams through the rink as I wait for my cue to help. I wait as Lewi rips off his glove and reaches up to his face. Red smears across his hand as I hear the commentators mention high sticking.

Gilly jumps over the boards and onto the ice with a towel in hand as Lewi slowly makes his way toward him. Once he's close enough to me, I can see he has a huge grin, with no care about the blood pissing down his face. I just shake my head. Damn boys. "Cover your damn nose before you turn the ice bloody."

He huffs, taking the towel from me and pressing it to his nose. I help guide him off the ice as the announcement is made of a double minor. The game is paused as the blood is cleaned up, and I make Lewi sit for a moment. He's still got a huge grin on his face when he says, "We can easily win this now."

Snapping on a pair of gloves, I pull the towel away to get a look at the damage. There's a slight cut on the bridge of his nose, so I press the towel back and grab some tape in hopes that will work. "I'm not sure a stick to the nose is worth the advantage."

He snorts out a laugh. "It is totally worth it, Ice Princess."

My brows knit at the nickname, considering the current company, but he just shrugs it off. He pulls the towel away, and I wipe up some of the blood. "I'll tape this better after the game, but the goal right now is to stop the blood pouring, so you can play."

He hums not moving as I continue to work on his nose. I look down once I'm done and give him a nod. "That should do for now." I give him a wink before saying, "You better get that goal like you promised."

He smirks as he jumps back on the ice. The game restarts, and even with our team with a man down, Lewi shows he has no doubt that we have the advantage. He sends a one timer from Taz right into the back of the net with only seconds left in the third. Burn it by The Fever 333 fills the rink as the fans go wild.

Dean will argue that the stick to the face is worth the winning goal. Though, I argued otherwise as I re-taped his nose after the game. The grin on my face most likely says otherwise.

Chapter Twenty-Eight

With our first game down, and a win nonetheless, we are working hard to prepare for our next game. My phone rings, and I look down to see my mother's smiling face on the screen.

I smirk as I accept the video call. "Hey Mom."

She turns the screen a bit so that my dad is in the video as well. I chuckle as I wave to him. "Hey Dad."

They exchange a look before grinning wide. "Happy Birthday!" they shout together.

I can't help but laugh as I realize I forgot my own birthday. I've been so focused on getting the team ready for the game tomorrow that I didn't think much about what day it is. I look at the calendar on the fridge that has everyone's schedule scribbled on it. Yep. It is October nineteenth.

I look back to my parents with a smile. "Thanks."

My mom arches a brow. "You forgot about your birthday, didn't you?"

With a shrug, I continue to get everything ready for tonight. They guys decided to do a movie night and chill before the game tomorrow.

"I've been busy getting everything ready for the season. I forgot what the date was."

She huffs a sigh. "At least do something other than your job on your birthday."

I laugh and give her another nod. "I promise, Ma. Love you both."

"Love you too," they say in unison before ending the call.

I shake my head and laugh. I suppose I have been focused more on work than anything else. How does someone forget their own birthday? I grab two bowls of popcorn for movie night. The others aren't due to arrive for another few minutes.

As I make my way out of the kitchen, I'm greeted with a loud, "Surprise!" I let out a loud squeal, the bowls of popcorn in my hands go flying, and it rains down all around me, some of it landing on my head.

I grab my chest as I look around and find the guys with wide smiles and hundreds of boxes of beads. What the hell are they planning now? "What the hell?" I shout because, damn, they almost gave me a heart attack.

Vicy and Taz give me sheepish smiles, and I should have known they would plan something like this. "We wanted to do something for your birthday, but we weren't sure what to do," Taz says with a shrug.

Vicy holds up a box of beads. "We figured a movie night and friendship bracelet making was safe the night before a game."

"Friendship bracelet making?" I ask with a snort.

Taz points a finger at me with mock anger. "Don't diss the power of a friendship bracelet."

I hold my hands up in surrender and laugh. "Not dissing the power of friendship, man. Just wondering why this was your first thought."

"We figured ten bracelets may be too many for you to wear all the time, so we agreed Lewi and Oli will each make you a bracelet. The rest of us will make one for you together," Vicy says with a slight blush on his cheeks.

Well damn. Who am I to say no to friendship bracelets. "Alright, fine. That means I can make each of you a bracelet then, right?"

Taz and Vicy both nod happily. "Yes."

With an eyeroll and a laugh, I make my way to the center of the living room. "Alright, let's get this party started then. But someone needs to make more popcorn."

Mac stands from the couch, heading toward the kitchen. "I got it."

Turning to look around at the boxes, I'm not sure where to start. I suppose I could start with Dean and Mac's, but I'm not sure what to do for them yet. I huff out a sigh and grab a box, deciding to work on the others' while I think of what to make.

I start with Perri. I'm going to pick his favorite colors and then spell out his name. It isn't very original, but it doesn't have to be. I grab several shades of red beads and pick out the letters for his name.

Moving onto Tuck, I decide to use Bobby instead. I grin as I pick out the letters and different shades of yellow. I even pick a sun to put in the spot of the 'O' instead of the letter.

For Merc's bracelet, I decide to make it in tribute to his twins. I do blue on one side with 'Seb' for Sebastian. Then separate it with a black heart with 'Sav' for Savannah. I add a few pink beads to finish up the bracelet.

Vicy and Taz's bracelets are easy. Vicy's is orange with the letters spelling 'Lil bro' and an orange heart separating the two words. Taz's is green with the same words but with a green heart.

Ozzy's bracelet is dark blue with the words 'Oz Man'. And I grin when I find a little hockey puck bead to separate 'Oz' and 'Man'.

Gilly and Fenni did a gender reveal a few days ago, and their wives talked about the babies' names. Fenni and Sam are having a boy named

Declan, so I make a purple bracelet with a purple heart on either side of the name 'Declan'. Gilly and Dannielle are also having a boy, who they named Rook. I remember Gilly having mentioned her favorite color once and hunt for the sage-green colored beads. Using the green beads for most of the bracelet, I put silver hearts on either side of 'Rook'.

Finished with the others, I move on to Dean and Mac's. I work on Dean's first, using black and blue beads. There's a little ghost bead, so I grab two and spell out his nickname, a little ghost on either side.

Switching to Mac's, I grab two little bear beads. I pull up the word I want on my phone to make sure I spell it right. I want to use a personal nickname for him like I did with Dean's. I'm not sure what to use for his bracelet until I find the French word for teddy bear. Mac always calls me Chérie, which makes me want to make his with a French name. I put together his bracelet with the word 'nounours'.

Once done, I look up to find the guys watching me, and I feel my cheeks heat with embarrassment. "What?"

Vicy snorts as he stands and makes his way over to me. He hands me three bracelets as he holds out his other hand. "You want me to hand them out?"

I grab the bracelets from him before handing over the ten I made. Before I look at the ones they made me, I watch the others as they receive their's.

Perri grins down at his wrist, then looks up to me with a smirk and a wink. "Thanks."

Tuck laughs when he sees I choose to put Bobby instead of Tuck. He points to the sun as he looks up at me. "I've got a sunshine personality, right?"

I laugh and throw a loose bead at him. He dodges it with a smirk. Merc is smiling down at his bracelet. When he glances up at me, he has a wide grin. "Thanks, Liz."

Ozzy snorts out a laugh, and I turn to see him showing off his bracelet. "Oz Man?"

I shrug. "It's a great nickname." My eyes jerk to Taz and Vicy who are pumping their fists in the air, chanting, "Lil bros for life!"

Gilly and Fenni are both caressing their bracelets with their sons' names. They look up at me with appreciation and say in unison, "Thanks Lizzy."

I chance a look to Dean and Mac and find them grinning wide. They point to the bracelets in my lap, encouraging me to check out what they made. I look down to find a baby-blue one with the words 'Ice Princess', a silver bracelet with 'Chérie', and the last one a rainbow of colors with 'Roe Roe'. I smile as I roll them onto my wrist.

"So, how's your birthday?" Perri asks with a hint of amusement.

"The best I've had in a while," I say with a smile.

Vicy claps his hands. "Movie night!"

Taz jumps up from the floor. "I'll get the cake and ice cream!"

I shake my head and lean against the couch. Dean and Mac come to sit beside me. They both bump into my shoulder before pressing a kiss to my cheeks at the same time. My face is squished, but I can't help but laugh.

"Happy Birthday!"

Our first away game of the season has me a bit rattled. I could have sworn I packed everything but, of course, I always forget something. Thankfully the home team's complex is accommodating, and they let me take what I need.

I clap my hands to get everyone's attention. This may not be our complex, but that doesn't stop us from our pre-game ritual. "Alright! It's our first away game of the season, but that doesn't mean there aren't people in those stands rooting for us. For you."

The guys howl in confirmation, getting hyped to hit the ice. I point to easch of them. "We have a plan, so let's stick to it." I point to Perri who will be playing tonight. "We've been working on that calf for the last few days, and you've looked great during practice. Don't—"

"—do anything stupid. I know, boss," Perri finishes for me.

I point to Dean next. "Let's not bloody the ice this time."

He gives me a cheeky grin, holding up his hands in surrender. "No promises, boss."

I roll my eyes but can't keep the smile off my face as I stare down at my boys from the bench. "Let's play our hearts out and take home another win. Now, get your asses into that locker room!"

Before they leave, Vicy holds up a carabiner with all the friendship bracelets I made for them attached. "We can't wear them out on the ice, so will you keep them safe?"

With a grin, I take it from him and clip it onto my belt loop. "I'll keep them safe. I promise."

He nods and turns to the others. "Alright boys, let's go!"

They all file out except for Mac and Dean. They look at each other, then take a step toward me. They reach down to take something off their wrists before holding them out to me. My eyes widen when I realize that they are the bracelets Mac's mom had given them.

"What—" Before I can finish the question, Mac interrupts me.

"We were wondering if you could wear these for safe keeping?"

I look between them before slowly reaching out a hand. "Why are you having me hold onto them? Where do you normally keep them?"

Dean shrugs as he backs away a bit. "We normally keep them in the locker room."

Mac backs away, following Dean with a shrug. "We figure they will be safer with you."

I slip them onto my left wrist—that is currently empty compared to my right, which has my watch along with the three bracelets I got for my birthday. I roll my thumb over the bracelets before looking back at them. "Are you sure?"

Dean grins as he takes another step toward the door. "No safer place than with you, Ice Princess."

"We trust you," Mac adds before he turns to walk out the door.

I watch as they leave unable to move from my spot. I'm left speech-less; this isn't just a simple act of trust on their part. These bracelets are a part of their very heart and soul. And... they left them with me to guard and protect.

I run my thumb over the beads again. "I'll protect them. I promise."

CHAPTER TWENTY-NINE

It's only the beginning of November, and the season so far has been brutal. As hard as Mac, Dean, and I try, we haven't found much time to spend together. We sneak kisses and touches here and there, filled with our need to be near each other.

The only time we've found to spend together is when we are at home. Which isn't a lot of time when we are all exhausted and fall asleep the moment our heads hit the pillows.

Next weekend, we have a few days off, and I am hoping we can plan something. I would be happy with just sitting at home and having a movie night, at this point. Maybe a 'Netflix-and-Chill', if you know what I mean.

I'm watching the team's post-game press conference from the sidelines as they answer questions for the press and public about the game in a few days. As much as I try to pay attention to all the guys, my eyes keep locking onto Mac and Dean. No matter how hard I try to keep my wandering eyes away from them.

I don't feel bad, considering they keep searching me out in the crowd of people.

Dean's eyes meet mine, and he smirks and winks in my direction as he answers a particularly beautiful reporter's question. I'm sure she thinks that it's meant for her but—as much as that irks me, we don't need anyone finding out about our secret relationship.

I glance around quickly, finding no one looking my direction, before blowing him a quick kiss. His eyes glitter with amusement until Mac snaps a hand in front of his face.

My eyes flick to him and he's also smirking. He pats his left pec before grinning wide my way. A female's voice snaps me back to reality when she asks, "Are you well, Mr. Oliver?"

He nods and replies, "Of course."

Dean bumps shoulders with Mac as he grunts in French, "Connard."

The reporter points between the two of them. "There appears to be some rivalry between the two of you. Is this normal?"

Mac throws an arm over Dean's shoulder as he laughs. "Lewi and I go way back. We like to have fun and cause some trouble."

"And you just stole a kiss from a fan. She blew that kiss to me," Dean growls.

The reporter's eyes widen, and she sucks in a breath. "Mr. Lewis are you dating anyone? You've never shown interest in the past."

Dean looks to the reporter, now realizing what he'd said. He briefly looks my way before looking back at the reporter. "Well, this fan girl is a bit special."

I bite my lip, wondering how he plans to get himself out of this situation. He just announced to the media that there is a girl he's interested in, and the press are going to do everything possible to find the girl who captured the bad boy's heart.

"We have a bit of a competition going to see who will capture her heart first," Mac adds.

I groan as the press roars with questions and squeals, everyone shouting over one another. I pinch the bridge of my nose when the reporter asks, "Is there any way you'll give us the lucky girl's name?"

Mac holds a finger to his lips and winks. "It's a secret. How are we supposed to capture her heart with the press is breathing down her neck?"

"Protecting her identity can only earn us brownie points, right?" Dean asks with a devilish smirk.

The reporter titters, but she moves on from questioning the mystery girl's identity. Thankfully, the reporters don't bring up the mystery girl again, but I have a feeling that while they may let it go for now, the question will be asked at future press conferences.

Danni bumps my shoulder with a snicker. "Do you know who their mystery girl is?"

I arch a brow. "What makes you think I would know?"

She rolls her eyes. "You are literally over there every day. You would be the first to know."

I shrug, neither confirming nor denying if I know her identity.

She looks me up and down with an assessing eye before smirking. "Sure you don't know who she is. I have a feeling I know, though."

"Who?" I ask, trying to sound uninterested and not give away how nervous I feel. I don't think she would tell anyone, but that doesn't mean I want others to know.

She presses a finger to her lips as she backs away. "It's a secret, didn't you know."

My brows knit as I frown. "Danni," I chastise.

She keeps a smirk on her face. "I'm not telling anyone. Not even you."

She turns and walks away, leaving me to wonder if she actually knows or not. Given how observant she is, it wouldn't surprise me if she's put it all together. So why hasn't she said anything? People have lost their jobs over speculation alone before, and this is definitely more than speculation.

Shaking my head, I turn back to the guys. They are wrapping up with the press. Once dismissed, Dean and Mac don't hesitate to get up. I watch as they make their way toward the exit. The meeting today was held in the Wraiths rink. Which means they have to head down the hallway of offices to reach the exit.

Sighing, I head in the same direction. If I can finish up an hour of paperwork before I leave for the night, I will have time to hang out with the guys.

I leave the press room, mentally going over the paperwork I need to get done, but squeal loudly when I'm jerked to the right and into a dark room. I open my mouth to scream as the door shuts, and lips are suddenly on mine. Making a fist to punch my attacker, I pause when I breath in the scent of cinnamon and cedarwood. Dean. My body relaxes as he kisses me breathless.

I pull away with a gasp, and he leaves a trail of kisses down my throat. Someone else's hand grips my chin from behind, gentle as he turns my face toward him and presses his lips to mine.

When the sharp scents of peppermint and pine mingle with the smell of Dean, I groan. Mac.

"Fuck, I've missed this," Dean mumbles into my neck as his hands tighten on my hips.

I pull away from Mac with a whispered gasp. "We can't do anything here."

Mac huffs in my ear before saying, "We know, Chérie."

Dean steps away with a pained look on his face. "We needed an uninterrupted moment with you."

"I can get leave early tonight. Let's spend some time together at the apartment," I say hopefully.

Dean and Mac both groan. Dean leans his forehead to my shoulder as Mac presses his into my hair.

"Wish we could, Ice Princess," Dean says sadly.

"Coach wants us to run a few more drills before we call it a night," Mac adds.

I sigh and nod. "Alright. But we can still meet up at the apartment tonight. I'll stick around until you guys are done. I know you don't want me at the apartment by myself, but we could use some alone time."

Mac and Dean both press kisses to my cheeks before backing away.

"Sounds like a plan, Chérie." Mac backs away slowly before opening the door.

"We'll see you after practice," Dean says gently pressing another kiss to my lips before leaving with Mac.

Standing there for a moment, I huff out another deep sigh. Dating hockey players is difficult because of their crazy schedules. As I look over my shoulder to the closed door, I can't help but smile softly. Those two? They are worth it.

CHAPTER THIRTY

I'm not sure how the boys managed it, but I have a funny feeling it involved all ten of them. Dean and Mac couldn't have pulled this off by themselves. There's no way. I wonder what made them think of renting the small cabin, so we'd have some alone time together. No. No, this had to involve all ten of them. I have a funny feeling Perri had more to do with it than he let on.

"So the boys are taking you on a trip." Perri grins as he looms over me where I'm sitting on the couch in the common house.

Looking up, I arch a brow when I see Merc, Gilly, and Fenni standing together. The four of them normally don't hang out in the house, saying it's too much like a frat house for their liking. "Boys?"

Gilly grins. "Mac and Dean are taking you on a trip."

"For some alone time," Fenni says as he wiggles his eyebrows.

I cross my arms as I, admittedly unconvincingly, say, "There's nothing going on between me and those two." That's a bold face lie, and everyone knows it.

Merc rolls his eyes. "We all know you have something with those two. We won't tell anyone, but the fucking sexual tension between you three is killing the rest of us."

I choke on my spit as I splutter, "What—no—there's—" My eyes flick between the four of them before I huff. "Is it that obvious?"

Perri laughs. "To the ten of us? Yeah. Definitely. I don't think management has caught on. But, to be honest, I don't think they will care so long as it doesn't affect how you treat the rest of us."

Gilly shrugs. "You're professional at work, not a puck bunny. That's all that matters."

Muttering behind me interrupts my response, and I look over the back of the couch finding the other six members of my group. They quiet down when they notice me eyeing them.

Mac and Dean are pushed to the front of the group, the two of them holding bags at their side. When my eyes meet theirs, I notice both have pink-tinged cheeks.

My gaze flicks to Vicy when he announces, "Alright! Let's go love-birds!" Furrowing my brow, I point to the extra bag in his hands. "What's that?"

Vicy grins. "Your clothes."

My eyes widen. My clothes? "You went to my apartment and packed clothes for me?"

He shakes his head. "Hell no! That's creepy. I called your mom and said that you were busy. Told her that you needed clothes for our trip this weekend."

"You told her what?" I screech.

He rolls his eyes, like it's totally normal for them to call my mom. "Don't freak out, Roe Roe. I told her it was a team trip. A short getaway to relieve some stress."

I pinch the bridge of my nose as I ask, "And what happens when she finds out that it wasn't the whole team?"

"Who's gonna tell her? No one here will."

I groan, realizing there is no way of getting out of this. "Where are we going?" I ask, resigned.

"I have a small cabin up North," Taz says with a grin.

"And whose idea was this?"

All fingers point at Mac and Dean. Hum... I have my doubts.

I'm standing in front of a frozen pond that sits behind the small cabin. Dean said he'll make sure everything is set up inside, so I dragged Mac with me to explore what's outside. The moment I see the pond I run back inside. "Did you guys grab my skates?"

Dean laughs. "The guys packed them before we left. I think I put them by the front door."

I race from the back of the house to the front, finding my skates next to the front door. Snatching them up, I race back outside.

Mac arches a brow as I make my way back to the pond. There's a small bench, so I sit to switch my shoes for my skates. "What are you doing?"

As I lace up my skates, I say, "I'm going to skate on the pond."

"Not sure that's safe, Liz."

Standing from my spot, I walk over to the ice-covered pond. "It'll be frozen solid by now. I'll be fine."

"Stay away from the center. There's no telling how solid that ice is."

I wave a dismissive hand. "Yeah. Yeah."

He huffs as he watches me glide onto the ice.

After skating for a few minutes, I look up to find Mac watching me. There's a content smile on his face as he tracks me across the ice. I skate past him as I call, "Come out here and skate with me."

He shakes his head. "I'm not getting out on that ice."

I huff as I circle around him again. "Oh, come on. It's not that scary."

"You are small and light; I am large and heavy. I will break that ice, Roe Roe."

Skating backward, I keep my eyes on him. "Don't trust me, Mac?"

His eyes soften. "I trust you with my life on a daily basis. I, on the other hand, do not trust that ice won't break under my weight. If you wanted someone to skate with you, you should have asked Dean while you were inside."

I pout a bit, but I understand. The ice could break under his weight. I slowly get closer and closer to the center of the pond when he yells out, "Too close! Get out of the middle!"

It looks sturdy out here, but I don't want to scare him. As I make my way to the outer part of the circle, I hear a crack. Now, when you hear the ice crack underneath you, you shouldn't stop and freeze where you are. I do, though. I freeze and lock eyes with Mac. He must have heard it too.

"Skate, Liz!"

I begin moving again, but as soon as I do, the ice shatters under me. My eyes meet Mac's as I scream. His eyes widen in horror as he rushes onto the very ice he refused to set foot on a minute ago.

Thankfully, I manage to catch the edge of the ice before I drop straight into the freezing cold water. Mac makes it to my side, falls onto his stomach, and slides closer to me. He reaches out to me as he says, "Grab my hand!"

My hand slaps into his, and he gradually pulls me out, being careful to avoid the ice breaking even more. As soon as I'm out of the icy water, my teeth chatter from the cold. We make it to a thicker patch of ice before Mac stands, pulling me up with him.

His breath fogs around me as he lifts me into his arms and runs toward the house. "Dean!" he shouts.

Dammit, I should have listened. I've already managed to ruin our trip.

His eyes meet mine as he runs. "We'll get you warm, Chérie. Hold on."

My teeth are chattering so badly that my words come out choppy. "I'm...s...s...sorry."

"No need to apologize." He rushes through the backdoor right as Dean opens it.

"What happened?" he questions, following behind us.

Mac moves closer to the fireplace. "She fell through the ice. Get a fire going."

Dean nods, rushing over to start the fire while Mac sets me down. "I need to undress you, Liz. We need to get these wet clothes off."

I nod. "O—okay."

He's gentle but rushed as he removes my wet clothes. He starts with my skates, throwing them to the side, then he peels off my socks.

"Fire's going," Dean says behind Mac.

"Get her some dry clothes," Mac says, and Dean rushes off to grab her clothes as instructed.

Removing my pants, Mac whispers, "I'll have to take off your underwear too."

I nod as he snatches a blanket off the couch to cover me once he has finished undressing me. He takes my shirt off and gives me a questioning look. I nod again as he removes my bra, shifting the blanket up to completely cover me.

Pulling me into his lap, he places me between him and the warmth of the fire. I feel a bulge under me and realize that it's him. He pulls me in closer, rubbing a hand up and down my shoulders, trying to get me warm. "Sorry," he whispers. I look up to find his cheeks bright pink. "Can't control that. Tends to have a mind of its own."

I can't help but tease him. "Ah, so removing a girl's clothes because she fell into a frozen pond is what does it for you."

"Liz," he groans.

"Just wanting clarification. I mean, if that's your thing no judgment."

He growls. "It's not my thing, Liz."

I snicker. "You sure? He seems to have other ideas."

He nips at my ear, making me yelp. "You are my thing."

I duck my head when I feel a blush heat my cheeks. "So it's not the wet clothes," I whisper.

He huffs a laugh. "I mean, the wet clothes certainly didn't help, but no. It's not the wet clothes."

"I've got dry clothes," Dean announces as he makes his way over to us. He sets them on the couch before grabbing another blanket. He sits next to Mac, pulling my exposed feet into his lap. He covers them with the blanket before rubbing a hand up and down my legs as well as over my feet. Trying to get warmth back into my limbs.

After a few minutes of silence Lewi asks, "Are you getting warmer?"

The teeth chattering thankfully stopped, and I can finally feel my toes again. I nod against Mac's chest. "Yeah."

"You want to get into dry clothes now?" Mac asks.

I shake my head. "Not yet. I'm comfortable like this." *And surprisingly, that isn't a lie. I am comfortable. Is it weird that I am completely comfortable sitting in Mac's lap, naked under a blanket, while Mac holds me, and Dean massages my legs and feet? Maybe. I can't say I care at the moment, though.* My eyes start to feel heavy, now that I am no longer freezing.

"Don't fall asleep yet," Dean's voice jerks me awake.

"Sorry," I whisper. "I don't know why I'm so tired."

"The cold zaps your energy. Should we give you a reason to stay awake?"

My body grows warm at the implication. "What do you have in mind?"

I shiver as his lips brush my ear. "We should check out the bedroom. What do you think, Liz?"

"I would love to check out the bedroom," I say breathily.

He hums before turning to Dean. "To the bedroom?"

Dean's grip on my feet tightens before he releases them and pushes off the ground. "Bedroom."

Maybe I didn't ruin our trip after all.

Chapter Thirty-One

Mac lays me gently on the bed as Dean closes the door behind him. My nerves get the best of me as I let out a nervous laugh. "We are the only ones here. I don't think the door being open or closed is going to make much of a difference."

Dean shrugs as he moves over to the bed. "I like the illusion of privacy."

They are both staring at me, and it only makes me more nervous. *Do they plan on doing something or am I supposed to make the first move?* I'm completely naked and, somehow, I'm still the only one unclothed. A few awkward minutes of silence pass, and I can't take it anymore.

I shimmy out from under the blanket, moving up the bed toward the headboard. Their eyes track my movement as, inch by inch, my body is exposed. "Are you two planning to stare at me the whole time?"

Mac gives me a devilish grin, then he reaches for his shirt. A bang on the window startles me, and I scream, grabbing the blanket again and looking over to find two figures. Two familiar figures. Their hands are cupping the glass as they try to peer in.

Another bang sounds, and Vicy yells, "What the fuck are y'all doing in there?"

I drop back onto the bed completely mortified. Did they seriously drive all the way here to check on us?

Dean yells back, "Fuck off, Vicy!"

"The sexual tension between y'all has been choking us for months! Fuck her already!" Taz yells.

"Fuck off, Taz!" Dean screams.

There's yet another bang on the window. "I can't hear anything. It's not that hard, just fuck her!" Vicy shouts.

Oh. My. God. Oh my *FUCKING* god! I really hope there aren't any people nearby to hear their screaming match.

"We don't need your help, Vicy," Mac says and growls.

"I can draw diagrams if you want!" Taz adds, unhelpfully.

Exasperated, I throw my hands into the air. Is this really happening? My embarrassment gets the best as I huff. "Do you need diagrams?" Mac and Dean both look at me with disbelief. I continue my embarrassed rant, "You didn't seem to have a problem finding it with your mouth."

I hear Vicy and Taz both yell, "Oh shit!"

From my position on the bed, I point to the window. "Those are tinted right? They can't see in here?"

Dean and Mac exchange a look at before Mac answers, "They can't see through, no matter how hard they try."

My body melts into the bed in relief. "Good. I don't think I could live through the embarrassment."

There's *another* bang on the window. "I don't hear any fucking! You guys must suck if I can't hear her making any noise."

Knowing they can't see inside, I jump off the bed and march to the window. I bang back as I shout, "Fuck off you two, or I'll make your lives a living hell on the ice."

The two of them look at each other before slowly backing away from the window. Vicy gives the window a salute. "Understood, Roe Roe."

Waiting until I'm sure they have indeed left, I turn around to face the guys. I attempt a sexy pose, but I'm not entirely sure I manage it. With my best siren eyes, I say, "Now. Who's fucking me first?"

They glance quickly at each other, then begin ripping off their clothes. They simultaneously yell, "Me!"

I squeal as they rush me. I manage to jump onto the bed before I hear a loud thump. Looking over my shoulder, I see Dean on the floor with his underwear around his ankles. Mac is frozen mid step. He looks over his shoulder when Dean groans, "Fucking hell."

I let out a snort, and Mac starts laughing. *"Frère? Tu es bon?"*

Dean thumps his head against the floor as he growls, "Fuck all the way off."

I can't hold back laughter anymore. "Did you seriously trip trying to get out of your underwear?"

He thumps his head against the floor again. "Fuck me..." he grunts.

"That was the plan. Are you okay?" I ask.

"Pretty sure I shattered my pride," he mumbles.

"Poor thing," I coo as I crawl off the bed and kneel beside him on the floor. "Come on, the night isn't ruined yet."

"I fell while getting out of my underwear, Liz," he groans. "I don't know how it can get any worse."

I poke his shoulder. "Don't say that. You know that's just asking for things to go wrong."

I push at him, trying to get him to roll over, but he huffs dramatically. "Leave me here to die."

I roll my eyes as I look up to Mac. "Help, please."

He shrugs. "If he doesn't want to fuck you, that's on him. I am completely fine with that. Leaves more time for me to ravage you."

My doe eyes are on point as I pout. "Please, Mac."

He immediately shuts his eyes. "That's not fair, Liz."

"Please," I whine.

He groans as he opens his eyes. "I'm only helping because I can't say no to you."

With a grin, I jump back onto the bed. "I love that you are such a cinnamon roll for me."

"Yeah," he grunts. "Not sure it's working in my favor at the moment." He pulls Dean from the floor grumbling, "If my dick touches your ass, it's all your fault for being a bitch."

Dean swats him. "Fuck off, man."

Mac points to the bed. "Get on the fucking bed," he demands.

Dean glares at him but does as instructed. I smirk as he collapses, refusing to make eye contact.

"*Imbécile,*" Mac mutters.

I pat the bed next to me. "If he wants to act like a baby, let him. I'll give you a little reward."

Mac arches a brow. "A reward?" He moves so that he can lie on the bed beside me.

Shifting, I straddle him and begin kissing down his chest. He hums as I trail kisses down his body.

"Liz—" He hisses my name when I wrap my lips around the head of his cock. He tangles his fingers in my hair as I suck.

I have to hold back a gag as his hips jerk. "Sorry," he pants. His grip tightens in my hair as I bob my head up and down. Sucking him as I hum around his cock. "Liz—fuck," he groans. "I-I'm not going to l-last much longer with you d-doing that."

I hum again and the vibration has his fingers tightening in my hair. I squeal as he rips me off his cock, and I look up to find his eyes scrunched tight as he pants for breath. I glance back down and see pre-come beginning to seep out the head of his cock.

When his eyes open again, they are no longer those of the soft cinnamon roll I've come to care for. No, these are the eyes of a famished man. He tugs my head to the side, and I roll with it as he suddenly straddles me.

"My cock will be inside you when I come, Elizabeth." He grunts.

A shiver shoots down my spine. He never uses my full name, and I fucking love the way it sounds coming from his lips.

He slides a hand between us, and his fingers dip between my folds. He chuckles. "So wet for me."

I suck in a breath as he slips a finger inside me. He pumps a few times before adding another. My arms wrap around his neck while my fingers tangle in his hair. My grip tightens as he glides another finger inside me, increasing his pace. "Mac..."

"Soak my fingers, Elizabeth," he growls.

My eyes fall closed as my pleasure builds but snap open when Mac snarls, "Eyes on me." He presses his thumb against my clit as he curls his fingers, and I scream with my release.

"Such a good girl," he praises. "Fuck, you soaked my hand, Chérie."

I'm not sure when I'd closed my eyes. His fingers slip free, and I open my eyes. I'm greeted with the sight of him sliding his soaked fingers into his mouth. He groans as he sucks them clean. Sticking his tongue out, he licks up his hand. With a wink, he says, "Delicious, *Chérie*."

"Fucking hell."

Turning to my left, I find Dean staring at us. My cheek burns hot when he continues to stare. His eyes finally meet mine, and he says, "That was hot."

I don't even get a chance to react before Mac is sliding inside me. He moves at an achingly slow pace. "Mac..." I whine.

"A woman like you should be savored like fine wine." He pants as he continues his slow pace.

I pull his face down, so his lips are close to mine as I moan. "I don't want to be savored." Once he's fully seated, I bite his lip hard. He grunts, and I suck his bottom lip into my mouth. Releasing it with a pop, I say, "I want to be ravished like you're a starving man."

"A starving man, *Chérie*?"

My eyes meet his as I smirk. "Like I'm your fucking oasis."

His eyes glitter with amusement as he slowly pulls all the way out. "As you wish," he grunts, then slams back into me.

I scream when his pace becomes brutal, but I fucking love it. "Yes!"

"*Putain, Chérie.*" He groans.

My eyes squeeze shut, and I can feel myself grow warmer with each thrust. "Fuck me like you need me."

He growls and fucks me harder and deeper. "*Tu es si belle. Tellement beau. Viens pour moi.*"

Fuck, he sounds sexy. I have no idea what he's saying, but his accent is thick with each word. He feels me tighten around him and huffs out a chuckle. "Do you love when I speak French, *Chérie?*"

"Yes," I pant.

He hovers over me, our lips almost touching, as he whispers, "*Crie mon nom quand tu viens.*"

"What does that mean?"

He doesn't answer me, instead he slips a hand between us and demands, "Scream my name when you come." He pinches my clit right as he thrusts deep into me.

I do as told; I scream his name, "Mac!"

"Tellement serré." He grunts, his hips lose rhythm before I feel him come. He presses his forehead against mine as he pants. *"Tu es si belle, ma Chérie."*

I groan, and I feel myself tighten around him again. He grunts. "You really do love when I speak French," he teases with a chuckle, pulling away to look at me.

Opening my eyes, I find him grinning down at me. "It turns me on more than it should," I admit.

He laughs as he slowly pulls out, flipping over to lie down beside me. "Are you done pouting, Lewi?" Mac asks.

I turn to look where I last saw him and find him wide-eyed, his chest rising and falling rapidly. I look down to find his cock standing at full attention and seeping with pre-cum.

I can't help but chuckle as I sit up. "Did you enjoy the show, Dean?"

"I swear to god if you touch my cock right now, I'll come." He warns. I begin crawling my way over to him, and he shakes his head, "Don't touch me! I've embarrassed myself enough tonight."

"Lie down."

He shakes his head. "Liz come on—"

"Lie. Down," I say more forcefully.

He gives in and closes his eyes. I can't wipe the grin from my face as I watch this grumpy hockey player whimper as I crawl closer. I throw my leg over to straddle him but make sure not to touch his cock yet.

"Liz," he pleads.

I smirk as I peer down at him. "Don't worry. You'll be inside me before you come." Positioning myself perfectly, I drop onto his cock. There's no resistance as I take him to the hilt.

His hands slap against my thighs as he yells, "Fuck!" And his fingers dig into my skin as he chants, "Don't move. Don't move. Don't fucking move, Liz!"

I steady myself, my hands on his bare chest. He's sucking in breath after breath like he can't get enough air. "I'm going to have to move soon."

"Ju-just give me another s-second."

I smirk as I lift up a smidge before dropping back down. He slaps my thighs and growls, "Sit fucking still for a second, Liz! Your cunt is wrapped so fucking tight around my cock that I am on the edge of coming right now! So. Do. Not. Fucking. Move!"

"Fine," I huff. I slip a hand between my legs and begin to rub my clit. Using my other hand, I flick at my nipples. I moan as I begin to massage my clit faster and pinch my nipple.

The feeling of him deep inside me as I play with myself is building that warmth back up. I can't stop myself as I wiggle on his cock, trying to help alleviate the ache of needing to come.

He growls as he slaps my thighs, making me cry out. I didn't realized I was so close, but Dean groans under me when my walls clamp down around him. "You better start bouncing," he instructs.

Rising up, I slam back down on him. His grip on my legs tightens and he meets my thrusts as I drop down making him hit deep. He growls. "You better fucking come again, Liz."

I moan as I bounce on his cock. He releases his grip on one of my thighs to slap my hand away from my clit, then pinches the sensitive nub while he slaps my thigh hard. "Drench my fucking cock!"

I scream as I see stars. He slams into me once more before snarling his release. I'm panting as I rest my hands on his chest. His heart beating frantically beneath my palms. His grip on my thighs loosen, and he begins rubbing up and down. "Fucking hell, woman."

"What?" I ask, my brow raised.

He smirks. "I've never come that fucking hard in my life."

I can't help but chuckle as I ask, "So... my pussy is just that good."

He reaches up, cupping the back of my neck to pull me down and press his lips to mine softly before pulling away. "You're just that good."

"Here you two go."

I look over to find Mac holding two washcloths and a towel around his neck. I slowly manage to pull myself off Dean, collapsing beside him. Mac throws one of the wash clothes at Dean before crawling onto the bed next to me.

He goes to wipe me down, but I grab his forearm. "I can do that, Mac."

"I know. But I want to."

"You want to?" I whisper.

He nods. "I want to take care of you, Lizzy."

My eyes burn as I release my grip on his arm. I give him a nod as I close my eyes. This is an intimate thing to do. All of this is intimate. This isn't just a fuck and flee sort of thing.

"Liz? Are you okay?"

I squeeze my eyes tighter. "Yeah. Yeah, I'm fine, Dean."

Mac settles on my other side. "In the history of all women, 'fine' has never meant 'fine' when a woman's face looks like yours."

"It's alright. I'm just being stupid."

"*C'est n'importe quoi, Chérie.* You are not stupid. Tell us what's wrong."

I huff out a breath as I word vomit, "This isn't a fuck and flee for you guys, is it?"

"Fuck and flee?" Dean asks.

Groaning, I open my eyes and find both of them looking at me with concern and confusion. "You know... now that you've finally fucked me, you'll leave."

Mac jerks back as if I slapped him. "Is... is that what you think we would do, Chérie?"

My cheeks heat, and I cover my face. I know they wouldn't do that to me, but it's easy to let my insecurities get the best of me. "No."

My hand is pulled away from my face, and I look up to find Dean's soft brown eyes. His brows are furrowed as he says, "I know I'm not the best with emotions and expressing how I feel. But I would never do that to you, Lizzy."

I turn when I hear Mac whisper, "Chérie." He takes my other hand into his, pressing a kiss to my knuckles. *Je tiens beaucoup à toi.*"

"What does that mean?" I whisper.

He gives me a wink. "For me to know and you to learn, Chérie."

Closing my eyes, I thump my head against the bed. "Can we cuddle now that I've managed to turn an amazing moment into me unloading my emotional baggage?"

They both chuckle and move in beside me, shuffling closer. Mac grabs a blanket, throwing it over all of us, before lying down.

Mac snuggles close as he whispers, *"Dors bien mon amour."*

My cheeks heat as I whisper back, "I know what 'mon amour' means."

He chuckles. "Good."

Chapter Thirty-Two

Tomorrow is Thanksgiving, and I am freaking out! Should I invite the guys to my family dinner? But that would probably be really awkward since I'm not exactly allowed to date them. Well... maybe I am, but not officially I suppose.

I facepalm as I debate whether to text my mom first to see if it's even okay for me to invite them. But it would be really weird if I asked, and she said it was okay and then the guys say they already have plans and can't come.

I'm... overthinking this aren't I? I hear a groan from the corner of the room and find Dean lounging on the loveseat. We spent the night at my apartment, so it's only us until we go back to the common house. Although, with everyone leaving to spend the holidays with their families no one will be there.

"What's up?" Mac asks.

Dean thumps his head on the back of the seat as he closes his eyes, looking pained. "Mom just texted me."

Mac huffs. "Let me guess, she wants you to come home, doesn't she?"

Dean's voice changes into a high-pitched, mocking tone as he answers. "Dean we expect you home tomorrow for family dinner. This is an occasion to be thankful for what we have. Do not disappoint me by not showing up."

Mac snorts. "God forbid you be ungrateful for your shitty parents."

"It's just going to be another shitty holiday where Dad praises the ground my sister walks on and points out all of my faults. Ugh!" He drops his phone as he covers his face and groans. "I don't want to go," he whines.

"I'll go with you if you want," Mac offers.

Dean uncovers his face. "As much as I would LOVE for you to come with me, you know my parents hate you."

Mac huffs out a laugh. "It's because they can't control me. I also don't care what they think about me and have made it very clear how I feel about them."

Decision made for Thanksgiving, I hop off the couch. Both guys look at me with wide eyes. "Give me a second, I have an idea."

"An idea?" Dean asks as I rush toward my bedroom.

"Give me a second," I yell over my shoulder. Bouncing onto my bed, I pull up my mom's number and text her. I'm too much of a wimp to call.

> Hey Mama, I have a question about Thanksgiving tomorrow.

A few minutes later, I see the little bubbles at the bottom of the screen that show she's replying. I feel like I'm about to vomit with nerves. Why am I so damn nervous about asking my mom if the guys can come? *Because you care about them, you dumbass.*

Mama

> **Please tell me you can still come!**

> *I can move some things around if you are go-*
> *ing to be late.*

I smile down at the screen. This will be the first holiday I will be home since I moved. I couldn't afford to go home for every holiday. Just from her text, I can already tell she is beginning to panic that I won't make it home because of work.

> *Mama I'll be home. I wanted to ask if it's okay to bring two friends with me?*

A few minutes pass before the dots indicate she's typing.

Mama

> *What type of friends?*

Damn her and her intuition. I've never brought a friend home for the holidays, let alone two. How can I put this so she won't ask more questions? Though, let's be honest, the questions would happen anyway.

> *A few guys from the team. They don't have anywhere to go.*

Mama

> *I know you are lying. But you know I won't say no to extra guests.*

> *Thank you, Mama!*

I jump out of bed with a grin and make my way out the door. Now, I just have to convince the guys to come. Considering how Dean acted about going home, I doubt it will take much convincing.

The guys look my way the moment I walk into the room. I grin as I hold up my phone, waving it. "So... I may have a way to get you out of going home."

Dean's eyes widen, begging for any excuse. "No way!"

My cheeks heat when I say, "This is an open offer, and it's only if you don't want to go home. You don't have to say yes."

Mac's grin widens as he asks, "What did you do, Chérie?"

Tapping the phone to my thigh, I shrug. "I may have asked my mama if you guys could come to Thanksgiving dinner, so you could avoid family drama."

"And your mom said yes?" Dean asks excitedly.

I nod. "Yes."

Dean hops up from the loveseat before jumping over the back of the couch. He lifts me into the air with a laugh. "Yes! I'm totally down!" He spins me around, then lets my feet touch the floor. Before I know what's happening, he smashes his lips to mine and then jumps back over the couch to smash his lips to Mac's cheek.

Mac laughs and shakes his head. "I've never seen you this excited about Thanksgiving before."

Dean points at Mac. "I've never had an excuse to tell my parents I couldn't go!" He pulls out his phone and his fingers fly across the screen as he types.

"What are you going to tell your parents?" I ask in curiosity.

"I'm telling them I can't come because I have to impress my girl-friend's parents." He replies distractedly.

"Girlfriend?" I squeak.

Mac snorts a laugh. "Did you think we considered you anything else?"

I shrug because I'm not sure how to reply to that. I plop down on the couch as I say, "I guess I don't really know what we are."

Mac leans over to press a kiss to my cheek. "You are our girlfriend. At least outside of work. Is that alright with you, Chérie?"

I can't do anything but nod. I like that I mean something to them. We are something to each other, but I'm not sure I should tell my parents that. "Do you mind if we keep it on the downlow with my parents for right now?"

Dean waves a dismissive hand into the air. "It's fine. I mainly want to rub this in my parents' face."

Mac weaves his fingers with mine before giving my hand a squeeze. "Don't worry. We won't embarrass you in front of your family."

I shake my head. "I'm not afraid of you embarrassing me. I'm just not ready to explain this"—I gesture between the three of us—"to my parents just yet."

"Do you think they won't except us?" he asks curiously.

I think on that for a moment. I think my mom would be okay with it, honestly. It's my dad I'd have to worry about. "To be honest, I think the only person who may freak out is my dad. But considering you guys play hockey, he may be okay with it." I smirk.

Dean jumps off the couch. "Let's get going!" he yells and runs off toward his bedroom.

I look at Mac with a smile. "He does realize we don't have to be there until tomorrow, right?"

He grins back. "I don't think he cares."

I yell over the back of the couch, "Dean, we don't have to be there until tomorrow!"

"These are your parents, Lizzy! We need to make a great impression. Let's go tonight and see if they need help with anything.".

"I don't think you are going to win this one, Chérie," Mac says with a huff of laughter.

Pushing myself off the couch, I look down at my pajamas, then back up to Mac. "I suppose I should get dressed, then."

Mac leans down to kiss my cheek. "I'll make myself presentable as well."

"You look fine," I say, then close my bedroom door behind me. Once in the walk-in closet, I pick out a baby-blue sweater dress and a pair of black leggings. I can finally wear the new pair of boots I got for the winter weather. It was a shock to my wardrobe having to change from sunscreen, sandals, and shorts to sweaters, boots, and beanie hats.

I quickly change before leaving to find the others in the living room waiting for me. I bite my lip as I look over my two boys. Dean has on a pair of dark-washed jeans with a black shirt and leather jacket. Mac contrasts his dark look with a pair of light-blue jeans and a crisp white shirt.

Mac winks when my eyes meet his. "Do I pass inspection?"

My cheeks heat as I roll my eyes. "I always think you look good."

Mac gestures toward the door. "I suppose we should be off."

Fifteen minutes later, we pull up to my childhood home. I let out a sigh as I take in the old house with a smile. "This place hasn't changed a bit."

Mac takes in the house. "Is this the house you grew up in?"

I nod as I unbuckle and open the passenger door. "Till the day I left for college."

Dean hums as we make our way up the drive to the front door. "It's cute."

I snort a laugh and knock. "Cute? I don't think I've ever heard you describe anything as cute."

"I think you're cute."

My eyes widen as the door opens, and my mother greets me with a look of shock. My cheeks are burning as I give her a shy smile. "Hey,

Mama"—I point to the guys—"these are the hockey players I invited for dinner tomorrow. They wanted to introduce themselves."

As if summoned by the word hockey, my dad appears in the doorway. "Well, this is a pleasant surprise, little bit."

I groan at the old nickname. "Dad…"

His gruff face softens before shifting to the guys. "Who's with you, Iz?"

Pointing to Dean first, I awkwardly begin introductions from the front porch, since they haven't invited us in yet. "This is Dean Lewis one of the players I'm in charge of and"—I switch to Mac— "this is Mac Oliver."

My dad's eyes widen as he shoves himself through the door. He jerks his hand out to Dean first. "It's a pleasure to meet two of the men on the Washington Wraiths."

Dean smiles as he shakes my father's hand. "It's a pleasure to meet our athletic therapist's parents, sir."

My dad waves a dismissive hand before turning to shake Mac's hand. "No need for formality. I'm Johanthan Monroe, but you can call me John."

My mother squeezes in front of my dad and smiles up at the guys. "I'm Katy Monroe, but you can call me Kate."

A few moments of uncomfortable silence pass, though I'm not sure if I'm the only one who feels that way. Considering the soft smile on my mom's face and the admiration shining through my father's smile; I think it's only me. I point inside of the house. "Could we possibly come inside?"

My mother gasps as she swats at my father. "Of course! Johnny, move out of the way so our daughter and her friends can come inside."

I never thought the word 'friends' coming out of my mother's mouth could make me feel like I was sixteen all over again, nervous to invite new friends over. The moment we step inside, it's like my father is a hawk, and he descends on the guys asking them non-stop questions about the season so far.

I shake my head with a smirk as I sit down beside my mom on the couch. The guys answer every question my dad throws at them with a chuckle or a smile. Mac must feel my eyes on him because he looks in my direction.

His wide smile turns soft as he gives me a little wave. I feel my cheeks heat as I can't help but smile back and give him a small wave. The gesture catches Dean's attention, and he gives me a wink before turning back to the conversation with my dad. I feel something poke my thigh, and I look over to find my mom smirking at me. She pulls back her foot and looks at the guys before focusing on me. "Is there something I should know, Iz?"

I bite my lip as I shrug. "We're friends."

She hums, but I'm not sure she believes me. "I'm sure. Do they know that?"

"Of course they do," I huff out.

She lowers her voice to whisper, "I'm not so sure. They way they look at you says otherwise." Something must change on my face because her teasing smile turns soft. "As long as you're not lying to yourself, that's all I care about. You look at them the same way they look at you."

"And how's that?" I whisper.

She taps the corner of her eye before whispering back, "The eyes are the window to the soul"—she points to the guys before pointing back at me—"and your souls show me everything I need to know." She presses a finger to her lips. "I won't say anything, Iz."

"Thank you." My chest fills with love for my mother.

"Are you happy?" she asks quietly.

I shift my gaze from her over to my guys before meeting hers once more. "Yes."

Chapter Thirty-Three

December is in full swing here in Washington. Today is my first game day off since the season started, and the wives have messaged me non-stop about the proper attire to wear to cheer on our boys. The knowing grins they've been giving me since the Fourth of July party makes me believe they know something is going on between Dean, Mac, and me. Though they haven't said a word about it.

My phone rings, and I roll my eyes, but grin, when Cheryl's name brightens the screen. That woman is dead set on dragging me along on their shenanigans for the day. "Hey Cheryl."

"Girl! Where the hell are you?" she asks with a huff.

"I'm at my apartment. Where else would I be?"

She groans. "You agreed to go with us to find a jersey for the game tonight!"

I laugh as I slip on my tennis shoes. "I never said I would go with you. *You* threatened to paddle my ass if I didn't go."

She hums. "I did say that, didn't I? Well, you already agreed to go."

Shaking my head, I grab my coat and slip it on. "I'm almost finished getting ready. You don't need to send in the cavalry."

"You've got thirty seconds to get your ass out the door or I'm sending in Karen." She laughs as she hangs up.

A snort leaves me as I grab my phone and purse before heading out. Locking the door behind me, I make my way downstairs before rushing to the parking lot.

Glancing around, I find Cheryl waving an arm out of her driver side window before rolling it back up. The rear door to the SUV opens, and Samantha hops out, though, I suppose it is more of a slip and slide down than a hop, from the seat with the size of her belly.

She points over her shoulder with a smirk. "You're between Dannielle and me."

Samantha climbs back into the car after letting me hop in the middle. I look between the hockey wives, taking in their large bellies; they are due any day now. "Almost to the finish line, right?"

They both nod as they rub a hand over their belly. "If the boys don't arrive in the next week, they will induce labor."

"I really hope it doesn't come to that," Samantha whines, patting her belly before adding, "I know it's comfortable in there, but Mommy wants you to come out and see the world. It's beginning to feel a little tight in there."

"I told you to try some of those old wives' tales to see if that helps," Cheryl says over her shoulder.

Samantha groans. "Ever since we had sex a few weeks ago, and he swore the baby grabbed his dick, he won't touch me."

I can't help but laugh. "He does know that's not possible right?"

She raises an irritated brow before saying, "I've tried to explain that to him, but he swears up and down that the baby grabbed his dick. The man is too stubborn for his own good."

I turn toward Dannielle. "What about you?"

She gives me a sour look. "Doug told Max what happened, and he's locked up his cock too."

The car erupts in laughter as we pull up to the shopping center and park. We begin to file out of the car, but before I get far Cheryl snatches my hand.

My eyes are wide as I meet her grinning face. "You're not getting out of this shopping spree."

I groan but let her drag me toward the shop where you can buy any jersey you could possibly want or need. "You don't think it would be weird for me to wear a jersey with just one of the guys' numbers?"

She clucks her tongue. "If you're sitting with us, you will be a proper cheerleader for your boys."

I grunt but accept that I'm going to be dragged into this no matter what I say. Though, to be honest, I don't hate the idea of wearing our team's jersey's. But how am I supposed to decide what number to wear?

Cheryl releases my hand and gently smacks my butt. I look over my shoulder with an arched brow, but she just grins. "Get shopping!"

Rolling my eyes, I look around. There are several jerseys with Dean's number as well as several with Mac's number. It feels like a betrayal to choose one over the other, though.

Continuing to wander around, I finally find a customizable jersey. Smirking, I decide that's the winner and make my way up to the woman at the counter. "Can I get this customized by tonight?"

She arches a brow before shrugging. "As long as it's not too difficult, I should be able to."

"Can you put Monroe as the last name on the back, along with the number sixty-nine?"

The woman smirks. "Sixty-nine?"

I nod and continue, "And can you put the number thirty-five on one sleeve and eleven on the other?"

Her smirk widens, but she nods. "Sure. I can do that. Give me a few hours to get it done. If you give me your phone number, I can text you when it's done."

I nod and pay, then give the woman my number to let me know when it's ready. As I make my way out of the store, my eyes meet Cheryl's. She arches a brow and says, "I don't see a jersey."

I point behind me as I reply, "I'm having it customized."

"Well, do we get to see it before tonight?" Samantha asks with a smirk of her own.

I shake my head. "You girls will just have to wait and be surprised like the guys."

It's odd being on this side of the boards. I'm impressed we were able to get seats in front, so the players will immediately see us as they skate in. Rock music blares through the rink, and I hold my breath as the players are announced.

The moment Dean's name is called, the crowd goes wild. He takes to the ice, his eyes searching the crowd before they land on me. He grins and makes his way over, taking in my jersey.

He bangs a hand on the glass before making a swirling motion, telling me to turn around. I spin, and when my eyes meet his again, he's sporting a wide grin before pointing to the sleeve with his number.

"I like it, Ice Princess. My number looks good on you!" he yells before backing away.

Mac's is announced, and it doesn't take him long to find me. He's slow as he makes his way over. I spin again before he even asks. He lifts his helmet, so his face guard isn't blocking his face. The smile he gives me is soft. *"Tu as l'air à couper le souffle, Chérie."*

I'm not sure what that means, but the way he says it makes my cheeks heat. I give him a shy smile. "I think I'm supposed to say thank you. But I don't know what any of that meant."

He taps the glass with his glove before skating to his post. I hear a woman's high-pitched voice yell, "Move out of the way!"

I turn and spot Danni attempting to move through the crowd toward me. "Danni?"

She squeezes through the last few people until she reaches me. Holding up a carabiner of bracelets, she says, "The guys wanted to make sure you held onto these for them. Apparently, it's a job they only trust you with."

I snort as I take it and clip it onto my belt loop. "Crazy men."

When I look up again she's holding out two bracelets. "Lewi and Oli said these had to be with you, as well, but couldn't be shoved with the others."

I take them from her with a nod, gently slipping them onto my wrist. As my gaze meets hers, I smile. "Thank you, Danni."

She nods and backs away. "Got to get back to work."

I cup my hands around my mouth as I shout, "Take care of my boys." She laughs and gives me a thumbs-up.

My attention is pulled back to the ice as the game begins. A player on the other team is slammed into the boards in front of me, and I laugh as Taz's eyes meet mine. He gives me a wink before taking off toward the puck.

I love the game and working on the sidelines as an athletic therapist. But nothing compares to being surrounded by screaming fans and watching the carnage from behind the boards.

Damn... I love hockey.

Chapter Thirty-Four

A few weeks into December, I'm back to work. I'm biting my lip as I tape up each of the guys. There's one missing. Glancing around, I still don't see Dean. *He should have been here by now.* Everyone besides him has been taped up, and they will need to head to the locker room soon. This is our ritual before every game. No one is late. *Ever.*

Looking up and down the hallway, debating which direction to turn, when I hear hushed but aggressive words. *Who the fuck?* I rush that direction, rounding the corner to find a gentleman scowling down at Dean. The look of resignation on his face makes my heart ache. *Does he get yelled at like this all the time?*

I catch the end of the man's words as I make my way closer. "We expect more from you, Dean. Do better."

"Excuse me, who are you?" I ask haughtily. Dean's eyes widen and snap to mine. There is panic in them now, as the man looks over his shoulder.

He gives me a once over before dismissing me. "It's none of your concern."

I pop my hip out and stand my ground. "It is if you are distracting one of my players who needs to get taped and ready for the game." My gaze shifts to Dean, as I point over my shoulder. "Get to the locker room, Lewis."

The man bristles when Dean gives me a nod and makes his way around to him. As he steps up next to me, the man huffs, "Do you know who I am?"

Dean freezes next to me as I straighten. There is nothing that flips my bitch switch faster than someone asking me if I know who they are. As if their attitude would be okay if I knew who they were.

Dean whispers, "He's my dad, Lizzy."

Well, that only adds fuel the fire. Giving the man my best bitchy glare, I say, "I don't give a *fuck* who you are. You could be the president for all I care, and that still wouldn't give you the right to talk to *my* player the way you have." I point behind him. "If you would be so kind as to leave the premises that would be great. If not, I won't hesitate to call security."

The man looks me up and down before rolling his eyes at me like I'm trash. "Whatever. Dean, don't fuck up tonight. You have a name to uphold." He turns and walks off like I didn't just threaten to call security on him.

I wait till he has disappeared to ask, "Are you alright?"

Dean shrugs. "I'm used to it."

Not liking the dark cloud hovering over him, I turn and wrap my arms around his neck. Pulling him down so I can hug him. He's stiff for a moment before he loosly wraps his arms around me. "You're amazing, Dean. Don't let him get in your head and convince you otherwise," I whisper.

He laughs, but it sounds hollow. "I am pretty amazing."

I pull back enough to cup his face. "I'm proud of you." I make a mental note to say those words to him more often. My thumbs caress his cheeks as I fill my words with every bit of adoration I feel for him. "I'm so fucking proud of you, Dean."

His eyes flick over my face, and his eyes shimmer with unshed tears. "Liz..." he whispers.

I pull his face down so my forehead can rest against his. "You are an amazing man as well as an amazing player. You can completely fuck this game up, and I will *still* be proud of you."

His breath hitches as he rests his face in the crook of my neck. His arms tighten around me, and his breathing is a little choppy. "You make it so hard," he whispers brokenly.

I try to lighten the mood with a joke. "Your dick? I think that's a bit inappropriate at the moment."

He chuckles and shakes his head while pulling away to look down at me. With a smirk and wet eyes, his voice is rough as he replies, "It's hard not to love you."

I smirk. "Well, I am loveable."

He leans forward brushing his lips across mine in a soft caress before he pulls away. "I'm *in* love with you, Liz." My eyes widen in surprise. He must see I'm about to say something because he presses his lips against mine again. When he pulls away, he whispers, "Don't say anything. I just wanted you to know."

I go to say something anyway, although, I'm not really sure what will come out of my mouth, but he presses a finger to my lips. "I said don't say anything you stubborn woman."

I roll my eyes with a nod. "Fine."

"Now, wish me luck."

I snort. "Good luck."

He takes a step away with a hum. "You know, I wish you could wear my number at work, Lizzy."

With a grin, I lift the edge of my team polo up to show him my undershirt. I have both his and Mac's numbers ironed onto to the other side of my shirt. His eyes widen before he lets out a loud groan. "Fucking hell, woman." He steps into my space again before slamming his lips on mine.

He pulls away, panting. His eyes still closed he says, "Yep. I fucking love you." He shakes his head before taking a step away and then another. "Okay, I need to get the hell out of here before I shove you in a closet and fuck you."

He smirks, and my cheeks heat. I stutter a moment as I say, "Y-yeah. Let's not get in trouble."

He winks. "You know me; I love trouble."

I huff and shoo him away. "Get. You're going to be late."

With a mock salute, he rushes away. Shaking my head, I huff out a laugh. *What are these boys doing to me?* Then I remember he hasn't been taped up. Fuck!

The boys look great out there! I watch as Dean whispers something to Mac, and by the grin on Mac's face, I'm guessing he told him that I was wearing their numbers. With that knowledge, they seem to be playing their hearts out to impress me. Which they don't even need to do, but it's amusing.

With each goal Dean makes, he looks my way. He waits until I give him a thumbs-up before he skates away with a wink. I've noticed that one of the rookie centers on the other team seems extra aggressive, but I try not to focus on it. Some players are just more aggressive than others, but there are rules put in place, so I try not to worry.

The other team is getting desperate. Our boys are getting slammed into the guards left and right. There's one player in particular I keep an eye on from the other team. I think he may be a rookie because I'd never heard his name before. As I watch, he skates fast and hard toward our goalie, which is confusing, considering he doesn't have the puck.

I gasp in horror, noticing what is about to happen before it does. I pound on the glass, trying to warn the guys. There are several un-written rules in hockey, but one is held above all else: **Don't touch the goalie.** The goalie is to be protected at all costs. This guy has no intention of stopping as he gets close to our goalie. *My* goalie. Mac. I scream as I bang on the glass, but my voice blends with the crowd's excitement. My breath catches when I see the two collide, and Mac is thrown into the net.

Before I know it, I'm already running in his direction. I watch as Samy, one of our defensemen, lifts the other player off Mac and pushes him aggressively, while several of our players converge on the rookie. My only thought right now is getting to Mac.

I slide as I come up beside him. His head is lying next to the goal post. Fuck! Breathing hard, I try to stay calm. "Oli? Oli, can you hear me?"

He groans as his eyes open. His gaze is unfocused as he looks around. "*Putain*," he huffs.

"Couldn't have said it better myself. Can you look at me?" His eyes try to focus for a moment but then they roll back. Shit, he's unconscious. "I need a medic!" I yell over my shoulder.

For the first time in years, my hands shake as I try to hold his head steady until the medics can get to us. Dean slides up beside me, falling to his knees. "Is he okay?"

I look up to find his helmet off and sporting a bloody nose. All professionalism leaves me. My eyes widen. "Dean! What happened to your face?"

He smirks. "So... I'm Dean now?"

Growling, I ask, "What the fuck happened to your face?"

He shrugs. "My face may have made contact with a fist... or two. I'm fine. How's our boy?"

Huffing, I look back down. "You're Dean when you are in trouble. Just like Oli is Mac when he's in trouble at work. Among other things. I think he has a concussion. I can't get him to stay awake."

"Coming through!"

I look up to find a few medics with a spinal board. They shuffle to slide up on his other side. The medic in front of me smiles softly as he says, "I got him."

I nod and allow the medic to take over with Mac. Just then he rouses, mumbling, "Chérie."

"It's okay. It's okay, the medics will take care of you now."

He's agitated as he pleads, *"Reste avec, moi Chérie."*

I've never hated not understanding French more than right now. Dean thankfully translates for me. "He said, stay with me, darling."

My chest tightens as Mac reaches out for me. I take his hand, giving it a squeeze which causes the medics to pause. "They need to take you to the hospital, Mac. I'll be there as soon as I can, but I need to take care of the other boys too. You listen to the doctors and do as they say."

His eyes are still unfocused when they try to meet mine. *"Promesse?"*

I nod. *"Promesse."*

Mac gives my hand another light squeeze before he lets go. His gaze moves to Dean beside me. *"Botter le cul."*

Lewi laughs. "Like I wouldn't kick their ass for hurting our goalie."

Mac attempts a grin as the medics take him away. Immediately, I'm engulfed in Dean's arms. My face smashed against his padded chest. I try to sound reprimanding as I say, "You shouldn't be hugging me like this in front of everyone."

His voice is soft when he says, "Shut up, and let me hug you."

My hands grip the back of his jersey as he holds me on the ice. A voice behind me yells, "We need to continue the game. Please, get off the ice."

Dean's arms tighten around me once more as he growls, "We just lost a goalie! Fuck off!"

I chuckle and pat his back. "It's okay. You need to finish the game. Win for Mac." I turn to the voice behind me to find the ref. "I'm sorry. I'll make my way off the ice."

He grunts and skates away. I head back to the bench when Manny, our other goalie, skates up beside me. He gives me a soft, playful shoulder punch. "Don't worry too much about him, Roe Roe."

Laughing, I give him a punch back. "Just protect the net. And don't get hurt. Danni can't afford to lose her goalie too."

He gives me a salute as he skates away. The players give me a pat on the back as I head to my designated spot to watch the rest of the game. Danni bumps my shoulder as she asks quietly, "You good?"

The adrenaline is starting to wear off, and my hands won't stop shaking. Shoving them in my jacket pockets, I give her a nod. "Yeah. I'm good."

She snorts. "No you're not, but I'll let you keep believing that. For your sake."

Biting my lip, I watch as the game continues. Shouts and screams surround us as I admit, "I think... I think I like him."

Danni laughs as she moves in closer. "Anyone with eyes can tell you like him. You'd have to be blind not to notice the way he looks at you. Even Lewi smiles for you, and that man doesn't smile for anyone."

I side-eye her to gauge her thoughts about the two guys who appear to like me. Her smile is wide, and she rolls her eyes. "I'm not going to judge you for liking them both if that's what you're afraid of. Nor am I going to tell anyone that there is something going on between the three of you. It's none of my business so long as you do your job. But don't lie to yourself. You more than like them."

"Ugh... this is turning into such a mess," I grumble.

She shrugs. "Love is messy."

"I could get fired for this! I shouldn't be with either of them, let alone love them!"

Her expression grows serious as she says, "Then switch them to my roster to train. You can take Manny and Langly. That way you'd still have a goalie and a center."

I arch a brow in question. "How would we go about asking Max for the switch?"

"Be honest. Bring the boys in with you for a meeting and tell him the truth; that you guys want a relationship. Explain that you and I have already talked and agreed to switch a few players we oversee so ethics won't be called into question. I think if you are honest and keep it professional, they will take that into consideration. It's probably better than keeping it a secret and them finding out later from some-one else."

Huffing out a breath I ask, "Do you think that will work?"

She bumps my shoulder. "You'll never know unless you try."

"I have a feeling the guys won't like switching it up."

Laughing, she says, "They will deal with it if it means you get to stay. You don't have a lot of options here. The pair are becoming too obvious about their feelings for you. The higher ups will notice soon if you don't do something about it now."

My shoulders slump as the adrenaline leaves my body completely wiped. "Soon." I hesitantly agree.

"Let's set up a meeting later this week," she says as the buzzer sounds, signaling the end of the game. She bumps my shoulder. "Now, go check on your boy."

I shake my head. "I need to make sure the rest of my boys are good."

She flicks my forehead. "What part of 'I've got you' do you not understand. Oli is the only one who got hurt, and I'm sure Lewi will be right behind you."

I rub my forehead as I narrow my eyes. "Was the thump necessary?"

"Yes. Now go!"

I smirk and give her a hug. "Thank you."

She hugs me back. "Anytime, girl."

I pull away and do a quick sweep around to find Dean staring at me. He points toward the locker room. I can't hear him so I watch his mouth as he asks, "Wait for me?"

I nod and point to the exit. "Hallway."

He nods, then rushes to the lockerroom. I make my way into the hall to wait for Dean to change. When I hear the door swing open, my head jerks up. My eyes widen when I see my nine boys step out.

Vicy smirks as he makes his way closer. Draping an arm over my shoulder, he asks, "Did you really think we would let you go to the hospital without us?"

My mouth gapes. "I figured you guys would come later."

Taz walks up to my other side with a smile. "We're family, right?"

My eyes burn but I grin. "Yeah," I rasp.

Vicy releases me and jogs forward. "Let's go check on our boy."

Dean twines his pinky with mine and says quietly, "They wanted to come to make sure it didn't look weird with only you and me showing up for Mac."

My gaze turn to Taz, and he smiles softly. He shrugs. "You're Roe Roe."

"And what exactly does that mean?"

I jump when I hear Perri's behind me. *"Famille."*

Family. My chest feels like it's about to burst. I never thought these boys would come to mean so much to me. "I love you guys. You know that?"

Perri ruffles my hair with a soft laugh. *"Je t'aime aussi soeur."*

"What does that mean?"

Taz yells, "He said 'I love you too sister'."

The grin that spreads across my face makes Perri roll his eyes. I poke him as I ask, "How do you say brother?"

"Frère."

I nod as we exit the building. "One of these days, I'm going to learn French."

Merc laughs. "It will be easier the longer you stick around; the guys that speak it fluently anyway."

I roll my eyes. "Curse words are not going to help me in a conversation."

Vicy claps his hands. "Alright, let's get going y'all!"

CHAPTER THIRTY-FIVE

I'm not sure why or what's going on, but the energy feels wrong. Peeking over my shoulder, I see that Perri is still following us. We don't all fit in one car, so we decided to take two cars to the hospital.

Maybe I'm just feeling jittery from the adrenaline after what happened to Mac and our win against the team that sent our goalie to the hospital.

A crash of thunder vibrates the car, making me jump. Dean slips his fingers into mine as he gives my hand a gentle squeeze.

"You okay?"

I nod. Not sure why I feel off. It's the same feeling I had at the game tonight but made the mistake of brushing it off. My dad always told me to listen to my instincts, and my mother told me many times that our bodies often know when something is wrong before the mind can catch up. Is this one of those situations?

Thunder sounds loudly around us as lightning flashes across the sky. The weather seems to reflect my mood as we make our way to the hospital. I stare out the window. Watching as dark clouds roll overhead. Blanketing over the beautiful sunset filled with oranges and pinks. It's ominous how fast the clouds are moving, as if they want to turn the world dark.

The air is charged with the coming storm, feeding my desperation to get to Mac. I need to make sure he's okay. Head injuries can turn horrible fast. My body tingles with awareness as a feeling of dread suddenly fills my chest, and another boom of thunder vibrates the car.

A shiver rushes down my spine, and I'm not sure if the dread is for Mac or for myself.

Dean bumps my shoulder. "You okay, Ice Princess?"

I'm still gazing out the window, wishing the dark clouds, or the bright colors of the sunset, would reveal what is making me feel this way. Nothing. Absolutely nothing. It only leaves me feeling more lost than I was before.

I turn to meet his gaze as my brows knit together. "I—I don't know. Something feels off."

He arches a brow. "What do you mean?"

A shiver runs down my spine as I mutter, "Something bad is going to happen."

His grip on my hand tightens. "We got you. Just stay with one of us, okay?"

I nod, taking a deep breath. I love that he doesn't discount my feelings. He doesn't laugh and say I'm crazy or give me empty platitudes of how everything will be okay. I squeeze his hand back, grateful for the reassurance, as I whisper, "Thank you."

He nods before talking to the others. Letting them know that I have a bad feeling, and that someone needs to always be with me. It doesn't lessen the feeling of dread in my body, but as long as I stay by their side I will be fine. Right?

Chapter Thirty-Six

I was wrong...

I was so... so very wrong...

I didn't even get the chance to tell them I loved them.

Chapter Thirty-Seven

I rush through the hospital doors with the guys following close behind. The ladies at the front desk look up in alarm as they see a woman with nine guys behind her enter.

"Um... ma'am is everything okay?" one of them asks.

I nod. "Yes! We're here for Mac Oliver."

She looks at us all before saying, "Alright. Well, may I ask who you are?"

"I'm..." What the hell am I supposed to say? His girlfriend? No, maybe they'll let me go back if I explain I am his athletic therapist?

Dean steps up beside me as he twines his fingers with mine, giving my hand a squeeze. "We're family. But if you want something more specific, we are his teammates."

One of the other girls quickly stands up with a wide smile. "Oh my god! You guys are the Washington Wraiths!"

He gives her his fake smile, the one all photographers and fans get. "Yes. If you wouldn't mind showing us where our brother is at that would be great."

She nods enthusiastically. "Of course!" Rushing around the desk she waves for us to follow.

"I don't think what she's doing is allowed," I whisper to Dean.

He smirks. "I don't think it really matters when we are getting what we want right?"

I hum in reply, too distracted for an argument. The nurse pulls the curtain separating the room from the hallway, and my eyes immediately zero in on Mac. He looks up at us with a grin. "Hey guys."

I release Dean's hand and rush over to him. He chuckles when I cup his cheeks, forcing him to look at me. "Are you okay? What did the doctor say? Can you focus on me? Did they say you had a concussion? What—"

Mac presses a finger to my lips with a chuckle. "That's a lot of questions for my rattled brain to follow, *Chérie*."

My eyes burn as I ask the only question that matters. "Are you okay?"

He sighs and wipes a few stray tears I didn't realize escaped. "I'm okay. *Ça va aller.*"

"I don't know what that means."

He cups my cheek, pulling me closer so our foreheads touch. "It's all right."

I bite my lip before whispering, "That really scared me."

"I'm sorry I scared you," he whispers.

A throat clears, and I look over my shoulder, finding the guys blocking the doctor from coming in. I can't help but smirk as I pull away and stand beside Mac. He slips his hand into mine before saying, "Sorry doc. You can let him in, boys."

The guys glance over before parting to let the doctor in. He nods to the others before looking at us. He gives Mac a smile before saying, "Your test results have come back. You do have a mild concussion, but other than that, you should be good to get back on the ice in a few days. But try to take it easy."

"Great," Mac huffs out. "Can I go home instead of staying here, doc?"

The doctor looks around the room and says, "Well, it seems you'll have enough eyes on you for the next twenty-four hours. You should be fine to head home. I'll make sure to send some information with you, so everyone knows what to look out for in case you need to come back."

"Sounds like a plan." Mac releases my hand and begins to sit up. "If all of you would be so kind as to leave, so I can change into something less revealing that would be great."

Dean snorts. "It's not like we haven't seen it all before."

"Not the point," Mac huffs.

"I can go get the car," I volunteer.

The guys' immediately yell, "No!"

I flinch at the barrage of ten men answering 'no' at the same time. "Someone can come with me, sheesh. I was only going to pull it around and wait."

Dean looks between Mac and me before huffing out. "Fine. I'll be down in a second. We'll help get Mac ready to go and make sure we have everything we need." He begins directing the others on what to do as I slip out of the room.

Walking back the way we came, I follow the signs to the exit. I know going outside by myself is a bad idea, especially since I still have the niggling feeling that something else is going to go wrong. So, I wait next to the door and pull out my phone.

I scroll through the posts on social media, most of them about the game tonight. Someone managed to get a photo of the rookie hitting Mac. How they got the photo? I'm not sure, but the sports photographers' are amazing at their job.

At the sound of someone shouting my name, I look up and see Dean heading down the hallway. I lift a hand in acknowledgement, then spin and begin making my way out the door. He yells my name again but more panicked this time. "Liz!"

I turn to look at him again in confusion and see the panic written all over Dean's face. He's screaming my name, but before I can figure out why he's yelling, I feel a sharp pinch in my neck.

My last thought before my vision darkens is, *well fuck*. The image of Dean running my way, panic clouding his face is the last thing I see before I'm pulled under.

Chapter Thirty-Eight

When you're stuck in the dark, it allows too much time to think. The one thing that keeps repeating in my head is how I'm a damn idiot for not trusting my instincts. I knew something felt off, and yet I still went off alone.

The image of Dean's face when he realized he wouldn't reach me in time will haunt me. His eyes wide with fear as he yelled out for me. I saw him rush my direction before the world went black.

"Izzy. Izzy. Izzy. Such a bad girl," a deep, distorted voice says from behind me.

My spine stiffens. There has only ever been one person who called me Izzy. "Emmitt?"

"Took you long enough to figure out who sent all those love notes. I told you you belonged to me. And what did you do?"

"What the fuck are you talking about?" Emmitt grabs a fistful of my hair, and I scream when he uses it to tug me up from my spot on the floor. My scalp burns with how hard he's pulling. He turns my face, so I'm forced to look up at a masked man. I know it's Emmitt, though.

The mask covers his entire face, but it has neon x's for the eyes and a wide joker smile. It's creepy as fuck. His head tilts as his distorted voice comes from the mask. "You belong to me. Me! And you went off and whored yourself out to those men."

Before I can stop the words from falling out of my mouth I yell, "I'll NEVER belong to you."

His head tilts to the other side as he shoves me to the ground. "We'll see how long that lasts." He turns and begins to walk away.

I rush after him but screech when my momentum suddenly stops and pain flares in my leg. I look down at the blasted ankle cuff keeping me here. I'd forgotten about it in my haste to get out of this place. "Where the fuck am I?" I yell after him.

He continues to walk away as he lifts my phone. My eyes widen when he looks over his shoulder. "If you think I'd let them find you easily, you're mistaken, Izzy."

I watch him drop my phone and stomp on it, shattering it so it can't be tracked. I glare up at him, his grinning mask mocking me as the last source of light disappears behind the closed door. I let the tears I'd held back flow. A choked sob makes its way out as I settle on the makeshift bed. I'm too afraid to close my eyes because I want to know the moment the light returns. When *he* returns.

Eventually, I feel myself losing the fight with sleep but startle when the door slams open. That stupid mask grins at me before he raises a gun. I scream as he pulls the trigger. Pain sears my shoulder, and I look down to find what looks like a dart.

I reach up and pluck it out of my skin, hissing at the figure moving toward me. A surge of panic fills me when one figure turns into two before blurring together.

Dark laughter greets me as I try to fight off whatever he dosed me with. "I had to make sure you wouldn't fight me. I couldn't knock you out the same way."

My words are slurred. "F-uck y-y-you."

"Such a dirty mouth for a beautiful snowflake, Izzy." I feel his disgusting hands on me, but I can't do anything to fight him. My body grows numb, and unresponsive to the commands my brain issues.

He positions my body on the bed, then ties my arms out to each side before moving and doing the same to my legs. They are spread wide as he ties my ankles down. Tears stream down into my hair, and all I can do is stare at the ceiling wondering what I did to deserve this. What does he plan on doing to me?

The clothes I've been wearing for fuck knows how long are ripped from my body. I whimper as he exposes my bare skin. The only things that prevent me from being completely naked are my bra and underwear.

I can't do anything but watch as he hovers over me. He removes the mask to reveal the muddy-brown eyes I remember. A dark glint that was never there before brightens as he takes me in, my body on display. With a salacious grin, he pulls what looks like a marker from his back pocket.

He taps it against his lips as he looks over me. "I don't want to mark up this beautiful body permanently by carving my name into it. But..." He bites the lid off the pen before spiting it across the room. "I can certainly leave my mark with this. Blood isn't really my thing, but you *will* remember who you belong too."

I want to writhe and fight and scream against the feeling of his hands on my body without consent, but my body refuses to do what it's told. All I can do is lie here as silent tears continue to fall. Each letter he marks on my skin makes my stomach turn, and the only thing I want to do more than run away is vomit.

He finally gives me a reprieve from the torture of his company when he stabs me with another dose of whatever drug he gave me before. "I do enjoy your silence much more than your constant shouting and screeching."

I watch as he walks toward the door. He glances over his shoulder one last time with a smirk. "I do love seeing my name all over your body, Izzy." He reaches down to cup his dick through his jeans and groans, his eyes closing in pleasure. "Fuck. The thought of you screaming my name."

His hooded eyes meet mine, and he growls. "Fuck it." When he turns back to head in my direction, my body floods with panic.

Is he going to rape me? Oh my god. Please. Please, don't do this. I can't even scream because the drug coursing through my body leaves me paralyzed. He stops beside me, quickly unbuttoning his jeans, slipping them down just enough to pull out his rock-hard cock.

He grunts as he grips his cock, tightening his hold when as he begins to stroke himself. His eyes, filled with pleasure, leer over my body. Using his free hand, he reaches out to trace the letters of his name that now cover my body. His breathing becomes labored as his thumb traces over my bottom lip.

"I can just picture your plump lips wrapped around my cock." He grunts as his thumb circles the head of his dick, pre-cum leaking from the tip. "Fuck," he says breathily. He shoves his thumb into my mouth, and I wish I so badly that I could bite him. My body won't listen to a single command as I lie practically naked and helpless while he jerks himself off.

His closed eyes open just enough to look down at me while he pumps his thumb into my mouth with the same rhythm he strokes his cock. "Your wet fucking mouth wrapped around me. Sucking me down like a good girl. *My* fucking whore." His breathing grows labored and his movements erratic. Pumping his cock faster he leans over me, his eyes closed as pleasure overtakes him.

"Licking me like the best fucking lollipop you've ever had. Fuck!" he roars as he comes all over my abdomen, jerking himself until his head slumps.

The need to vomit is so overwhelming that I'm sure if I had any control over my body, I would have already vomited all over this man. When he opens his eyes, I know in this moment that he will never let me go. The look of pleasure and total control in his eyes tells me that I'll be strapped to this bed for the foreseeable future.

He smears his cum over my skin before backing away. "My Izzy. Forever."

My vision blurs as I watch him leave, silent sobs wracking my body as the door to my freedom closes behind him. Left in the dark with nothing but my tears and memories of the two men I wish I had told how much I loved them.

I'm not sure how long it's been since Emmitt brought me here, but I refuse to sleep more than a few moments. I jerk awake whenever I hear a creak in the floor or voices talking behind the door. I'm so fucking exhausted.

Emmitt forces me to drink broth so I get some nutrition. But he refuses to give me more than a few seconds before dosing me again and again, paralyzing me so I can't put up a fight. I doubt I'd be able to anyway, considering how weak I am. I haven't moved from this bed; I'm still tied in the same position.

I feel the drugs start to wear off, and I know he will be back soon to dose me again. I stare up at the ceiling as my mind drifts to the only two things keeping me sane.

Dean and Mac. I wonder how they are doing? How's Mac? I don't know how long I've been here, but I hope he has recovered after the concussion. Hopefully Dean isn't beating the shit out of anyone right now. His anger often gets the best of him. Who's taking care of my guys while I'm stuck here? Danni. I know Danni will be taking care of them.

A smirk briefly creases my face as I think of the fiery woman. I'm sure she's giving them hell, trying to keep their focus on the upcoming games.

I wiggle my toes, enjoying the small win I feel at being able to do something other than lie paralyzed in this disgusting bed. My brows furrow as I look at the door. He usually doesn't leave me alone long enough that I recover some feeling. My fingers come alive, the pins and needles feeling tingling my extremities. What's going on?

A loud thump sounds above, and I look up at the ceiling, not that I can see anything, considering I'm in a dark basement. I hear someone yell 'clear' before there's a rush of thundering steps above me.

Is that... help? I open my mouth to yell, but nothing comes out from disuse. I hear someone yelling my name, my eyes widening when several different voices call my name. It's the boys! It's my boys!

My body comes alive with hope, and I begin to struggle against the ropes tying down my ankles and wrists. Steps thunder down the stairs, and I look at the door before it's kicked open.

I squint against the sudden light since I've been kept in the dark as two figures fill the doorway. I can barely make out guns and realize they're police officers. I force the word through my dry throat, "Help!"

My voice is raspy, but one of the officers hears it and asks, "Elizabeth Monroe?"

I whimper as I tug at my restraints. "Yes," I rasp back.

"Liz!" My name is yelled from the doorframe, and I look over to find Dean, Taz, and Vicy fighting to get through the door first.

Something inside me breaks, and I begin to thrash and screech, wanting desperately to be free. "Let me out! Let me go!" My throat burns from yelling so much, but I don't care.

I watch as Dean takes a hesitant step in my direction, but the officer beside him shakes his head. "You need to stay here, sir."

I have no idea how the guys convinced the officers to let them in the house, and I don't care. I just want out of this fucking place. I want to be free.

"She's hurting herself!" Taz yells at the officer.

The sound of a females voice makes me pause. When I look in her direction, I see she's slowly making her way toward me. I hiss at her and keep tugging at my restraints. She raises her hands in surrender as she says softly, "Hi, Miss Monroe. I'm here to help get you out of here, but I need you to stop fighting your restraints."

"I want them off," I grunt.

She nods. "I understand, but we need to take a few pictures and gather evidence first, okay?"

I bite my lip but still as I process her words. Pictures? I peer down at myself as best I can, and I'm disgusted when I get my first glimpse. Being kept in the dark meant I had no way to tell how bad I looked. My eyes sting with tears as I look back up at her. "I don't want them to see me like this."

She gives me a sad smile. "We are going to do everything we can to put this man in jail for a long time. After we take pictures, I'll cover you, alright?"

I nod as I look back up at the ceiling. "Hurry."

She shouts orders to a few people, and camera flashes fill the room as I'm subjected to pictures and them gathering evidence. One of the male officers moves in my direction, and I snap. I scream and tug at my restraints again. "Get away! Get away from me!"

He pauses before backing away. Through the fog of my panic, I hear a familiar voice. "Ice Princess. Lizzy, baby. Try to stay calm." His broken voice cuts through my panic. I turn in the direction I heard his voice and see Vicy holding him back. He pauses his fight to get to me when he sees me looking at him. He blinks, and I watch as a few tears stream down his cheeks. With a sad smile, he meets my gaze. "I'm here. I'm not going anywhere. Keep your eyes on me, okay?"

I feel something cover me, and I go to look, but Dean's voice stops me. "Eyes on me, princess. Don't look away."

My eyes never stray, but exhaustion fills me as the adrenaline leaves my body. "Ghost?" My voice is brittle as his nickname slips over my dry lips.

A wet laugh escapes him as he nods. "Yeah, baby. It's me. I'm here."

I let his dark eyes be my escape while the officers do what they need. Never letting my gaze stray from his. He looks so tired. I can see dark circles under his eyes.

When I hear the female officer beside me, I startle. "Miss?"

I let my gaze move from Dean to look to her. "Yes?"

She stands and backs away. "We have everything we need. Your wrists and ankles will need to be looked at, but you are free."

Before I can make a single move, I'm wrapped in Dean's arms. I'm engulfed in his warm scent, and my body melts into his. I slowly wrap around him, and I feel my eyes burn. Relief fills me, as tears slip down my cheeks. I feel him shaking as his wet breath brushes across my neck.

"I was so fucking scared. I've never been so afraid in my life than when I saw you ripped away from me." His arms tighten around me as he huffs. "I fucking love you, Elizabeth."

With as much strength as I can, I tighten my grip on him and whisper, "I love you, too, Dean."

It's not long before I lose the battle to stay awake. I haven't slept much since being brought here and knowing I'm safe means my body needs rest. I was too afraid to sleep with Emmitt; I didn't know what he would have done if he found me asleep.

Dean must feel my body go limp, and he pulls away just enough to look at me. "Lizzy?"

My head lulls as I lose the fight completely. "So tired," I mumble.

I can hear his panic as he yells, "I need help!"

Words are yelled around me, but I can't make most of them out. *I'm sorry, I'm making you worry. But... I'm so... tired.* The last thing I feel before darkness consumes me is my body being lifted in the air.

CHAPTER THIRTY-NINE

T he first thing I remember after was waking up in a hospital bed with the steady beep sounding around the room. I wince when I open my eyes, hoping the room isn't too bright. My boys must have already thought of that because the room is warmly lit, and I can see the bright daylight mostly blocked behind the curtains.

When I finally focus, I see there are eight bodies slumped around the room. Dean and Mac are on either side of the bed, their heads resting on the edge of my bed. Each has a hand on my thighs. I can't stop myself from weaving my fingers into their hair.

Dark, licorice locks cover my right hand as wavy dark chocolate strands cover my left. Damn, I love their hair. How do they keep it so soft and fluffy? They start to stir under my touch, and their eyes slowly open.

"Morning, sleeping beauties," I say in a rough whisper.

Their eyes pop before Dean jerks up with a shout. "You're awake!"

I wince, and Mac swats him with a grunt. "Stay quiet, you asshole!"

Dean looks thoroughly chastised as he whispers, "Sorry, Liz."

"You guys look rough. How long have I been out?" I grunt as I try to sit up in the bed.

Mac jumps up to press a button on the side of the bed. It slowly lifts, and I don't have to work so hard to sit up. "You've been out for a few days. The doctors said you needed the rest, and they set up an IV for nutrition stuff."

I grin at his description. "IV nutrition stuff?"

He shrugs with a small smirk. "I guard a post and hit hockey pucks."

I hear shuffling and notice the others moving in closer. There are two people in particular I notice missing. "Maxy and Fenni!" My eyes widen in realization that Samantha and Dannielle were supposed to be induced a few days ago.

Taz smiles. "They're good. The babies are great, and Moms are healthy. They wanted to wait for you to wake up before they visited."

"Right, that makes sense. What is today?" I have no sense of days or how long I'd been gone.

"It's been about a week and a half since you were kidnaped and brought to the hospital. You've only been here for three or four days, I think," Dean says helpfully.

I groan and close my eyes. "You've had two games since then."

"Don't worry. Danni has been taking care of us. She says your notes are always helpful," Vicy says from his spot on the edge of the bed.

It's been weeks since the incident, but the guys haven't left my side for even a moment. Emmitt was taken into custody, but his dad is trying to work his magic and grease some palms to get him out. With the amount of evidence against him, though, I don't think it will happen anytime soon. To be honest, I just want it over and to forget everything.

Today is the day before Christmas, and all I want is to get back to work with the team. Since I left the hospital, the guys have had several games, and I had to watch with the wives. I don't mind watching or the wives, but I miss my guys and working with the team.

I'm jerked from my thoughts when my phone rings. I look down to find Max's face on the screen. When did I take a picture of my boss to put in my phone? Then, I remember that Taz had stolen my phone to take pictures of everyone so their face would pop up when they call.

"Hey, Boss," I say with a laugh. "What are you doing calling me the day before Christmas?"

"We've got a problem, Elizabeth," he says seriously. I start to worry, but I see a smirk pulling at his lips even though he tries to hide it.

My brows still knit in worry, and I sit up straighter. "What's wrong? Did one of the guys hurt themselves? I can head right over if you need."

He chuckles before saying, "Always ready to work. I hope you can keep up that same energy when you come back to work after New Years."

I let out a squeal and do a little happy dance in my seat. "Are you serious?"

"Danni has done a great job with your boys, but it seems they want their athletic therapist back." He huffs out a laugh. "They've come into my office enough times, pleading for me to bring you back. I told them you needed some time to recover and heal."

Oh my gosh! This is the best Christmas present ever! "Yes! Yes, I would love to come back."

"Good. I'm tired of having ten hockey players traipsing in and out of my office, constantly bothering me. I'll see you after New Years, Elizabeth."

"Thank you, Max!"

He hums before saying, "I should be thanking you. I've never seen my boys as loyal to anyone as they are to you. You should count yourself lucky."

My cheeks hurt from grinning so wide. "I'm the lucky one, boss."

"I'll see you then, Liz," he replies before hanging up.

I jump from the couch with a squeal of happiness and do a dance in the middle of the common house's living room. The guys have practically refused to let me out of their sight or move too far away. And it's not even Mac and Dean who are the overbearing ones.

Doors slam in the hallway, and I look over my shoulder to find six guys standing in the hall staring at me, eyes wide.

"What the fuck was that about?" Taz waves a frantic hand in the air, gesturing wildly.

Vicy presses a hand to his heart. "You cannot scream like that."

"What had you screaming like that, Roe Roe?" Tuck asks.

I lift my phone in the air with a wide smile. "Max called and said he wants me to come back to work after New Years!"

The guys cheer as Dean and Mac come up to me with a smile. Both squishing me in a group hug. Mac chuckles and whispers, "I'm glad you're coming back."

Dean hums. "We've missed you."

"I have a question for you guys," I whisper back.

"What's that?" Mac mumbles into my ear.

"Do you want to come to Christmas with me tomorrow? As my boyfriends." My cheeks burn with the question.

"We went with you for Thanksgiving as your boyfriends," Dean says with an edge of mischief.

"As in my official boyfriends. I would tell my parents."

Mac kisses my cheek and pulls away with a smile. "I would love that, *Chérie.*"

"Official boyfriends, eh?" Dean teases with a grin.

I swat his chest as I huff, "Are you coming with me or not?"

He presses a soft kiss to my lips and says, "There's no place I would rather be, Ice Princess."

Christmas Day

My hands are beyond sweaty as we make our way up the drive to the front door. Why am I so nervous? Oh yeah... I'm about to introduce the two men with me as my boyfriends. I really hope my dad takes this better than my imagination keeps coming up with.

Fingers glide between mine before giving my hand a sure squeeze. I look over to find Mac smiling down at me. "Everything will be fine, Lizzy."

I bite my lip before confessing, "I'm starting to dislike you using my name. Which is not saying to not use it, but..."

Another hand tangles with my free hand as Dean says, "You like our nicknames for you, Ice Princess?"

I sigh as we reach the front door. "It seems I've grown attached to them."

Mac kisses the side of my head as he whispers, "Take a deep breath, *Chérie*. Everything will be okay."

I do as he says, and he knocks on the door, still keeping his grip on my sweaty hands. Good lord, why the hell is he holding my sweaty-ass hands? Before I can panic over my sweaty palms, the door opens to reveal my mom.

I give her a smile before saying, "Hi, Mama. I hope you don't mind I brought Mac and Dean with me again?"

She takes us in before looking down at our joined hands. A knowing smile graces her lips before she meets my eyes. "I don't mind, Iz. I had a feeling they would join you." She lifts a hand, and a frosting covered spatula suddenly appears, in which she proceeds to use to boop both Mac and Dean on the nose. "Hope you boys are treating my daughter right."

Mac is the first to recover as he lifts a hand to remove the dollop of frosting on the tip of his nose. "Of course, Mrs. Monroe."

She boops him again and chastises, "It's Kate to the men who are my daughter's boyfriends."

He doesn't clean his nose this time as he nods. "Yes, ma'am."

Dean is frozen still, gaping with wide eyes. To which my mother chuckles. "You alright there boy?"

He shakes off his thoughts before nodding. "Yes, ma'am."

My mother sighs. "We will work on this ma'am thing." She gestures over her shoulder with the spatula. "Your father is in the living room watching hockey replays from the last few weeks."

I release my grip on the guys as I push them into the house. They look at me with raised brows, and I grin. "Go keep my dad company. I'll help my mom with the food."

A look passes between them before they turn back to me. They each lean forward, kissing opposite cheeks before pulling away. Mac smiles softly. "If you need anything just yell."

Dean smirks before following Mac into the living room. "Don't push yourself, Ice Princess," he yells over his shoulder.

"Don't tell me what to do, Ghost." I grunt. A deep laugh echoes after him as I follow my mother into the kitchen.

The moment we are hidden in the kitchen, my mom drops the spatula on the counter. She turns to me suddenly and wraps me in her arms. It takes me a moment to realize what's happening before I wrap my arms around her in return.

"What's this for?" I ask in a hushed voice.

She pulls away from me with tears in her eyes. "I knew the moment I saw you with them on Thanksgiving that they were meant for you. I could see it in the way they looked at you and the way you looked at them in return." She pulls away, cupping my cheeks as she continues, "I was so afraid after what happened with Emmitt when you were younger and what happened a few weeks ago that you would strengthen the walls around your heart."

My eyes widen at her words. "Mom?"

"I'm so happy for you, baby." She presses a kiss to my forehead before backing away.

I'm still reeling from my mom's confession before I'm jerked out my thoughts. An apron is thrown over my head, covering my face, and I can't help but laugh. "What was that for?"

She gestures to my face as she grins. "You had this shocked, then dreamy look on your face. Either help me or get out of my kitchen and go to your boys."

I bump her hip with mine and chuckle. "I'll stick with you."

Hours of laughing and eating passed joyfully. There was a minor bump at dinner when my dad found out the two guys he'd been bonding over hockey with are my boyfriends. He opened his mouth like he was going to say a few words, but with one look from my mom, he'd shut his mouth and gave me a tight smile.

"Alright, are there any more presents?" My mother announces. It doesn't sound like a question but rather a prompt. All presents have all been opened, so I'm not sure why she's asking.

As if that's the magic word, my boys get up and pull two boxes from behind their backs.

Mac smiles down at the small box in his hands. "This one is from the team, well your team."

I reach out hesitantly. "This is from all the guys?"

He nods as he hands it to me. "It took forever for them to agree on something to get you."

"I should probably warn you that there is also a box set of a certain anime show that I'm not allowed to reveal from Vicy," Dean adds.

I snort as I open the small box. Inside is a shimmering silver necklace with a figure skate charm and a blue diamond set in the middle. "Oh... my..." I glance up at the guys before looking back down at the beautiful piece of jewelry. "This is beautiful guys."

"Would you like me to put it on you?" Mac asks.

I nod enthusiastically. The moment it's around my neck I reach for my phone. I quickly send a 'thank you' text in the group chat before shifting my attention to Dean. He's smiling, but it looks a bit nervous as he hands it over. "I hope we didn't go over the top with this gift, but I hope you like it."

I quickly open the box and gasp. My eyes meet a pair of custom, baby-blue ice skates. I slowly take one out for a closer look. My eyes catch on the blades, and I bite my lip when I see 'Ice Princess' etched into it. I gently lay the skate down and take out the other one. It's getting harder to hold back the barrage of emotions as I see '*Chérie*' etched into it.

The guys are watching me nervously when I look up. Mac gives me a hesitant smile. "Did we do okay?"

I set the other skate down and launch myself at them. I wrap my arms around both as I choke out, "That's the best gift anyone has ever given me." This will go down as the best Christmas a girl could wish for.

CHAPTER FORTY

The first of the year is finally here, and I'm beyond excited to get back to work. But getting back to work means it's time to disclose my relationship with Dean and Mac, so I don't lose my job.

My hands are clammy as I try to get my nerves under control. I refused to let the guys come with me, they would have fought any negative decision, and I need to do this for myself.

My fingers curl into a fist, and I knock on the head-coach's office door. A meeting between Mason Fernandez and Max Spencer is a bit intimidating. But I need to discuss this with them, considering Max is my direct manager in a way.

"Come in," Mason's deep voice greets from the other side.

Slowly opening the door, I greet the two of them with a smile. "Good morning."

Max smiles. "Morning, Elizabeth."

Mason gestures to the chair in front of his desk as he says, "Have a seat, Elizabeth."

I nod as I do as requested. I take a deep breath before diving into the reason I'd asked for this meeting. "So, I asked for this meeting because there is a situation that needs to be addressed within the group of guys I am in charge of." I look down at my sweaty palms in my lap as I continue, "A... romantic relationship has grown between me and two of the players I train. I would like to request those players be traded to work with Danni, and in turn, I would train two of her players of equal status."

"Who are the two players you wish to trade?" Mason asks. My eyes jerk up to meet his. He's arching a brow in question, and I'm surprised they haven't heard about our relationship yet.

Clearing my voice, I say, "Mac Oliver and Dean Lewis. I can discuss with Danni which players she wants to trade. I have notebooks on all my players, so she won't have an issue taking over. She's also been taking care of my guys alongside Max while I've been… away."

Max jumps in before Mason can say anything. "Danni has been doing great with Elizabeth's players, and I don't foresee an issue with this."

I bite my lip as I nod toward Max in thanks. I didn't expect him to go to bat for me, but I'm thankful he is.

Mason is quiet for a moment before he leans back in his chair. His dark eyes meet mine as he says, "I get the feeling this relationship has been going on much longer than just a few days."

I hesitate before nodding. "It has, sir."

His fingers tap on the top of his desk before he turns to Max. "Has she been professional and treated all of the players equally?"

Max nods. "I haven't seen her show any favoritism toward Dean and Mac compared to the others." His gaze turns to me before a smirk pulls at his lips. "All of her players love her and speak very highly of her."

Mason hums before he turns back to me. "I want you to understand that in these situations we would normally put you on probation as an investigation is conducted." He huffs out a sigh. "But I have a feeling I will have a riot in my office, if I do that, and I need my players focused on the game instead of how I put you on probation because of protocol."

"I understand, sir."

He knocks on the desk before grunting. "Your relationship doesn't appear to have reached the ears of the higher ups, so I'll make you a deal."

I nod. "Anything."

He points at me. "You get together with Danni and switch two of her players with Dean and Mac. And make sure your quality of training doesn't suffer just because you are switching around players."

"Yes, sir," I say enthusiastically.

"Talk of your relationship will not enter my locker room, is that understood?"

I agree immediately. "Yes, sir."

His tapping increases on the desk before he pushes away and stands. "Alright, as long as we are all in understanding. Dismissed."

I jump up from my seat as well. "Thank you, Coach!"

He hums before clapping a hand on my shoulder. "It's been hard to find an athletic therapist who can match Danni's gusto for the team. But it seems we've found her equal, and I'm not about to lose you over matters of the heart. We can compromise."

"Thank you," I breath out.

He claps my shoulder again with a smile. "You better get to work, Elizabeth. I have it on good authority that your boys have missed you."

I nod and rush out of the room. The first place I head is to find Danni. The moment I burst through the doors of the training room, twenty pairs of eyes turn their attention to me. Danni is helping Trav, one of her players, in mid-stretch as her eyes fall on me. Her mouth gapes in surprise before shifting into a smile. "So... did it go well?"

My grin is wide as I yell, "Yes!"

She squeals in excitement, but in turn accidentally presses down too hard on the Trav's legs, making him grunt. "Danni! You're going to bend me in half if you keep doing that."

She jumps away before muttering, "Sorry, Trav."

He groans and lets his legs fall to the ground. "It's fine, Danni." His attention shifts to me. "So, what's the verdict?"

My grin is still plastered across my face as I explain, "Two of my guys for two of yours. As long as our relationship doesn't enter the locker room everything is fine!"

Danni claps in excitement. "I prepared for this very thing!" She rushes off to the closet where we keep all our equipment and medical stuff. It only takes her a few minutes before she rushes back to me, holding out two notebooks. "I made sure I had journals made for them just the way you like it. Everything from previous injuries and stats to their favorite snacks and color."

My eyes widen as I grab notebooks with Manny and Langly scrawled across them. "You... you made notebooks for your players?"

She shrugs. "It was a great idea actually. After weeks of looking over your notes, I decided to make some of my own."

I throw my arms around her, wrapping her in a huge hug. I can't believe how supportive the team has been and how they've been in my corner every step of the way. I never thought that the Washington Wraiths would become my second family, but here I am. "I fucking love you," I whisper to her.

She chuckles and pats my back. "Love ya too, girl." With a harder pat, she barks, "Now, we need to get back to work."

I release her as I nod. "Right. Back to work."

She smirks. "You have been slacking lately. Do you even remember how to do your job after so much time off?"

I'd throw the notebooks in my hand at her, but then I'd just have to go pick them up. I roll my eyes as I clap to get my guys' attention. "Let's prove to Danni that I haven't forgotten."

"Yes, boss!" they yell in unison.

CHAPTER FORTY-ONE

The guys asked for a karaoke night as their reward for last night's win. I couldn't argue otherwise, once I saw how excited Vicy and Taz were. So here I am getting ready. I wouldn't normally dress up as much as I have, but I am officially going out for the first time as Dean and Mac's girlfriend.

I'd decided to get ready at the common house since we all planned on heading to the bar together. I still have an honorary room here, even though I spend most of my time at my apartment. I'm not alone though. The moment Dean, Mac, and I became official, they moved in with me.

I give myself one last look in the mirror before making my way out the door. While it is cold outside, I know it's going to get warm with so many bodies crammed in a small area.

I feel sexy in my skinny jeans, black heels, and baby-blue dressy tank. I paired my outfit with my leather jacket. I chose to go with light makeup, and my hair curled and pulled up into a high pony.

Heading into the living room, everyone turns at the sound of my heels clicking across the hardwood floor. Ten pairs of eyes widen, making me smirk, as I gesture toward the door. "We ready to go?"

Vicy jumps up from the couch with a yip. "Damn, Roe Roe, you clean up nicely."

I laugh. "Thanks Vicy."

Taz bumps Deans shoulder as he loudly whispers, "It's a good thing you locked her down. I'd be tempted to steal her from you if I were a dishonorable man."

He rolls his eyes before giving me a smile. "You look beautiful, Ice Princess."

"Thank you."

Perri claps and calls, "Let's get going before all the good spots are taken!"

Dean and Mac move over to me, and we make our way out the door. Mac twines his fingers with mine before lifting my hand to his lips. *"Tu es à couper le souffle, Chérie."*

I smile. "I haven't got that far in learning my French yet. Considering it's you who said it though, *merci.*"

He smiles and helps me into the back of the car. "You'll be fluent by this time next year."

Squished between Dean and Mac, I laugh lightly. "That's the hope."

Ten or so minutes later, we arrive at the karaoke bar; another few minutes and we are heading inside to find a spot. Before I can even take a seat, I'm thrown over one of the guys' shoulder.

I let out a squeal of surprise before looking over my shoulder to find that Vicy carrying me, and Taz leads the way to the stage. "Guys! What the hell?"

Vicy laughs. "It's been months since we've done karaoke! We need to hear you sing."

I roll my eyes as I let whatever this is happen. There's no chance I'll be able to escape once these two are set on something.

Vicy sets me softly onto the stage before he looks to Taz with a smirk. "She can sing to Lewi and Oli."

Taz laughs and points to the computer that holds thousands of songs. "You should pick out a song that tells them how you feel."

I huff out a sigh. "Are you guys seriously trying to play matchmaker? I've already got the guys."

Vicy boops me on the nose. "But have you told them that you love them yet?"

"Yes..."—but then I think about it before groaning— "I told Dean, but it was while you guys rescued me from that house. I never told Mac."

Taz gives me a sad smile. "This is your chance to tell them in a way that's a bit easier."

Nodding, I walk over to the computer and scroll through the songs. Dibs by Kelsea Ballerini pops up, and I can't help but smile at the thought of singing that song. I tap Vicy and Taz before pointing to my choice. They give me enthusiastic nods and get into place onstage.

Of course, they want to sing with me, but to be honest, it helps my nerves that they are up here with me. I click select, and the thump of the drums begins, and the guys in the crowd go wild with hoots and hollers.

I grin out at the audience as the verse begins. My eyes meet Dean and Mac's eyes. The chorus starts, and I look over my shoulder when I hear Taz singing along. Vicy yells, "hey," along with the song. And they repeat the same thing on the second line before joining with the rest of the chorus.

I pop the microphone off the stand, and make my way off the stage, singing the post-chorus. I stand between the two men who stole my heart as the second verse begins. I press a quick kiss to each of their cheeks, leaving a red lipstick mark behind. I am all about marking my boys as mine now.

The chorus begins, and I make my way back up onto the stage. I clip the microphone back onto the stand, then with my hands free, I gesture along with the post-chorus as the song draws to its end. Pointing to my lips, I blow them a kiss. I point to my wrist as if I had a watch before pointing to my two guys. I make a heart with my hands and press it to my heart.

I do that again as it repeats before it ends with me pointing to my guys as I sing, "Dibs."

The room is silent a moment before it erupts in cheers. I laugh and try to catch my breath as Vicy and Taz attack with a dual hug. I'm squished between them but the smile on my face is there to stay when I see Mac and Dean hold up their hands in a heart.

Vicy grabs the mic and calls out, "Lewi, it's your turn!"

He doesn't argue as he makes his way up onto the stage, which surprises me. He presses a kiss to my cheek before his hand presses to my back. "Go sit with Mac." He gives me a wink and goes over to pick a song.

I take Dean's seat next to Mac and hum in satisfaction when Mac leans forward and presses a kiss to my cheek. With his lips next to my ear, he whispers, "Now it's our turn to show you how much we love you, like you just did for us."

My eyes widen as I hear the beat of Pretty Please by Dutch Melrose, and the moment Dean opens his mouth to sing the first verse, my body tingles from his deep voice. Damn why does he have to sound so fucking sexy? Vicy and Taz are singing back up, which quickly makes this song my favorite.

His eyes are dark as he stares directly at me while he sings the pre-chorus, pointing at me when he sings the last line. He moves into the chorus, then the second verse with his wrists crossed in front of the mic. He raises them above his head as he belts out the first line.

I'm not sure if I black out for the rest of the song or am so entranced by his voice and dark eyes that I don't realize it's ended until everyone erupts around me.

Dean smirks my way before announcing, "Your turn, Mac."

Mac chuckles and says, "I'm not sure I can top that performance."

Before I can say anything, he and Dean have switched places. His lips stop next to my ear, and he whispers, "Love you, Ice Princess."

"Love you too, Ghost," I whisper back.

My attention turns to Mac as he starts to sing 24/7 365 by Elijah Woods. I bruise my bottom lip between my teeth as his voice slips over the words. His voice is soft and soothing.

My eyes begin to burn as he sings the verse because this is the sweetest damn song he could have picked. He holds up the number he's singing as he moves onto the chorus.

The rest of the song is a blur as I feel tears slide down my cheeks. How did I get lucky enough to have not only one, but two men love me the way I always craved. The moment the song ends he steps off the stage, making his way to me.

He kneels in front of me with a soft smile and reaches up to brush the stray tears with his thumb. *Je t'aime, Chérie.*

I grin as I reply, *Je t'aime, Nounours.*

He brushes his lips softly against mine then pulls away just enough to say, "My language passing across your lips is the sexiest thing I've heard."

"Then I'll make sure to practice as much as possible," I say with a laugh.

Chapter Forty-Two

Three Months Later...

It's the last game of the regular season, and I can feel everyone's nerves. We need to win this one if we want to make it to the playoffs. I take a deep breath as I wait in the crowd for the players to be announced. Danni said that I needed to be part of the fans for the last game, so I could cheer on my boys.

I'd wanted to argue but the look on Dean and Mac's face at her suggestion had me thinking better of it. She'd done amazing taking care of my guys, and I hoped I'd done the same for her.

Daisy bumps my shoulder as she holds her daughter Aspyn on her shoulder. "Should I really be here?"

I snort as I take in both her jersey as well as Aspyn's. Daisy is sporting the number nineteen on her back which happens to be Vicy's number, while Aspyn is wearing number eight for Taz. They are going to lose their shit when they see these two wearing their numbers.

They know exactly where I'm sitting because I'd told Dean and Mac where I would be. I point to her jersey, then Aspyn's. "They will love that you are supporting them."

She bites her lip and huffs. "This doesn't mean I like them, okay."

I grin as I placate her with a nod. "Of course, it doesn't. My mistake." I doubt the guys will see it that way. As if on cue, music blares through the speakers, and they begin announcing the players. I play with the bracelets on my wrist. I didn't put them on the carabiner like I normally do, wanting to use them to distract me from my nerves.

Ford—our left wing, and Samy—our defenseman, are announced as they skate out, and the crowd goes wild. The night is special and helps boost the crowd. We have home team advantage, and we want this win. Vicy is announced, and it takes him a few minutes to find me in the crowd. He grins before his eyes shift to the woman beside me, and his eyes widen. He skates over until he's against the boards and bangs on the glass.

I laugh when he points to Daisy's jersey, yelling, "That's my number!"

Daisy's eyes are wide as she takes in Vicy's excitement. His gaze shifts to me as he yells again, "That's my number!"

I nod with a laugh. "I know!"

He begins skating backward, pointing at Daisy. "I'll make sure to win for you!"

"I didn't expect him to be that excited," she whisper-yells because the crowd is rowdy tonight.

I shake my head. "Then you haven't been paying attention to how much that man likes you."

She doesn't get a moment of rest before Taz is announced next, and it doesn't take long for him to spot us. He grins when he sees Daisy and Aspyn. His eyes are locked on Aspyn as he yells, "You cheering for me, little one?"

Aspyn squeals, "Tazzy!"

He's smiling widely as he backs away. "I'll get you a puck after the game, Aspyn!"

She squeals again, clapping her little hands. "Mommy! Did you hear that? He's going to get me my very own puck!"

Daisy smiles and replies, "I heard, baby girl."

Lewi and Oli are announced and they quickly skate by, blowing me a kiss. My heart starts to race as everyone gets into position for the faceoff. The puck drops, the game begins, and then we lose the puck. The away team's center, number thirty-four, shoots it back to one of their defensemen, number eighty-four, before he passes it to their left wing, number twenty-one, making it cross the blue line before dumping the puck into the far corner. Our defense tries to keep him off Oli as they chase the right wing, number fifty-seven, who now has the puck. Taz and Samy work as a team to avoid letting him have a direct shot.

He attempts the shot, but Oli anticipates the quick top-shelf shot and saves it with an amazing catch. Our team gets the puck, and Ford tries to get out from behind our post as their number twenty-one forces us back. Ford is slammed into the boards, but he refuses to give up the puck as he forces his way around and slaps it toward Vicy.

Vicy slaps it down the ice racing after it. The other team's second defenseman, seventy-two, races after Vicy. Seventy-two manages to get the puck, but Vicy slams him into the boards and steals it from him. Vicy passes it to Lewi, who manipulates the stick and puck to line up the perfect shot, making the buzzer sound and Burn it by The Fever 33 explodes around us. Cheers echo around the rink as Lewi lifts a hand in victory.

The first period ends in a draw, each team with a single goal. The next period is brutal with us down a player for a bit due to injury. Ford got slammed into the boards too hard, which smashed his hand between his body and the boards. The medics were quick to take him off the ice, and Danni evaluated him while the game continued. The other team became savage as we each fought to get an edge in the second period. The puck managed to slip right between Oli's legs before he could block it, giving them the lead. It's time for our fifteen-minute break, and the guys were all panting as they step off the ice.

I'm pretty sure the nails on both of my thumbs have been obliterated by all the nail-biting I've done. We need to score two goals in period three to win. I see the fire in our team's eyes as the last period begins. Our boys will leave everything out on the ice as they fight and claw to get the puck through those white posts.

Ford and Vicy work together to get Lewi down the ice. Taz and Samy pushing everyone they can away. While all eyes are on Lewi, he quickly passes it to Ford as he makes his way behind the net. Ford passes it back to Lewi, before he slaps it to Vicy, who manages to strike it right into the corner of the goal post.

Power Ride by Fred Coury blasts through the speakers as Ford and Lewi attack Vicy with a hug. With only a few minutes left on the clock, I watch the opposing team's goalkeeper go to the bench for an extra attacker. I know this is a common tactic, and I hope it works in our favor.

The puck is dropped in the center of the ice, and we win possession. I watch in suspense as a battle rages along the boards in the back corner of the opposite end. I bite my lip in worry, hoping we can score while their net is empty. It's hard to make out whats happening on the other end until the other team manages to shoot the puck down the ice. I watch as it flies down the ice toward Oli.

The puck slows, and Oli gathers as he skates a few feet away from his post. He waits a few seconds to let the clock run down, then scoops the puck into a lifting pass down the ice to get it over the oncoming players. I gasp as I watch the perfect pass as it slides past the defense. I hold my breath as I watch the puck fly down the ice, the opposing team fighting to get to it in time. Their goal is completely empty. Time seems to slow as seconds feel like minutes.

The puck slides into the net and Popular Monster by Falling in Reverse explodes from the speakers. GOALIE GOAL! It was a fucking goalie goal for the win! I jump up and down, screaming as our boys' attack Oli.

When I look up, I see there are only ten seconds left on the clock. The guys line up for a face off, and the puck drops. Before the puck makes it too far down the ice, the horn blasts, echoing around the rink. The clock hits zero, and we win the game! The Washington Wraiths are going to the playoffs! It's almost deafening how loud everyone is screaming before they disperse to drink and be merry about our win. I grab Daisy's hand and usher her toward the exit that leads to the locker room.

The hallway close to the locker room is clear, and I stop when I see Dean standing there getting berated and lectured by his father. I whisper to Daisy, "Go ahead of me."

She gives me a questioning look but nods. I turn my attention back to my boyfriend. He doesn't appear to be listening to a single thing his father says. His eyes roam the area, and when they catch on me, he smiles. A genuine, no shit smile. I can't help but smile back, offering a subtle nod of encouragement.

He holds up a hand to stop his dad, which seems to shock his father into silence. "Sorry to cut this lecture short, Dad, but I have places to be."

He begins walking my direction when his father recovers enough to sputter. "Dean! Do not walk away from me, I wasn't done speaking."

Without taking his eyes off me, he yells back, "Well, I'm done listening. Not that I was doing much of that anyways." I watch some sort of realization flashes in his eyes, and he stops to look over his shoulder. "You've been telling me how to do my job as a hockey player for years. Yet you have no idea how to play the game or how the game works. You have no idea how relationships between the players work to play the game, nor do you care. If you want a pliable Lewis you can control, maybe you should make another one because I'm done. I'm done trying to make you proud and hoping you'll give me even an ounce of the respect you give my sister. I don't *need* you to be proud of me anymore, Dad. I don't even need your attention." He turns back to me with a soft smile. "I have people in my life who care no matter I win or lose." He rushes to me now, and once he's in front of me he wraps me in a huge sweaty hug.

I laugh as I hug him back. "I was about to step in, but it seems you had things handled."

"I don't care about his opinion anymore. He's not the one I'm trying to impress," he whispers.

I squeeze him tighter and say, "You don't have to impress me. I'm proud of you either way."

"Then say it," he demands, though it sounds more like a plea than a demand.

I pull away so I can look up at him. I give him the most genuine smile I can muster, which isn't hard. "I'm so proud of you, Dean."

He hums before pressing his lips to mine. I chuckle into his mouth when I hear, "Well, where is my congratulations kiss?"

I look over Deans shoulder and find Mac standing there with a grin. "Get your ass over here, and I'll kiss you too."

He doesn't hesitate, making his way over to position himself at my side. He doesn't seem bothered that I'm still in Dean's arms as he presses his lips to mine. He smiles down at me. "I love you, Lizzy."

I grin up at him as I reply, "I love you too, Mac."

Dean nips the lobe of my ear to get my attention, and he grunts, "I love you, too, you know."

I press a quick kiss to his cheek. "I love you too, Dean."

Pulling out of Dean's arms, he reluctantly releases me. I give them both a wink as I back away. "Who wants to celebrate at the apartment?"

The guys look at each other before Dean asks, "What type of celebration?"

I grin as I pull down the top of my jersey enough so they get a glimpse of the baby-blue lace bra I'm wearing. "The type where whoever catches me first gets me all to themselves for the night."

Mac smirks and asks, "What if we catch you together?"

I shrug. "Then, I suppose you both get me."

Dean bumps Mac's shoulder as he groans, "Let's get our girl." They begin taking large steps toward me, and I turn around with a squeal and take off toward the exit.

My love story may have started with betrayal, but it ended with two men who showed me what love could be if I gave them a bit of trust. The ice will always be my first love, but it introduced me to true love and family.

EPILOGUE

I can see the team's defeat in their eyes as the game ends. We were down by one point, in game seven of our journey to the Stanley Cup finals. The moment Dean is close enough, I wrap him in my arms. He's on the ice while I'm still in the bench area which puts me in the perfect position for him to bury his face into my neck.

"I'm so proud of you," I whisper into his ear.

"We lost..." he mutters into my neck.

"That doesn't make me any less proud of you. There's always next year."

He hums into my neck as he pulls me closer. My eyes meet the rest of my boys' as they skate closer. I open my arms with a grin. "I'm proud of you guys. You did amazing!"

Mac gives me a small smile as he joins the hug with Dean and I. Taz and Vicy pat the top of my head as they make their way toward the exit. I notice Daisy waiting there for them. Aspyn is in her arms as she gives them both a side hug. I don't know what she's saying, but I can see their spirits lifting in her company as Aspyn reaches out for Taz.

He smiles as he takes the small girl into his arms, and they head toward the locker room.

Mac's voice jerks me out of my spying. "Are you trying to play matchmaker, Lizzy?"

I give him a crooked smile as I reply, "I don't think there's much I need to do."

Dean pulls away, looking in the direction Taz and Vicy just left. "I hope they don't fuck it up. That girl is a spitfire."

"I'm sure they will do just fine." I lift on my tiptoes to kiss both my boys on the cheek. "I guess figure skaters can't help but fall for you hockey players."

Dean smirks. "Well, we are pretty irresistible."

I smack his pec as I roll my eyes. "If I remember correctly, you were an asshole at first."

Dean shrugs as Mac says, "True love has bumps and hurdles. If they believe it's worth it, they will fight for it just like we did." He looks at me with a soft smile and rubs a thumb over my bottom lip. "A love worth fighting for and all that, right?"

"I hope their journey is smoother than ours," I say with a sigh.

Mac leans forward and presses a soft kiss to my lips. *"Ça vaut tout."*

And it was. It was worth it all. Every bump. Every bruise. I love these boys with every beat of my heart. *"Tu es mes cadeaux les plus précieux."*

Mac grins against my lips as he says, "I love when you speak French."

I laugh and push them both away. "Go get cleaned up, so we can go home and celebrate."

They grin and skate toward the locker room. I jump when I hear a feminine voice beside me. "So, how's life with your harem of men?"

I laugh as I turn to face Danni. "It's not a harem, there are only two men."

She shrugs. "Same thing if you ask me. Anyways, how's life?"

"I love it."

She arches a brow and asks, "Any issues with the whole Emmitt thing?"

I shake my head. "He was found guilty and will spend a few years in prison. He accepted a plea bargain and will be placed in a psychiatric hospital once he's served his time in confinement."

"The nightmares?" she asks softly.

I shrug as I look in the direction the guys left. "I have my good days and bad. But the guys are there to make it better." I give her a soft smile. "All of them help, actually."

She returns the smile. "That's good. I'm glad you're doing great."

I point to her. "What about you?"

She shrugs. "I haven't found the right one yet. But I'll let you know when I do."

I jump when I hear my name yelled. I look over to find Dean and Mac waiting at the exit for me.

Dean cups his hands around his mouth as he yells, "Let's go home, Ice Princess."

I look at Danni and she gives me a shooing motion. "Go get your men."

Laughing, I jog toward my guys. We have some celebrating to do, and I do love the way we celebrate.

ALSO BY

<u>Books Also by Ivy Cole</u>

Underground Syndicate Series:

Underworld

Tartarus

Why Choose Fables:

Meddling with Madness (Wonderland Retelling)
The Stolen Throne: The Villainous Reign (Snow White Retelling)

The Washington Wraiths

Ice Me Baby (Liz, Mac, Dean)

About Author

Ivy Cole is a long time lover of writing and has wanted to publish her books for years. She love Reverse Harem of many kinds. She's a indie author and can't wait to share future books with you.

Want to follow Ivy Cole and see future books? Follow her at:

https://www.facebook.com/groups/508646927449550/